CHABLIS AND THE TERRORIST

Who Resurrected the Spirit of Che Guevara

By

J. Wayne Frye

Chablis and the Terrorist
Who Resurrected the Spirit of Che Guevara

The Author

Wayne Frye's *Aaron Adams, Girl* series books and *Lynton* adventures are popular among mystery readers. He provides satirical political commentary to many Canadian newspapers, and his books on politics have created a great deal of controversy. He has written marketing/advertising textbooks, been a highly successful U.S. university hockey coach, professor, university president and served as a marketing consultant to hockey teams and motion picture companies. He has been cited for his work with inner-city gang children in the Los Angeles area and been active in the anti-globalization movement. He became a Canadian citizen in 2003 and lives in Ladysmith, British Columbia and Cavite, Philippines.

Other Books by J. Wayne Frye

Hockey Mania and the Mystery of Nancy Running Elk
Something Evil in the Darkness at Hopkins House
How Hockey Saved a Jew From the Holocaust:
The Rudi Ball Story
The Catastrophic Calamities of a Village Idiot
Fighting for Justice in the Land of Hypocrisy
Guide to Alternative Education (13 Editions)
Cataclysmic Dreams in Black and White
The Girl Who Stirred up the Whirlwind
The Girl Who Motivated Murder Most Foul
The Girl Who Said Goodbye for the Last Time
Fall From Apocalypse
Armageddon Now
Worth
When Jesus Came to Jersey as the Son of Thunder
When Jesus Came to Canada to Lead an Indigenous Rebellion
Canadian Angels of Mercy – Nurses in Times of Peril
Points of Rebellion: Aboriginals Who Fought for Justice
Lynton Curls Her Hair
Lynton Buys a New Cell-Phone and Hears the Voice of Doom
Lynton Walks on Water
Lynton and the Vampire at Tagaytay Manor
Chablis: Avenging Angel for the Forgotten in the
City of Lost Hope

Chablis and the Terrorist
Who Resurrected the Spirit of Che Guevara

TABLE OF CONTENTS

Chablis and the Terrorist
Who Resurrected the Spirit of Che Guevara

TO: My Buddy Jeff Garfield
Affectionately Known as Dry-Waller to the Stars

Catalogue Number: 2014-2453569
ISBN: 978-1-928183-04-4

Fireside Books – Victoria, British Columbia
Part of the Peninsula Publishing Consortium

Chablis and the Terrorist
Who Resurrected the Spirit of Che Guevara

PROLOGUE
I CAME NOT TO BRING PEACE
BUT A SWORD

His name is a whisper on the wind.
Yes, listen to the whisper on the wind.
Che Guevara is more memory than man.
He never bowed in supplication to the mighty.
Wild eyed and fiery with passion he stood tall,
Fighting bravely to make the arrogant fall.
A legend who lives in the hearts and minds
Of all who long for freedom and justice,
Idealism eventually cost him his life.
But today, those who face poverty's strife
Can hear that whisper, that whisper on the wind?
"Che lives. Che Lives. Che lives."

Jose Juan Martinez was born in the ghetto of Spanish Harlem. He lived there all his 30 years, but journeyed all over the world in his mind. A voracious reader, he consumed three or four voluminous books each week. And these were not inconsequential manifests of insignificance. He poured over volumes by men of letters from the early beginnings of America like Thomas Paine, Benjamin Franklin, Hector St. John de Crèvecoeur, Philip Freneau, Charles Brockden Brown, Washington Irving, Henry David Thoreau and James Fenimore Cooper. His quest for learning had an obvious left of centre vent as he enthusiastically sought out the works of Aristotle, Plato, Aldous Huxley, Eugene V. Debs, John Paul Sartre and W.E. B. Dubois. However, he was also fascinated by the modern writers who had great insight into the plight of those enslaved by the falsity of the American ideal that was more words than reality. A T-Shirt he saw hanging in a clothing store at 134th Street and Lenox Avenue, however, was what changed his life. There, printed in bright red on a white T-Shirt was a photo of Che Guevara with his trademark beret and cigar. Obviously, Jose Juan, who was generally referred to as J.J., had come across the name many times in his reading, but for some reason, he had never read anything specifically written by Che. Anyway, in the USA, Che was the antithesis of everything the country stood for. What place did the musings of a wild-eyed idealist have in a society where greed was aggrandized as a favourable trait? Though a socialist at heart, J.J. knew that in America there was no hope for any modicum of social justice as poverty was your own fault. Helping the poor with a government handout was nothing but evil socialism, according America, which guaranteed continued dependence rather than independence. Despite his penchant for left wing ideals, even J.J., amidst all the poverty that kept him in bondage, felt that too many people were not willing to help themselves, but once he got hold of Che's writings, his attitudes slowly began to change.

He was 25 when he saw the T-Shirt, and he had just struggled through the completion of his Ph.D. in Urban Studies with straight A's. Supporting himself by working odd jobs for minimum wage, along with massive loans and help from his mother and sister, he was now ready to join that venerable thing called "the middle class." However, that day, as he stood staring at that T-Shirt, something strange happened.

All around him there was a sudden quietness, and it was as if everyone there became frozen in time. People were not moving, and J.J. felt a presence next to him. He turned to his right and saw the rough outline, almost a ghost like figure of a man in army fatigues wearing a beret and smoking a cigar. He blinked his eyes and the figure was gone. People began to scurry about again, and J.J. took a deep breath, shook his head as if it needed to be cleared of cobwebs, sighed and from that day forward read everything written by or about Che Guevara.

He took a low-level job in the New York Department of City Planning, and worked diligently to repay all the loans that had forced him deep into debt in order to finance an education. In European countries, the playing field was levelled for the poor, as everyone was entitled to a free university education, but in the USA, only the rich got out of university debt free. Inequity was built into the system, so that the poor, for the most part, were denied the same privileges as the wealthy. Safe neighbourhoods, grand homes, good schools, prestigious universities and an instant slot as a VP at Dad's firm upon graduation were not for people like J.J. Oh yes, there were the exceptions. Hey, a black man (actually a Mulatto) had even been elected President, but his sojourn as leader of the so-called greatest democracy was marked by stark racism and inertia promulgated by the right wing to make sure he was as ineffective as possible.

Chablis and the Terrorist
Who Resurrected the Spirit of Che Guevara

Ironically, Barrack Obama was a centre-right thinker, but the colour of his skin kept the majority from realizing that.

The next five years were relatively insignificant, as J.J. continued to live in the roughest section of Spanish Harlem, but vowed to his mom and sister that he would get them out of the ghetto once his loans were paid off and he could save enough for a down payment on a co-op in Queens.

All this time, he continued to ponder the writings of Che Guevara, and he painstakingly consumed volumes on Che's philosophies of how to effectuate social change in a world where the rich ruled with the iron fisted economic policies that perpetually trapped 99% of the world's population in servitude to the top 1%.

Many nights as he lay contemplating what one person could do to change things in a country where change was equated with anarchy, he would drift off, but awaken suddenly as he felt an unearthly presence by his bed. On occasion, he would see that ghostlike figure, more mist than man, by his bed. He would blink his eyes and the mist was gone.

So, as J.J. approached his 30th birthday, like Jesus did on his 30th birthday, he was about to begin his ministry – a ministry of blood. He often thought of what Jesus said in Matthew 10:34: "Don't imagine that I came to bring peace to the earth! I came not to bring peace, but a sword."

Chablis and the Terrorist
Who Resurrected the Spirit of Che Guevara

CHAPTER 1
THE TERROR OF JOSE JUAN MARTINEZ

Hope was slain by the CIA in Bolivia
But Che's spirit still rides high and free.
Yes, this man was the Jesus of the modern age,
Crucified with a bullet fired from Washington.
The tiger was murdered by the worms
To protect the status-quo.
When they put him in an unmarked grave
Justice and hope were laid low.

In order to understand the metal state of Jose Juan Martinez, we must first explore, in a cursory manner at least, the legend of Che Guevara, because everything J.J did was based on his growing fascination with Che. Therefore, to understand, Jose Juan, we must first attempt to understand the man who was the guiding light that would lead Jose Juan down a path of murder and destruction as he attempted to emulated a man who has been called *the most complete human being who ever lived.*

The legacy of Argentine Marxist revolutionary Che Guevara (June 14, 1928 – October 9, 1967) is constantly evolving in the collective imagination. As a ubiquitous symbol of counterculture worldwide, Guevara is one of the most recognizable and influential revolutionary figures of all time. However, during his life, and even more since his death, Che has elicited controversy and wildly divergent opinions as to who he was and what he represented. Mostly revered and occasionally reviled, he is passionately characterized, even by most detractors as a heroic defender of the poor. Admired, sanctified, romanticized and, of course, derided by those who embrace unfettered capitalism and unbridled exploitation of the masses, his crystallized status as a brilliant intellectual idealist or a violent ideologue is usually dependent on where one falls along the left and right of the political spectrum. The debate around his legacy is further complicated by the fact that Guevara exists simultaneously as several different entities, both literal man and global emblem, leading to disputes between what people contend he did and what he now represents.

Che's practical and theoretical work had a profound political impact around the globe during the second half of the 20th century, especially in the developing world, where revolutionary organizing and anti-colonial struggles were inspired by his thought and example. As a consequence, his writings have been translated into hundreds of different languages, and he became an icon to the oppressed of the world that yearn for justice in an economic system that has enslaved most to the oligarchs and the corporations they own. These captains of capitalism have become the modern day lords of the manor while the rest of us are the serfs bowing and scraping for a pittance from those at the top of the economic ladder. Che wanted to change this economic slavery and offer everyone fairness and compassionately provide healthcare, shelter and an opportunity for a job that allowed the workers to share in the fruits of their labour rather than the rewards only flowing to those at the pinnacle of wealth. He was an idealist, who dreamed of a world where the least among us was treated with respect and afforded an opportunity to excel and reap the same benefits as those born with a silver spoon in their mouths.

He saw the workers as the real producers of wealth, but who garnered few of the benefits of wealth, as all the real money flowed to those at the top, who never had to toil on the factory floor or worry about putting food on the table. The few who made it to the top from the lower economic rungs of the ladder were ballyhooed as the reason why capitalism was so great since it made it possible for every man to succeed. However, Che saw through this fallacy, as he understood that those with money, power and prestige were a clique that effectively barred most from the lower classes from making it to the apex of success reserved for those who came from wealth. If your father is Chairman-of-the-Board of a corporation, you start out as a vice-president, whereas, if your father is a millwright who managed to send you to university, you have to start out much lower and chances are, you will never make it to the presidential suite, because that is reserved for family. In a just world, that phrase in the U.S. Constitution about "all men being created equal" would be true. The suggestion that a child born in the Watts ghetto has an equal opportunity with the one born on Beverly Hills is a farce, and Che Guevara realized that until the playing field was levelled for all that there could be no justice for the economically deprived. That is why he devoted his life to rectifying unfairness.

Chablis and the Terrorist
Who Resurrected the Spirit of Che Guevara

Ernesto Guevara was born in 1928 into a wealthy family in Rosario, Argentina. Referring to Che's "restless" nature, his father declared "the first thing to note is that in my son's veins flowed the blood of a rebel."

Very early on in life, Ernesto developed an affinity for the poor and had problems, even as a child, understanding why the rich were treated better by the government than the impoverished. As a child he once said, "A government that ignores poverty is not a government of the people, because most people in Argentina are poor."

Despite suffering crippling bouts of acute asthma, he was an accomplished athlete and was a world-class rugby player as well as an avid cyclist. This penchant for cycles would eventually lead to a journey of discovery that made him realize that he was destined to be a revolutionary.

During adolescence and throughout his life he was passionate about poetry, especially that of Pablo Neruda, John Keats, Antonio Machado, Federico García Lorca, Gabriela Mistral, César Vallejo, and Walt Whitman. He could also recite Rudyard Kipling's "*If—*" and José Hernández's *Martín Fierro* from memory. The Guevara home contained more than 3,000 books, which allowed Che to be an enthusiastic and eclectic reader, with interests including Karl Marx, William Faulkner, André Gide, Emilio Salgari and Jules Verne. Additionally, he enjoyed the works of Jawaharlal Nehru, Franz Kafka, Albert Camus, Vladimir Lenin and Jean-

Chablis and the Terrorist
Who Resurrected the Spirit of Che Guevara

Paul Sartre; as well as Anatole France, Friedrich Engels, H. G. Wells, and Robert Frost.

As he grew older, he developed an interest in the Latin American writers Horacio Quiroga, Ciro Alegría, Jorge Icaza, Rubén Darío, and Miguel Asturias. Many of these authors' ideas he catalogued in his own handwritten notebooks of concepts, definitions, and philosophies of influential intellectuals. These included composing analytical sketches of Buddha and Aristotle, along with examining Bertrand Russell on love and patriotism, Jack London on society and Nietzsche on the idea of death. Sigmund Freud's ideas fascinated him as he quoted him on a variety of topics from dreams and libido to narcissism and the Oedipus complex.

Typical of American racism, a declassified CIA report about him in 1958 had the following notation: *Guevara has a wide range of academic interests and is quite well-read and intellectual for a Latino.*

In his late teens, he went to Chile where he became enraged by the working conditions of the miners in Anaconda's Chuquicamata copper mine. On the way to Machu Picchu high in the Andes, he was struck by the crushing poverty of the remote rural areas, where peasant farmers worked small plots of land owned by wealthy landlords. Later on his journey, Guevara was especially impressed by the camaraderie among those living in a leper colony, stating "The highest forms of human solidarity and loyalty arise among such lonely and

Chablis and the Terrorist
Who Resurrected the Spirit of Che Guevara

desperate people." Guevara used notes taken during this trip to write an account titled *The Motorcycle Diaries*, which later became a *The New York Times* best-seller. This was a time when America almost changed as people took to the streets to demand justice. Unfortunately, it would not last.

The journey took Guevara through Argentina, Chile, Peru, Ecuador, Colombia, Venezuela, Panama, and Miami, Florida before returning home to Buenos Aires. By the end of the trip, he came to view Latin America, not as collection of separate nations, but as a single entity requiring a continent-wide liberation strategy. His conception of a borderless, united Hispanic America sharing a common Latino heritage was a theme that recurred prominently during his later revolutionary activities. Upon returning to Argentina, he completed his studies and received his medical degree in June 1953.

Guevara later remarked that through his travels in Latin America, he came in close contact with poverty, hunger and disease, along with the seeing that peasants could not get treatment for their children's diseases because of a lack of money. It was these experiences which Guevara cited as convincing him that in order to help these people, he needed to leave the realm of medicine, and consider the political arena of armed struggle. It was then when he issued one of his greatest edicts, *"I could have become a physician and helped a few thousand people, or I could become a revolutionary and help millions. The choice was obvious."*

Chablis and the Terrorist
Who Resurrected the Spirit of Che Guevara

On July 7, 1953, Guevara set out again, this time to Bolivia, Peru, Ecuador, Panama, Costa Rica, Nicaragua, Honduras and El Salvador. Guevara was appalled by the United Fruit Company and how it treated its employees in South and Central America like slaves, which convinced him how terrible the capitalist monoliths of evil that gobbled up everything in sight were.

Guevara arrived in Guatemala where President Jacobo Árbenz Guzmán headed a democratically elected government that, through land reform and other initiatives, was attempting to end the serf-like system. To accomplish this, President Árbenz had enacted a major land reform program, where all uncultivated portions of large land holdings were to be expropriated and redistributed to landless peasants. The biggest land owner, and one most affected by the reforms, was the United Fruit Company, from which the Árbenz government had already taken more than 200,000 acres of uncultivated land. Pleased with the road the nation was heading down, Guevara decided to settle down in Guatemala so as to perfect himself and accomplish whatever might be necessary in order to become a true revolutionary who could stand by the poor and lift them to freedom.

In Guatemala City, Guevara established contact with a group of Cuban exiles linked to Fidel Castro through the July 26, 1953 attack on the Moncada Barracks in Santiago de Cuba. During this period he acquired his famous nickname, due to his frequent use of the Argentine diminutive interjection *che*,

Chablis and the Terrorist
Who Resurrected the Spirit of Che Guevara

used to call attention which is similar to U.S. expression *bro* or the Canadian phrase *eh*.

Upset with the appropriation of United Fruit Company property and what it considered a drift into socialism, the United States CIA sponsored an army that invaded the country and installed a right-wing dictatorship in 1954.

Guevara was eager to fight on behalf of Arbenz and joined an armed militia organized by the Communist Youth for that purpose, but frustrated with the group's inaction, he soon returned to medical duties. Guevara's repeated calls to resist were noted by supporters of the coup, and he was marked for murder. Guevara sought protection inside the Argentine consulate, where he remained until he received a safe-conduct pass some weeks later and made his way to Mexico. The overthrow of the Arbenz regime cemented Guevara's view of the United States as an imperialist power that would oppose and attempt to destroy any government that sought to redress the socioeconomic inequality endemic to Latin America and other developing countries. He saw the USA as a nation willing to commit cold premeditated aggression to ensure that corporations were allowed to exploit Third World countries and the workers. This experience convinced him that the only avenue to assure social justice was armed struggle.

Guevara arrived in Mexico City in early September 1954, and worked in the allergy section of the General Hospital but he made a promise to an old scrub woman there to fight for a better world and a better life for all the poor and exploited.

He became friends with Cuban exiles and became friends with Raúl Castro and Fidel Castro. During a long conversation with Fidel on the night of their first meeting, Guevara concluded that the Cuban's cause was the one for which he had been searching and before daybreak he had signed up as a member of the July 26 Movement to free Cuba from American domination and the dictatorship of Fulgencio Batista. Despite their contrasting personalities, Che and Fidel began to foster a revolutionary friendship that would change the world, as a result of their mutual disdain for imperialism.

By this time, Guevara was convinced that U.S. controlled corporations installed and supported repressive regimes around the world. In this vein, he considered Batista a U.S. puppet.

On November 25, 1956 they landed in Cuba and were immediately attacked by Batista's military and most of the 82 men were either killed in the attack or executed upon capture. Only 22 found each other afterwards. During this initial bloody confrontation Guevara tossed aside his medical bag and took up arms, vowing that he would die fighting.

The survivors retreated to the Sierra Maestra mountains, where the author of this book's father once flew in guns to this band of brave men who were trying to free Cuba.

Chablis and the Terrorist
Who Resurrected the Spirit of Che Guevara

During Guevara's time living hidden among the poor subsistence farmers of the Sierra Maestra mountains, he discovered that there were no schools, no electricity, minimal access to healthcare, and more than 40 percent of the adults were illiterate while Batista and his American cronies dined on caviar and sent their children to exclusive private schools in other countries.

Guevara set up factories to make grenades and other armaments, built ovens to bake bread, taught new recruits about tactics, and organized schools to teach illiterate peasants to read and write. He established health clinics, workshops to teach military tactics, and a newspaper to disseminate information. He was promoted by Fidel Castro to *Comandante* (commander) of a second army column and thus began his career as Castro's strong right arm.

Although he maintained a demanding and harsh disposition, Guevara also viewed his role of commander as one of a teacher, entertaining his men during breaks between engagements with readings from the likes of Robert Louis Stevenson, Cervantes, and Spanish lyric poets. Committed to literacy for all, Guevara ensured that his rebel fighters made daily time to teach the uneducated with whom they lived and were taught to read and write, in what Guevara termed the battle against ignorance.

To quell the rebellion, Cuban government troops began executing rebel prisoners on the spot, and regularly rounded up, tortured, and shot civilians as a tactic of intimidation.

The greatest and most decisive battle for Cuban independence was led by Guevara in the attack on Santa Clara. Che's eventual victory despite being outnumbered 10 to 1 remains in the view of military strategist as one of the most remarkable achievements in modern warfare.

Upon hearing of Che's victory, Fulgencio Batista boarded a plane in Havana with hoards of money, diamonds and gold valued at around 6 billion dollars in today's funds and fled to the Dominican Republic, where another U.S. installed dictator, Rafael Trujillo, was in power.

The following day on January 2, 1959 Guevara entered Havana to take final control of the capital. Seeing that victory against capitalist exploitation was possible with armed conflict, Che wrote a book that became a bible for guerrilla warfare that is still used today, and was a favourite of Jose Juan.

In the summer of 1959, Castro sent Guevara on a world tour to showcase the new Cuba. Guevara spent 12 days in Japan, participating in negotiations aimed at expanding Cuba's trade relations with that nation. During the visit, he refused to visit and lay a wreath at Japan's Tomb of the Unknown Soldier commemorating soldiers lost during World War II, remarking that the Japanese imperialists had killed millions of Asians. In its place, Guevara stated that he would instead visit Hiroshima, where the

Chablis and the Terrorist
Who Resurrected the Spirit of Che Guevara

American military had detonated an atom-bomb 14 years earlier in the most deadly terrorist attack of all time.

The USA began almost immediately to denounce Castro for appropriating land from the wealthy and corporations to redistribute to the poor. In fact, Castro appropriated his own family property in order to illustrate that no one was excluded from doing the right thing. This was the act of a true revolutionary. With U.S. support, terrorist acts were a regular occurrence in the Havana area. In one such incident, 76 civilians were killed.

Along with land reform, Guevara stressed the need for literacy. Before 1959, the official literacy rate for Cuba was around 70%. Thanks to the efforts of Che, today, Cuba has the highest literacy in the world at 99.8%. Accompanying literacy, Guevara was also concerned with establishing universal access to higher education. To accomplish this, the new regime introduced affirmative action to the universities and made all education completely free to citizens all the way through university.

One favourite Che quote of J.J.'s came from this era. *"The merit of Marx is that he suddenly produces a qualitative change in the history of social thought. He interprets history, understands its dynamic, predicts the future, but in addition to predicting it (which would satisfy his scientific obligation), he expresses a revolutionary concept: the world must not only be interpreted, it must be transformed. Man ceases to be the slave and tool of*

Chablis and the Terrorist
Who Resurrected the Spirit of Che Guevara

his environment and converts himself into the architect of his own destiny."

To Che, man truly achieves his full human condition when he produces without being compelled by the physical necessity of selling himself as a commodity.

In an effort to eliminate social inequalities, Guevara and Cuba's new leadership had moved to swiftly transform the political and economic base of the country through nationalizing factories, banks, and businesses, while attempting to ensure affordable housing, healthcare and employment for all Cubans. However, in order for a genuine transformation of consciousness to take root, Guevara believed that such structural changes would have to be accompanied by a conversion in people's social relations and values. Believing that the attitudes in Cuba towards race, women, individualism and manual labour were the product of the islands outdated past, Guevara urged all individuals to view each other as equals. To accomplish this, Guevara emphasized the tenets of Marxism-Leninism, and wanted to use the state to emphasize qualities such as egalitarianism, self-sacrifice, unity and freedom. He viewed capitalism as a contest among predators where one wins through chicanery. A primary goal of Guevara's was to reform individual consciousness and values to eliminate greed. To quote Che: "There is a great difference between free-enterprise development and revolutionary development. In one of them, wealth is concentrated in the hands of a fortunate few, the

Chablis and the Terrorist
Who Resurrected the Spirit of Che Guevara

friends of the government, the best wheeler-dealers. In the other, wealth is the people's patrimony."

On April 17, 1961, 1,400 U.S.-trained Cuban exiles invaded Cuba at the Bay of Pigs. Guevara did not play a key role in the fighting, as one day before the invasion a warship carrying Marines faked an invasion off the West Coast of Pinar del Río and drew forces commanded by Guevara to that region. However, historians give him a share of credit for the victory as he was director of instruction for Cuba's armed forces at the time. Unlike America's leaders, who send others out to die, Che and Castro were in the front lines fighting.

The revolutionaries won because Che Guevara had trained the army to be a cohesive revolutionary unit. Che sent a personal note to American President, John F. Kennedy thanking him for the invasion. "Thanks for Playa Girón (Bay of Pigs). Before the invasion, the revolution was shaky. Now it's stronger than ever."

Guevara antagonistically attacked the United States claim of being a democracy, stating that such a system was not compatible with financial oligarchy, discrimination against blacks, and outrages by the Ku Klux Klan. He insinuated that the United States was not interested in real reforms, only maintaining the status-quo so that corporations and the oligarchs could continue their dominance.

Guevara arranged for the Soviet nuclear-armed ballistic missiles that precipitated the Cuban Missile

Chablis and the Terrorist
Who Resurrected the Spirit of Che Guevara

Crisis in October 1962 and brought the world to the brink of nuclear war. A few weeks after the crisis, Guevara was still fuming over the Soviet betrayal and said that if the missiles had been under Cuban control, they would have fired them off, because Cubans would not bow in supplication to a tyrannical country like the USA.

Che Guevara had emerged as a revolutionary statesman for the oppressed who saw through the lies promulgated by capitalist propagandists who worked diligently to convince everyone that there was equal opportunity, when the truth was that there was very little opportunity for anyone but the well-connected oligarchs.

He saw the amount of poverty and suffering required for the emergence of people like the Rockefellers, and the amount of depravity that the accumulation of a fortune of such magnitude entails, as an affront to human decency.

Guevara dropped out of public life in 1964, and then vanished altogether. His whereabouts were a great mystery in Cuba, as he was generally regarded as second in power to Castro himself. On October 3, 1965, Castro publicly revealed an undated letter purportedly written to him by Guevara some months earlier which was later titled *Che Guevara's farewell letter*. In the letter, Guevara reaffirmed his enduring solidarity with the Cuban Revolution but declared his intention to leave Cuba to fight for the revolutionary cause abroad. Additionally, he resigned from all his positions in the Cuban government and communist party, and renounced his honorary Cuban citizenship.

In early 1965, Guevara went to Africa to offer his knowledge and experience as a guerrilla to the ongoing conflict in the Congo. Guevara led the Cuban operation in support of the Marxist Simba movement, which had emerged from the ongoing Congo crisis. Dismayed by the lack of commitment from the rebel forces, Guevara declared you can't liberate a country that does not want to fight for freedom. Dejected, he simply seemed to disappear.

On November 3, 1966, Guevara secretly arrived in La Paz, Bolivia on a flight from Montevideo under the false name Adolfo Mena González, posing as a middle-aged Uruguayan businessman working for the Organization of American States.

Three days after his arrival in Bolivia, Guevara left La Paz for the rural south east region of the country to form a guerrilla army. Guevara's guerrilla force, numbering about 50, scored a number of early successes against Bolivian army regulars.

On October 7, 1967, an informant on the CIA payroll apprised the Bolivian Special Forces of the location of Guevara's guerrilla encampment in the Yuro ravine. They encircled the area with 1,800 soldiers triggering a battle where Guevara was wounded and taken prisoner. Guevara was tied up and taken to a dilapidated mud schoolhouse. He refused to be interrogated by Bolivian officers and would only speak quietly to Bolivian soldiers. In defiance, Guevara spat in the face of Bolivian Rear Admiral Ugarteche who attempted to question him.

On October the 9th, Bolivian President René Barrientos, with tacit approval from the USA, ordered that Guevara be killed. A little later, Guevara was asked by one of the Bolivian soldiers guarding him if he was thinking about his own immortality. "No," he replied, "I'm thinking about the immortality of the revolution."

A while later, a soldier came in and Che said, "You've come to kill me. Shoot. Do it." When the soldier hesitated, Che said, "Shoot me, you coward! You are only going to kill a man! You can't kill the ideals for which I stand."

He was shot nine times. Each bullet was a tyrannical symbol of the attempt by the USA to destroy hope for the oppressed. Guevara had written his own epitaph months earlier by stating *"Wherever death may surprise us, let it be welcome, provided that this our battle cry may have reached some receptive ear and another hand may be extended to wield our weapons."*

J.J. had remembered almost by heart Castro's eulogy. "If we wish to express what we want the men of future generations to be, we must say: Let them be like Che! If we wish to say how we want our children to be educated, we must say without hesitation: We want them to be educated in Che's spirit! If we want the model of a man, who does not belong to our times but to the future, I say from the depths of my heart that such a model, without a single stain on his conduct, without a single stain on his action, is Che!"

Buried in a mass grave at the end of an abandoned dirt airstrip to make sure no one would discover his body, while pictures of the dead Guevara were being circulated and the circumstances of his death were being debated, Che's incredible legend began to spread. Demonstrations in protest against his assassination occurred throughout the world, and articles, tributes, and poems were written about his life and death. When a few months later riots broke out in Berlin, France, and Chicago, and the unrest spread to the American college campuses, young men and women wore Che Guevara T-shirts and carried his pictures during their protest marches. Thus Che Guevara was not dead. He was very much alive.

In July 1997 a team of Cuban geologists and Argentine forensic anthropologists discovered the remnants of seven bodies in two mass graves. Bolivian government officials with the Ministry of Interior later identified the body as Guevara when the excavated teeth "perfectly matched" a plaster mould of Che's teeth made in Cuba prior to his Congolese expedition. On October 17, 1997, Guevara's remains, with those of six of his fellow combatants, were laid to rest with military honours in a specially built mausoleum in the Cuban city of Santa Clara, where he had commanded over the decisive military victory of the Cuban Revolution.

Chablis and the Terrorist
Who Resurrected the Spirit of Che Guevara

His heroic status grows with each passing year all over the world. He remains a national hero in Cuba, where his image adorns the 3 peso banknote and school children begin each morning by pledging "We will be like Che."

Slowly, methodically, without realizing it, Jose Juan was also reciting in his head, "I will be like Che."

J.J. had tried to believe in America. As a child, he dutifully stood every day in school, hand over heart, and recited the Pledge of Allegiance. His little voice would crack with emotion as he believed that he was lucky, even though poor, to live in great nation where he could accomplish great things. Only later in life did he began to ask why children of colour and poverty were supposed to recite a pledge that promised liberty and justice for all, when the truth was that liberty and justice was only reserved for the privileged class. The brainwashing of America's youth was simply a way to guarantee a patriotic slew of naïve young men to fight wars of conquest, believing they were defending freedom, when what they were really defending was the right of corporations to exploit Third World countries for profit.

Watching with concern as his neighbourhood continued to deteriorate as a result of the Reagan Revolution, which turned the country over to corporations and the wealthy, he realized that social programmes had been sacrificed so the wealthy could accumulate more riches through lower taxes.

Chablis and the Terrorist
Who Resurrected the Spirit of Che Guevara

He began to see that the system was rigged to benefit the few at the expense of the many. Each day, as he walked home from work, which was on Broadway, to uptown Lenox Avenue in Harlem, he saw the stark contrast between the haves and have-nots and wondered why the poor were too complacent to demand fairness. They were afraid to walk into the corporate owned giant grocery stores and start taking food off the shelves, because they knew that the police worked for the corporations and the privileged as their salaries and parsimonious benefits were afforded them so they would stay loyal to the ruling class. It was their job to keep the middle class and poor in line – make them afraid and complacent.

For J.J., it was gradually becoming crystal clear that what the modern world needed was a new Che Guevara who could lead the people out of bondage. His obsequious manner had gone on for too long, and one event made him tumble off the precipice of complacency into the abyss of despair that would snap his fragile mind and lead to a cataclysmic series of actions that would make part of the world tremble in fear and the other glorify the terror of Jose Juan Martinez.

Chablis and the Terrorist
Who Resurrected the Spirit of Che Guevara

CHAPTER 2
THE NEXT INSTALMENT OF KILL A C.E.O.

How terrible is the pain of the mind and heart
When freedom is so unceremoniously suppressed.
Those who wallow in the misery of poverty
Are the most oppressed people of America.
The price they pay every day is a result
Of a system where those with the least
Are looked upon as malignant cancers
And discarded with contemptuous disregard
By a society that is itself diseased with greed.

In America's ghettos, the police are not looked upon as saviours, but rather as oppressors. They are not there to reach out with a hand of compassion and assist those who need a hand up, but rather, they are assigned the task by authorities to keep the poor and marginalized from spilling out into the wealthy suburban enclaves of exclusivity and disturbing the lifestyles of the affluent. So, all his life, being a brown-skinned man, Jose Juan had suffered the indignities of harassment by the police who were paid exorbitant salaries and furnished with parsimonious benefits to keep poor people of colour in line. Their billy-clubs and tasers were not weapons of protection for the populace in the "hood" but they were instruments of sadistic retribution meted out with dispassionate disregard for whether someone was guilty or innocent. In "the hood" you were always guilty – guilty of being poor and a person of colour. In the USA, the truth of discontent lay in that which every oppressed individual feels within himself but hasn't the courage to express. However, J.J. was about to explode with a ferocious fury that would shake the very foundations of a society that had for far too long disregarded common decency when it came to compassion.

America was filled with complacent people who refused to demand fairness and justice, because they had been so suppressed, so brainwashed in American superiority of opportunity propaganda that they had forgotten that a society that gets rid of all its troublemakers goes rapidly downhill as there is no one who will rock the boat of the status-quo which represents the moneyed interests. This was about to change, as a result of one event in the hood which would kindle the smouldering ember of discontent that had been simmering within J.J. and make those embers reignite to light a fire that would consume those obsessed with greed in a country that had simply lost its way.

J.J.'s sister, had unbeknownst to him, been fired by her employer, Kimberline Commodities Trading. Now, how the firing came about must be explained so that everything can be put in perspective.

His sister, Keita, had worked for Thomas Kimberline as a janitor for almost 10 years. She was paid slightly above minimum wage and though looked upon as an undeserving underling, and treated with general disrespect by the traders and the executives of the corporation, she felt fortunate to have a job, because the unemployment rate in her neighbourhood was almost 30%. Like most poor people of colour she suffered demeaning treatment as a condition of a system that froze out those who did the real work while rewarding those who simply shuffled papers. She jokingly said she was a paper shuffler too – she shuffled paper from the floor into trash cans.

J.J. had noticed that Keita was always sitting out on the stoop the past three nights when he came home from work. This was unusual, because she usually worked in the office building cleaning up from 6:00 PM until 2:00 AM. He sat down beside her and said, "What's up sis? You've been home the past three nights, something's up at work, right?"

Dejected and despondent, she began to cry as she said, "They replaced us all with a private subcontractor, who refused to take any of us on, because they already have enough employees and, anyway, they pay only minimum wage. Ten years I have worked hard for these people and just like that, without even two weeks notice they say, 'don't come back, we don't need your services anymore.' Why are they allowed to treat us this way? It isn't fair."

Furious, J.J. said, "They treat you that way, because they can, because the government doesn't give a damn about people like us, because business isn't about rewarding your employees for making you money, its about rewarding the stockholders, the people who sit on their asses and do nothing for their goddamn money." He got up and almost shouted, "Fuck America and fuck capitalism."

Chablis and the Terrorist
Who Resurrected the Spirit of Che Guevara

He glanced to his right and there was that mist that often appeared, and in the mist was a faint outline of a bearded man wearing fatigues and a beret. He had a cigar in his mouth a look of determination on his face. J.J. looked down at Keita and in a whisper said "Keita, look, look beside me and tell me what you see."

Keita turned as did J.J and the mist was gone. Keita said "What you mean? I don't see anything."

J.J., realizing that he must be imaging things, shook his head, turned and as he started walking into the apartment building barked, "Nothing, just my furtive imagination. Don't worry sis, those bastards will pay. Thomas Kimberline has fucked over his last employee."

Keita, almost pleading, said "You aren't going to do anything stupid?"

Very determined, as he stood in the entryway, J.J. replied "I have been doing stupid things all my life. Not anymore, I am tired of this bullshit life, this bullshit economic system, this bullshit country, this bullshit oppression we suffer day in and day out. You get freedom by letting your enemy know that you'll do anything to get your freedom; then you'll get it. It's the only way you'll get it. I know who the enemy is. It isn't the government as they are only the tool used by the wealthy and the corporations to enforce their sick, evil, lying system of greed that devours all goodness through the avaricious pursuit of more and more. C.E.O.'s and the bloodsucking vampires of commerce are the real culprits who put a price tag on everything, even human beings. Goddamn it, Jose Juan Martinez is not for sale as of right now. I am tired of bowing before the arrogant assholes that run this country with their greed based economic system that takes from the middle-class and poor to give to the rich."

J.J. walked into the building as a dumbfounded Keita sit bewildered by her brother's wild reaction to her firing. She looked at him walk down the hallway, and he seemed different in his physical appearance. There was a swagger to his stride, a bearing of determination. This was no longer the meek, mild mannered man who was just another in the countless millions of ghetto dwellers hanging on precariously to a life on the edge. That night, feeling his sister's pain, J.J. was determined to take on the cruel, inhuman system that used people as commodities by whatever means it took to show the U.S.A. and the rest of the world where greed ruled supreme that there was a big cost to pay for subjecting people to the cruelties of a system with no compassion and no heart. Hell was about to be unleashed.

Chablis Louise Chavez (pronounced Sha-blee) had no idea what was happening with J.J., as she was dealing with deep personal problems. As detailed in her previous adventure *Chablis: Avenging Angel for the Forgotten in the City of Lost Hope*, she was recovering from a bad experience with a philandering husband who had been falsely accused of murder. Having secured his release by finding the real culprit, she was now back in the private investigation business and free of the cheating bastard, returning to work as an operative and partner with her old mentor, Aaron Adams.

For those readers unfamiliar with Chablis, a bit of explaining might be necessary. This was a most unusual woman. Born in a small Mexican village, she realized at the age of 14 that her sexual prowess was a ticket out of poverty and she used it willingly. She would often, with her sheepish smile, say, "I am so good at giving blow jobs I could suck the chrome off a bumper." Perhaps she was so good, because she thoroughly enjoyed the experience, and more than the physical pleasure sex brought to her, it was the psychological effect of knowing that she had complete control over men through her sexual manipulation. She thoroughly enjoyed being a woman, and what a woman. At a mere 5:2 and 50 kilos (about 110 pounds), her long silky smooth coal black hair cascaded like a serene waterfall over her shoulders and went all the way down her back resting gracefully at her waist. She exuded an air of carefree confidence that was most noticeable in her serene alluring brown eyes outlined with a dash of mascara. Her soft face with rounded cheek bones, proportionally slim but slightly flat Asian-type nose, high trimmed brows, soft pouty ruby red lips, and rounded chin was complimented by her easy, charming smile that slowly crept across her lips and lit up a room like a bright beacon of sexual energy. Wondrous gently rolling waves of delight seemed to undulate out in playful curiosity as she mischievously giggled. There was a hint of a wild wantonness that seemed to be lingering behind those delicately fluttering eye lids that appeared to be whispering "I am hot to trot, baby."

Chablis' slightly unruly hair seemed to offer a hint that she had just enjoyed a roll in the hay with a lover. She had a soft neck and athletic broad shoulders that formed into equally lithe arms and hands. Her breasts were not the silicon enlarged variety that so often grace women today, but were perky little hills that jutted out defiantly with perpetually erect nipples that made a man want to return to infancy so that he might nurse serenely on them and coo with delight. Her midsection was toned but had a just ever so slight protrusion that was muscularly taunt like an archer's bow. Her dark brown skin gave her an exotic aura that seemed to glisten like the sun peeping over the horizon in the morning bringing the shimmering light of the coming glorious day. Her muscular thighs and calves made a man's mind run wild with fanciful thoughts of what it would be like to have them wrapped around him as she brazenly pulled him further and further into that gap in her body that was split to accommodate the male love instrument that palpitated with desire.

Oh, and this was a woman who looked as good going as she did coming. The sway of her magnificently proportioned hips was hypnotic and the perfectly shaped derriere jiggled with each stride as if begging for a man's attention. And could this woman use her ass! It was her love tool of desire as men craved to kiss it, lick it, suck on it and pound it into oblivion. It was what she affectionately called her ass-pussy, because Chablis had no real pussy. You see, Chablis was a pre-op transsexual!

The fact she was a transsexual rarely made any difference to men, as they saw in her more woman than they had ever had in their lives. At 29, she was at the very peak of her sexual attractiveness, and you just knew that this was a woman who would improve with age. What you saw now would ferment like a fine wine and only get tastier, smoother and mellower with time. She had survived the ravages of poverty, ignorance and bigotry in a small Mexican village to become a tasty Boudreaux wine made from the fine vines grown in a valley where you knew that the grapes offered sweet ambrosia of taste like nothing that had ever been on your palate before. Sipping from her nectar of desire was like a misty morning that was ready to dance with mirth and song. She was full of depth, warmth and desire with beaded bubbles bursting at the brim from which her lover might drink and leave the world unseen and fade away into the dim, peaceful, serene, ecstasy-laden forest to dwell in sweet harmony with all desire satiated from the embrace of an angel.

Chablis' physical attributes often detracted from her depth of intelligence, as she was an educated woman, having graduated from the University of Mexico City with the financial assistance of a lover who willingly took care of her, because of a deep abiding love. Yet, she had never deceived him. This

Chablis and the Terrorist
Who Resurrected the Spirit of Che Guevara

was a woman who always laid her cards on the table and never wavered in her commitment to being above board and honest in her relationships. She left Mexico for New York City, where she became an operative for Aaron Adams, New York's premiere private eye. When she married, she became a U.S. citizen, retired from her job and devoted herself to a man who thought cheating was just part of being a man. He found out the hard way that Chablis, although enjoying her beauty and sexuality to its fullest, respected her marriage vows implicitly without any reservations. His lack of respect for those vows cost him dearly, and now Chablis was free of him and once again exploring her sexual freedom with vigour.

Everyone goes through hard times at some point. Life isn't easy, and Chablis knew that, because she had struggled through poverty and bigotry to stand astride the mountain of self-respect and confidence that made her a revered and respected figure in her career and as a woman of quality and exactitude who was always reaching out with compassion to those who needed a hand up. Like her mentor, Aaron Adams, she had a soft spot for those at the bottom of the socio-economic ladder who were the victims of a cruel system based on greed. She was not afraid to stand-up to authority as she saw authority as an institutionalized way of suppressing those who dared challenge the norms of society. She saw the U.S.A. as one of the worlds most suppressed societies where people were fed a steady diet of propaganda to convince them how free they were and how lucky they were to be Americans. In fact, she knew that America was not free, and was not the guiding beacon that so many in the country thought it was. She understood that the government had been turned over to corporations carte blanche by the second worst buffoon to ever inhabit the White House, Ronald Reagan, and that there was no core left to the country. There was now an emptiness of heart and spirit that had been sacrificed at the altar of greed. Add to that an acquiescent church that was, itself, nothing more than a giant corporation of control with a steady stream of donations extracted from those who equated capitalism with Christianity and the result was a nation that was the greatest danger to peace in the world, because it saw itself as morally superior with the right to impose its will on other countries with impunity. Chablis saw through this façade of arrogant self-righteousness and never wavered in her commitment to justice that most times eluded those trapped in economic servitude.

J.J. lived in Upper Harlem, and Chablis resided and primarily worked in Lower Manhattan, but the two were actually similar in the perception they had on the way of the world. This similarity, however, would be like the distance between Lower Manhattan and Upper Harlem, a gulf that would make the earth shake as these two people went about challenging authority in two very different ways in a city where the wealthy were royalty and everyone else was a serf. The individual reader will be left to decide for himself or herself whether what J.J. did was terrorism and murder or rather just a justifiable way of trying to right wrongs that were caused by individuals who simply took no prisoners in the economic war of the mighty against the poor and discarded people when they had been used up by a system that saw people not as human beings, but as commodities.

Thomas Kimberline became an obsession with J.J. He had met him only once several years ago, but came away with the impression that he felt his family name somehow made him more important, more exalted than the average man. He had graduated from Harvard, so his intelligence was unquestionable, but upon his graduation, he immediately moved into an executive suite at his father's corporation, and began his rise among the financial elite. J.J. could not help but think of all the people he had been in university with who were just as smart, but did not have the connections or family name to start out at the top. That was what was wrong with capitalism. It had built in nepotism that rewarded people based upon family name and connections rather than on merit. President George W. Bush had derided Affirmative Action for minorities, but it was the Yale policy to give priority to the sons and daughters of alumni in admissions that got a mediocre student like him in. Affirmative Action for the wealthy was something Bush had no problem with, as his own father had used it to get in also. Equality was only a hollow word in America. It had no core to its meaning, because equality of opportunity was a farce promulgated by propagandists. It was easily swallowed by a gullible public that gobbled up patriotic tripe like it was a four course meal in a five star restaurant.

In the USA they make it easier to buy a gun than to vote. They love the 2nd Amendment almost as much as they love Jesus. These are the people who don't want a woman to own her own uterus, but she can sure own a rod to protect herself from rapists, because if she gets knocked-up, the right-to-lifers want to force her to have the baby. These blooming idiots actually think arming themselves with rifles or assault weapons is going to protect them from a tyrannical government. They believe a rifle is a match for military tanks. They live in a fantasy world where a gun and a bullet are as sacrosanct as the Holy Bible.

J.J. had never fired a gun, but as he lay in bed one night, that mist seemed to creep all around him, and a cloudy outline of a man could be discerned. A faint whisper said, "Power comes from the barrel of a gun. You change things, not with rhetoric, but with violence. The establishment uses violence, and the time honoured tradition of the revolutionary is to meet violence with violence. Those who beg for justice only get a small dose of it from the ruling class. Those who demand justice with violence to back up the rhetoric will stand victorious in the arena of hope."

J.J. knew that it was not Martin Luther King and his peaceful disobedience that had altered America, but, rather, it was the boldness of the Black Panthers and other organizations like it that forced the ruling class to offer accommodations in order to avoid a revolution in which they would lose their privileged status. Violence and the threat of violence had been the ace-in-the-hole for civil rights in America, not the meek marching hordes who sit in streets meekly begging for justice from "the man." The only justice "the man" meted out came from the end of a billy-club.

J.J. got up the next morning, went defiantly into his supervisor's office and handed in his resignation with a bold, brazen statement. "Mr. Caruthers, in the words of an old country boy, take this job and shove it."

Take this job and shove it
I ain't workin' here no more
I'm tired of working for no reward.
I can't even afford a used Ford.
I wonder what I'm working for.
Watch me walk out that door.

You better not try to stand in my way,
Cause I only got one thing to say.
I do all the work while you sit and read.
Just cause your uncle got you the job,
They pay you so much more.
Yeah, I'm walking out that door.

Been working here now for five long years,
Every day I go home and drown myself in tears.
Lots of good folks just like me are slaving away,
But others get the rewards at the end of the day.
And all I have is more bills piling high.
Hell, they even charge you when you die!

Chablis and the Terrorist
Who Resurrected the Spirit of Che Guevara

I've been waiting to get the guts to say:
Take this job and shove it.
I ain't working here no more.
Mess with me man and I'll have a fit
Take this job and shove it.
I ain't working her no more.

The bosses get their jobs by nepotism,
But each and everyone is a goddamn fool.
They prance around with noses in the air.
They think they are so damn cool.
I'll look at 'um and say, "Take this job and shove it.
I ain't working here no more."

For the first time in his life, Jose Juan Martinez felt genuinely free. Actually, more than free – he was genuinely alive for the first time with a purpose, a cause.

He had perkiness to his stride and a swagger like a cowboy in a western movie going out to face someone in a shoot-out at high noon. J.J., also, for the first time, genuinely felt like a man. He had no fear of anybody or anything. People on the streets stared in wonderment as he passed them by with an intense look of determination that said, "Don't fuck with me."

His first stop was the Oliphant Gun Shop, but thanks to a modicum of intelligence, even when a Republican was mayor, New York City did not just hand out guns like so many other places. The owner was willing to sell him whatever he wanted, but there was a three day waiting period. Realizing registration meant the gun would be easily traceable, J.J. elected to go to another state to buy the guns he needed. He rented a car and headed to Delaware, where rifles were readily available with no waiting period and no background checks. Like most other states, the rights of gun owners precluded the rights of the victims of gun violence. Delaware was home to corporations because they had no corporate tax, and neither did they worry about the proliferation of guns, as it was every Americans God-give right to be "packing."

Delaware required no permit to purchase rifles and shotguns? No registration or permits required to own or carry them. And the same applied to handguns. Yeah, thought J.J., you often wondered what Americans loved more, Jesus or guns. Hell, if Jesus had just been packing an AK 47, he could have blown away Pontius Pilot and the rest of those bastards who crucified him. It wasn't America and apple pie. It was America and guns. Rather than the eagle, they should have had a machine gun as the national symbol.

J.J. bought the kind of firepower that would rattle the establishment and bring terror to a nation that had been exporting terror for its entire history. Like the Canadians who came down after the Plains of Abraham victory over the Americans in Ontario in 1814 and burned the White House as repayment for invading Canada, J.J. was about to lay siege to a nation that had simply pissed him off for the last time. Only this would be the most unique act of terrorism ever devised and it was all courtesy of

Chablis and the Terrorist
Who Resurrected the Spirit of Che Guevara

Che Guevara, whose rhetoric of revolutionary hope was now playing in J.J.'s head like a sweet melody of retribution for all the ills perpetrated by a select group of capitalists who thought money, power and position made them above the law. They might be above the U.S. law, but they were not above J.J.'s law.

Going to 12 different gun shops, J.J. was amassing enough weapons to serve his needs. In the trunk of the car were weapons that Americans thought were necessary to keep themselves safe, but in their idiotic concerns with 2nd Amendment rights they were actually making it possible for almost anyone to walk in and buy weapons that could be used to wreck havoc on a society that valued guns more than people.

He stopped in the New Jersey marshlands on the way back to Manhattan. In a desolate area off the beaten path, as the sun came up over the horizon, he was busy sawing off the barrels of several shotguns. He had learned on-line how to convert high-powered rifles from semi-automatic to fully automatic. He also filed down the fine site of four Hogan semi-automatic sniper rifles that were, according to accomplished assassins, the best long distance killing machine available over the counter that with proper ammunition can almost make a chest explode from a distance of 1 kilometre (6/10's of a mile). The massive barrel was a bit heavy but at 6:2 and 90 kilos (about 190 pounds) J.J. had the upper body strength and arm extension to easily shoulder the weapon .

Chablis and the Terrorist
Who Resurrected the Spirit of Che Guevara

J.J. rented a nearby hotel in the marshlands and for three days he intensely practiced shooting the various weapons. He got so good with the Hogan that he could hit a watermelon from 1 kilometre away. He returned to Manhattan and stored the weapons in a Lock and Leave facility in Yonkers. He used a fake ID to buy a 1997 Ford Crown Victoria and began to plan the murder of Thomas Kimberline.

His mother and sister were surprised when he told them he had quit his job, but he explained that he had a job with a firm in Connecticut, and that he would be driving up to Westchester daily for work. He was going to Westchester alright, but he had plans to work only one day. He was going to rob the Connecticut National Bank to finance his upcoming killing spree that would not be as catastrophic as 9/11 in numbers, but it would be even more damaging, because he was going to kill the rich, the powerful and the well-connected. The idea had come to him when Thomas Kimberline had fired Keita. It was something that Che Guevara had written in 1963: *"America's imperialism will not be halted by killing the President. It will not be stayed by killing congressmen or senators. It will not be abridged by the killing of any government official, because they are only the mechanisms used to carry out the policies of the ruling class. You strike at the heart of American imperialism by killing the presidents of Exxon, Mobil, Lockheed, General Dynamics and the rest of the bottom feeders who gorge on taxpayer funded defence contracts to spread their insidious evil that binds the Third*

Chablis and the Terrorist
Who Resurrected the Spirit of Che Guevara

World in slavery to the fat cats of greed. After you finish with them, next on the list should be the barons of Wall Street who worship money as their God and expect the rest of the world to humbly beg for a crumb from their table of plenty."

Thomas Kimberline was not a billionaire, nor a defence contractor, but he was an immensely rich commodities trader who made money betting on both success and failure. The reason you paid more for food was because he was a middle man who got his cut without ever producing anything but paper to scribble down the bids. Like the bankers and hedge fund managers who crashed the economy with the willing acquiescence of the Bush Administration in the early 2000's, he was one of those who could, with impunity, steal and laugh all the way to the bank. Rob a 7/11 of $50 to put food on your family's table and you were shipped off to the slammer for 10 to 20 years. Rob people of their life savings to put billions in your pocket and you were fined. Steal 100 million and they will fine you 50 million while you are relaxing on your yacht in the Mediterranean. Now that is rich man's justice, American style! Well, Thomas Kimberline was about to get a special kind of justice, not just for the money he stole daily, but for the indignities he perpetrated on those who toiled for him in obscurity so that he could live a life of luxury in a gated estate walled off from the riff-raff. He was about to reap what he had sowed.

Each day Kimberline rode from his home in Westchester to his posh offices in Manhattan. In his

Chablis and the Terrorist
Who Resurrected the Spirit of Che Guevara

chauffeur driven limousine, he passed on the periphery of some of America's worst slums to which he was oblivious, because he had his tinted windows rolled up as the air conditioning whirred while he read the Wall Street Journal to see how much money he made on stocks the previous day while he sat on his fat ass in a $5000 Corinthian leather chair admiring the Picasso original he had hanging on the wall across from his leather trimmed, gold-plated desk. If he was a little more frugal about the 2 million dollars he spent remodelling his office that money could have gone to the people who toiled in obscurity to make him rich. They did the work. He did the counting of the money.

As J.J. was contemplating his assault, he began to develop a historical perspective, realizing that people who thought they were either social or economic royalty or both, assumed their blood line would continue ad infinitum as they assured their progeny a place at the table of plenty just because of whom their parents were. The royal leeches of England had been guaranteed an exalted status for hundreds of years and the ignorant masses lined up to cheer and wave with adulation as the royal carriage carrying the snobbish blue bloods passed by them. People had actually been propagandized into believing that somehow royalty was actually better than they were.

When the Bolsheviks overthrew the Tsar, they did not stop at killing him, they killed his wife and children to assure that the bloodline was wiped out, and that there would be no returning to the days when so-called royalty would rule by right of birth. They ended, for once and all, any possibility of a return to rule by right of inheritance. Furthermore, in a bold move to assure that the rich could not assume power under any other auspices, they confiscated the wealth and redistributed it fairly to the masses. Every man was now a capitalist and could share in the bounty, rather than all the proceeds going to those at the top of the economic ladder. Those who did the work were rewarded, not those who made fortunes on the backs of others.

Yes, thought J.J., most of the offspring of the rich were arrogant usurpers who felt entitled. George Bush II, thought by virtue of his father being President and his grandfather being a Senator that he, by right of his royal blood, was entitled to the presidency. Even the majority of blue bloods on the Supreme Court felt the same way, so they handed the election to royalty rather than to the poor guy. Of course, no politician is really poor, as exorbitant pay and parsimonious benefits assured they would be taken care of by the taxpayers the rest of their lives. Welfare for the poor was a waste of taxpayer dollars, but lavish benefits, perks and retirement were acceptable, if it went to those at the top. All paid for by those at the bottom.

Should he or shouldn't he contemplated J.J. Was it right to kill the offspring of those at the top? He could justify killing those at the top, but if the children were young, he simply could not bring himself to do as the Bolsheviks had done. No, they would be spared his wrath. He would not kill innocent children, who, though no fault of their own, happen to be born into wealth. Perhaps, seeing what their parents had reaped would make them realize there was a better way. Yes, for now, he would spare the children.

Thomas Kimberline was just a practice run. He would be the first to fall and J.J. would find that Kimberline would make it possible to forget about robbing the bank. J.J. kept the Crown Victoria parked on a nearby street. He had been to Lock and Leave facility and removed the Hogan. However, that would only be a back-up, because he wanted to kill Kimberline close up and personal. He wanted him to know that he was not being killed just for his merciless stealing from the poor and middle class, but for what he did to his employees. This was not just about retribution for economic sins, but for the sins of indifference when it came to employees. Yeah, thought J.J., most companies had stopped calling the workers employees, and started using the more benign term, associates. That way, the public, and the employees, were supposed to actually believe that it was a cooperative effort where everyone was respected and treated with dignity. That everyone was a key part of the team and that everyone was more than just a commodity to be used by the corporation. It was just another brilliant marketing move that guaranteed subservience from those who really did the work.

J.J. knew the truth and the truth was not pretty. Associates or employees, it was all the same. In the end, everyone in the corporation, even the customers who thought they could buy happiness neatly packaged to satisfy their whims for that which was promoted as a necessity, were all slaves, slaves to the bottom lines of corporations that controlled people's lives, and the fools willingly lined up for their chains and shackles.

People had been so brainwashed that they actually believed they had a choice when the went into a store, but they failed to realize that their choices were basically only two or three, as all the brand names were owned by the same corporation which had gradually gobbled up the little guys until they controlled the market. The same corporation sold several brands to fool the consumer into thinking he or she actually had a choice and that there was competition. Competition had been killed long ago when Ronald Reagan, as President, green lighted mega-mergers so a few large companies could create monopolies. In America, free enterprise had been dead for a long time. It had been killed and buried, and people didn't even realize it, so complacent were they as they sat in front of their giant screen televisions watching the mundane pabulum that passed as entertainment. Sure, they had 350 channels, but 350 channels of junk is still junk. Well, J.J. was about to give the masses some real entertainment, and like 9/11, people would be glued to their televisions, waiting for the next instalment of *Kill a C.E.O.*

CHAPTER 3
PRISONERS OF THEIR OWN MINDS

Fate is a silent hunter
that perches in the dark.
On each individual
it leaves its mark.

It's calling when least expected,
and may cut you in two.
Do you even know when
it is whispering to you?

Take it to the real world,
then break it in half.
Just roll life's dice
and that will suffice.

Sense it in your heart.
Don't take it for granted.
On a precipice you stand.
It will use you if it can.

When fate comes calling,
what can you do?
When fate comes calling,
what can you do?

Chablis Louis Chavez's high heels clicked a tune of morning mirth as she nonchalantly walked into Aaron Adams Investigations, said a casual hello to Myrna, the secretary, and asked, "Is the sultan of investigations, the sheik of shylocks and the potentate of peepers in yet?"

Chablis and the Terrorist
Who Resurrected the Spirit of Che Guevara

Smiling, Myrna replied "He's in and pissed about the Myerson case, so watch out."

Chablis winked at her, gave her the thumps up and didn't bother to knock on Aaron's door. She strolled in with that swagger that always disarmed men and got their hearts to palpitating as they gazed upon a woman who was so cool she could disarm a bomb while giving a blow job. She eased into the chair across from Aaron's 1940's style oak desk, crossed her legs seductively to show a bit of upper thigh because of her short skirt and lit up the room with that slow, gradual smile that crept across her lips as her eyes twinkled mischievously.

Aaron, who had been intimate with Chablis once but knew that would be the only time, was still not immune to enjoying her seductive machinations that were always distracting. He smiled at her, eased back in his chair, rocked back and forth a bit, licked his lower lip slightly as she gave him a wink and in almost a whisper said "Morning boss. I hear you are a bit perturbed. If I wasn't such a lady I would crawl under the desk and give you a blow job to relax you and get your mind of your troubles."

"Chablis, you are all talk and no action with me. You gave it to me once just to see how I would react to sex with a transsexual. You are more tease than action with me, and we both know it."

Chablis let out a little chuckle and said, "I like to make you older men squirm. It gets me off. Why I am almost squirting right now."

Chablis and the Terrorist
Who Resurrected the Spirit of Che Guevara

Aaron got up, walked over to the window, stared out at the street for a couple of seconds, turned and barked at her. "Cut the crap and tell me what you found out about Myerson yesterday. I hit a brick wall."

Chablis, feeling playful, replied "Why a brick wall is not a barrier. It is just a temporary hindrance. You can go over it, crawl under it or go around it. I simply went down to Myerson's Wall Street office and asked to see him on some important business. I said I was a techie with an IPO I wanted him to handle. Fortunately, he had a male secretary, so I flashed a little tit, wiggled my ass nicely, gave him that come-hither look and just like that," she snapped her fingers, "I was in Myerson's office."

She uncrossed her gorgeous shapely legs, took a deep breath and said, "Hey, maybe you need sex reassignment surgery. It would make things a lot easier for you. Men are such ninnies. They are, well, except for the gay ones that is, easily manipulated with a wiggle, a little thigh, some cleavage and a bit of sexual innuendo. You all think with your dicks."

"OK Chablis. We all know how stupid men are when it comes to tits and ass. Get to the point. What did you learn?"

"The guy is a gold-plated, arrogant, bombastic jerk who steals people's life's savings with no compunction at all. He thinks it's funny that he got slapped with a 28 million dollar fine when he stole nearly 100 million. I laid out an elaborate plan for raking in 50 million, and while he was ogling my tits, he was telling me how we could make it 100 million of which he would, of course, take 40%. He said there were ways to make the, as it put it, stupid morons who are always looking for get rich quick schemes to take the bite out of the apple and swallow the worm."

"So, our client wants proof that Myerson is a charlatan. How close are we to proving his intentions? Your word that he intends to fleece somebody is not good enough to go into court with."

Chablis, her playful nature set aside now, replied "Not close at all. This guy is good, so good he covers his tracks extremely well. When he was talking about fleecing people, he did it in a creative way to mask any outright statement that we would steal from people, and he always moved over toward the window, far away from me just in case I had a recording device. I used the name Charlotte Rampling, but I am sure he will check it and see she is an English actress from the 70's and 80's, so my cover is blown. I got nothing on the recorder that he said in an incriminating fashion." She reached in her purse and took out the nickel size device and tossed it on Aaron's desk and continued, "There you go. It's nothing concrete but file it away. I will work an angle, don't worry. I am nailing this son-of-a-bitch."

Aaron smiled and said, "Of course you will."

Chablis and the Terrorist
Who Resurrected the Spirit of Che Guevara

Chablis winked at him and asked if he wanted to go down to Willie's in the lobby for lunch. Shaking his head, Aaron replied, "Not today little girl. I have a meeting with the Merchants Council. Looks like we are getting some background checks thrown our way."

"Pays the rent," she said as she moved over to the less than tidily dressed Aaron, brushed off his coat and straightened his tie.

She turned and as she walked out the door, her magnificent ass swaying provocatively, Aaron thought to himself "that woman looks just as good going as she does coming. Damn, what an incredible ass and her cheeks swivel like hot buttered toast tantalizing your taste buds. That was one hell of a woman!"

There is an old saying, especially by those prone to religious pronouncements' that things happen for a reason. Yeah, maybe so. Maybe God, if you believed in him, does have a plan, but he, as Chablis always said, "Sure has a damned weird ass way of implementing it."

We are not here to debate whether there is a God or not, nor are we going to discuss the role of fate. However, it must be said that there are certain times in everyone's life when all the stars of heaven above seem to be absolutely perfectly aligned, and the fact Aaron had an appointment, and the fact that Chablis came in late that morning, all seemed to point to perfect timing for the clear skies of chance to be but throbs of opportunity timed to a common pulse.

Walking down the two flights of stairs, Chablis was reflecting on the enormity of Myerson's crimes that had placed people's futures in jeopardy because of his greed. An elderly couple who hired Aaron and Chablis had invested nearly $400,000 with him, their entire life savings. They were, themselves, afflicted with greed, but at 75, all they wanted was to leave their children a legacy of financial hope. So, it was not greed for themselves that made them trust Myerson with their money, but greed to provide for those they loved who lived in a country where no help, no compassion, no fairness prevailed. You either looked out for yourself or no one else would. Government was not there to protect the average person. It was there to do what it always did, protect the wealthy, the corporations and the privileged. So, because of inane government polices and corporate selfishness that cut benefits for the middle class and poor, they felt compelled to gamble their savings to help secure some modicum of financial security for their two children after they were gone. There were no more fair pensions as a result of labour unions being destroyed, and there was no hope for a secure old age, because government had sold out to corporations, increased the retirement age, all while continuing to provide lavish salaries for politicians, parsimonious benefits and outlandish retirement.

All things considered, despite her most recent flirtation with misery when her husband had cheated on her, been accused of murder, been freed by Chablis' stellar detective work and dumped the minute he was free, and then her boyfriend was now up the river doing time, this would be the most momentous day of her life. Why it should be so styled is not at once apparent. Chablis had made her way out of poverty, managed to fight the bigotry of those who somehow thought religion should trump her right to be who she wanted to be and was a resounding success in the profession she had wanted to be in since she was a child.

On this afternoon as she sat down at the corner booth in the coffee shop, she noticed a good looking man of maybe 30 in the booth next to hers looking over at her. Now, she was used to men staring at her, and freely admitted to liking it, but this man seemed special. There was a certain aura about him that appeared to give him an almost celestial glow. Hell she thought, "If this is Jesus, I might get religion!"

In the dull, dingy, severe-looking quarters of the old coffee shop romance was not commonplace, but Chablis felt a slight erection between her legs and an obvious palpitation of her heart. She smiled and said to him, "You could see me better if you came over and joined me."

There was a determined manner in his stride as he walked over smiling, sat down and said, "I suppose you are used to men staring at you. I beg your pardon, but I am sure you know that you are an extraordinarily beautiful woman. Sincerely, I do want to say I am sorry, but the truth is that I am not. I simply could not help myself."

Smiling provocatively, Chablis said, "Well, if you knew a little secret I have, you might not be so enthralled. I am not a perfect specimen of a woman you know."

The man, very deliberately said, "Don't tell me you are a man."

Still smiling, Chablis said "No, I am not a man, but I do have male genitals."

The man's eyes glistened a bit and he sighed. "Well, I am a reasonably educated man, and I am familiar with gender dysphasia, so I understand that you have a birth defect. Hey, I am not perfect either." The he laughed and continued, "I know you look at this virile looking, handsome, suave, debonair man and think he is perfect, but I do have my physical flaws."

They both laughed and Chablis extended her hand and said, "Chablis Louise Chavez. Please to meet you Mr.......?"

"Rodrigo Rodriquez, pleased to meet you."

They shook hands across the table, and although Chablis generally preferred her sex partners cut, and she suspected this man wasn't because he was obviously Puerto Rican, she still felt a strong physical attraction to him.

Chablis and the Terrorist
Who Resurrected the Spirit of Che Guevara

Rodrigo, articulate and precise with his diction said, "I know you Ms. Chavez."

Chablis immediately said, "Chablis, please."

"Sure, Chablis. You are actually a very famous person here in the city. I thought I had seen you before. I must say that I was enthralled by your last case, where you freed your, I assume since there is no ring on your finger, now ex-husband from prison on a bum rap when he was accused of killing that woman with whom he was cheating. Damn fool man I might add – cheating on a woman like you."

"Right on both accounts; he is now my ex-husband and he certainly was a fool."

They shared mutual laughter. Now, it would behove the reader to bear in mind that a lever, insignificant in itself, switches an express train off one track on to another. In a like manner a very insignificant interlude switched Chablis off from the tracks of an ordinary work-a-day mortal into a woman who was about to become part of an elaborate plan to make America's captains of finance pay the ultimate price for the greed which they had allowed to rule their lives; and thereby, to ruin the lives of others in the process.

You see, into this café walked none other than Bob Myerson who spotted Chablis right away, walked over and said, without even looking at Rodrigo, "So, nice little play bitch. I know who you are and what you are up to."

Chablis and the Terrorist
Who Resurrected the Spirit of Che Guevara

Rodrigo very calmly placed his hand on the sleeve of Myerson's $3000 dark brown suit and said, as Myerson turned toward him, "This lady can obviously take care of herself. However, I am not prone to sitting idly by and having a man call a woman with whom I am conversing a bitch. If you prefer to exit this place with all your teeth, I suggest you turn around and walk out that door now. I am asking you very politely, but I am only asking once."

Chablis, who was more than capable of taking care of herself, was nonetheless, impressed with the calm but forceful manner in which Rodrigo was handling the situation. She immediately knew that through his sophisticated calm exterior beat the heart of a lion. He was not a man you wanted to mess with.

Myerson, lowered his head, took a deep breath and left with a look of fear on his face. He might have been a match for any man on the floor of the stock exchange when dealing with matters of finance, but he was no match for a man as physically capable as Rodrigo.

Chablis, in a cursory manner, explained the story behind Myerson, and found Rodrigo a genuinely astute individual when it came to comprehending the way America worked for the benefit of the few at the expense of the many. One thing he said made Chablis think this was a man with a heart. He, with emotion, said, "You know, someone needs to really bring down all these arrogant financial manipulators and make them pay for their malicious disregard for fairness. It all started with Ronald Reagan's destruction of the unions and turning the country over to banks and corporate thief's, and reached its apex with Bush and Cheney who should have been prosecuted for war crimes as well as financial chicanery. There is no justice in this country, none whatsoever."

Chablis, a strong adherent of fair-play was impressed with Rodrigo's passion for justice. "So, you want to round up the peasants and lead an assault on the White House?"

"Hey, the Canadians were successful back in 1814. Burned the thing down as repayment for America invading Canada. If a few more countries would have the courage to take a stand against the tyranny of greed and self-righteousness, this nation might think twice about sticking its nose into other people's business."

Chablis, impressed with his passion, smiled and offered an observation. "Your passion is admirable, but we live in an era when people have been brainwashed into flag-waving hysteria rather than using logic and common sense."

Rodrigo smiled and replied, "Chablis, why don't we use some common sense and make a dinner date. I can assure you that I will be a gentleman."

Chablis, smiling broadly, replied, "Well, as long as you don't let that gentlemanly thing go too far."

Chablis and the Terrorist
Who Resurrected the Spirit of Che Guevara

He laughed and said "Well, I will let you control when you want me to stop being a gentleman."

"OK, how does 8:00PM sound? I'm in the Lower Eastside. 4385 Minerva, Apartment C on Floor 3, near Washington Square. You know it?"

"I do, see you tonight."

He got up, and as he walked out he stopped at the door, turned and waved good-bye, and Chablis observed his determined swagger that indicated not arrogance, but confidence. This was a man of no pretentions whatsoever, and he had an air about him that simply indicated he was fair and just, but that crossing him was not a good idea. She shook herself just a bit while an anticipatory tingle coursed through her body as she thought about what lovemaking would be like with him. She wondered what he did for a living.

This was a fascinating man thought Chablis. He stood a good 6 feet 2 and his upper body was not muscular, but he had definitely been an athlete at one time.

Thomas Kimberline was on the FDR Expressway going to a meeting and he noticed an old Ford Crown Victoria seemingly keeping pace with him as his chauffeur cruised along at 100 Kilometres an hour (about 62 mph). J.J. looked over at him and smiled. It was a sinister smile and Kimberline felt a cold chill as J.J. eased off the accelerator and fell in behind the Mercedes Limo, slowly dropping further back but not losing sight of him. As they exited at East 34ᵗʰ Street, J.J. followed at a reasonable distance. They pulled into a parking garage at Fulton, and J.J. waited patiently for them to park. Kimberline got out, walked in the building and the chauffeur waited.

J.J. was a man of many talents, and he had studied theatre in undergraduate school, entertaining thoughts for awhile of being an actor. He was a master at makeup, not just the kind that was used on the stage, but the kind that could completely mask your identity with a rubberized face. He had put a portable air conditioner in his Lock and Leave storage unit and had spent three hours preparing for the role of his life. He was now going to be an assassin.

He walked up to the limo and tapped on the window. As the driver rolled it down the soft whir of the power window mechanism just reminded J.J. that everything connected to the rich had that special look, and along with the look, even sound was somehow better modulated, almost as if it was a whisper saying "look, even the sounds around me speak of affluence."

J.J., noticed the Smith and Wesson M&P 40 felt warm and snug with his hand wrapped around it in his coat pocket. For a second, he could understand the euphoric power gun-lovers felt with a gun in their hands. You had the power of life and death. It was almost like smoking, there were little neurons firing in the brain giving you a subdued high.

Chablis and the Terrorist
Who Resurrected the Spirit of Che Guevara

He very carefully pulled the gun from his pocket as he said to the chauffeur who had a quizzical look on his face, "how is it going?"

Still with a puzzled look, he responded, "Fine, fine. What can I do for you?"

J.J. slowly pulled the gun from his pocket, levelled it at him and said, "It is what I can do for you that counts, my friend" as he cut his eyes downward toward the gun, he continued "and I want to get in the back seat. Unlock the door."

Visibly shaken, a sudden snap indicated the back door was unlocked. J.J. slowly opened the door, all the time keeping the gun levelled at the chauffeur. He slid in the back seat, reached over with his left hand and padded the chest of the chauffeur. He reached inside and pulled out a gun and tossed it on the floor of the backseat. "So, you ever use that thing?"

"No, it makes Kimberline feel safer knowing I have it. I ain't no bodyguard man, just a chauffeur who packs because his boss wants him to pack. Whatever you want – take. I got a few dollars. That's all."

J.J. leaned slightly forward as the driver kept looking straight ahead. "I don't want your money. I want justice."

The driver, his voice quivering, replied "I haven't done anything man. I'm just a chauffeur."

Chablis and the Terrorist
Who Resurrected the Spirit of Che Guevara

"Put your hands on the wheel."

J.J. reached into his pocket and brought out a pair of hand cuffs. He handed them to the chauffeur and had him handcuff himself to the steering wheel. He eased back into his seat and said very calmly, almost as if they were just having a casual conversation, "So, is Myerson a nice guy to work for?"

His voice really quivering now, he replied "He's an asshole, but I make good money for a poor man. Man, I got a wife and two kids. Please."

"Don't worry, I'm not going to hurt you. Unfortunately, you'll be out of a job in a few minutes, because I'm killing Kimberline. I apologize for putting you in the unemployment line, but the few jobs Kimberline gives people aren't worth the price his victims of deceit have to pay. I am going to deliver the justice today that our government should have delivered long ago."

Shaking his head as he looked in the rear view mirror, the driver said, "I'm a survivor man. You got a grudge against the son-of-a-bitch, then kill the asshole. He has been fucking over people for years and laughing about it. I am not going to interfere. I am just another one of his fucking slaves. I work for him, because I ain't educated and can't always get the best job. I make $800 a week, and for me that is good money, but is still poverty wages here in New York City. If things were fair, "I'd be making twice that. So pop the bastard. I don't give a damn."

Chablis and the Terrorist
Who Resurrected the Spirit of Che Guevara

J.J. leaned forward and said, "I'll pop him alright, and he'll know why. I hope you stay mellow man, because I don't want him tipped off when he gets here. The dark tint on the windows will keep him from seeing me, so just be cool."

"Yeah, but if I don't open the door for him, he'll know something's up. He expects to be treated like those arrogant royal leeches in England. The asshole hasn't opened a car door in years."

J.J. knew life was a gamble, so he reached over the seat and handed the driver the handcuff keys. "Unlock yourself, and open the door for him. Then walk inside the building. By the time you call the cops, I'll be gone. If you are messing with me, you'll be dead, too."

As he unlocked the cuffs, he said, "Not messing with you man. I figure you for a righteous dude who is just repaying Kimberline for ripping you or somebody you know off. This is the kind of justice these guys should be getting from the government, but all they get is a slap on the wrists, and they laugh all the way to the bank." Just as he finished, he saw Kimberline coming their way and said, "Here he comes. I'm cool man. I'll give you 10 minutes before I call the cops. Good luck."

J.J. simply said, "Thanks, and the same to you."

The chauffeur got out, opened the backdoor and Kimberline stood in shock as he looked down at J.J., gun levelled at his midsection in a manner that seemed to intonate it was an instrument of retribution. The chauffeur said, "You've had it coming asshole. I hope you suffer before you die." He then looked at J.J. and said, "Adios amigo."

As the chauffeur very casually walked out of the parking garage, J.J. just stared at Kimberline who was standing there shivering with fear. In a quivering voice, Kimberline said, "I got plenty of money. Name your price"

J.J. showing no emotion, replied, "There is no price on dignity Kimberline. There are some people left who can't be bought. I'm one of them." He motioned for him to get out. "One day, the few of us left will band together and bring down people like you once and for all. I am punching your ticket today for many reasons and for many people, but especially for my sister Keita, whom you don't even know and for the millions of Keita's who make people like you rich while they wallow in poverty. This is day one of retribution for the sins of greed."

He pulled the trigger and was surprised at how muffled the sound was in the concrete structure. It was just a little pop, like someone opened a can of soda. Kimberline grabbed his stomach, desperately trying to hold his insides in. He dropped to the concrete floor and J.J. slid out of the car, looked down at him and said, "That pain is nothing compared to the pain you have caused."

Kimberline looked up at him pleading with his eyes. J.J. had no sympathy and no regrets as he said,

Chablis and the Terrorist
Who Resurrected the Spirit of Che Guevara

"That's it Kimberline. You're a dead man, and guess what. I am killing your wife, your children and anybody else who might inherit your ill-gotten gains. Go to hell thinking about that, thinking about how your greed destroyed your entire family. Remember, justice cannot be for one side alone, but for all sides. Today the other side wins, not you."

"This is justice," he said as he aimed the gun at his head, pulled the trigger and brains splattered all over the garage floor, even against the concrete column a few feet away. J.J. strolled over to his car and thought to himself, "that is pretty good. *Justice cannot be for one side alone, but for all sides.* Yeah, I think I'll send that to the *New York Times.*"

J.J. felt no remorse whatsoever. In fact, he felt exhilarated, as if he had struck a mighty blow for justice. He looked to his right and he saw a faint image of that same man who had so often appeared to him in a mist.

He drove out of the parking garage singing "Rock of ages, cleft for me, let me hide myself in thee."

Donald Beckman was a young reporter who felt privileged to be working at the *New York Times.* The day following the murder of Kimberline, Donald was sitting at his desk, waiting patiently for his next assignment. His boss, Harry Roberts, who was the City Editor, told him to pick up the morning mail and go through it. As he did, he noticed one envelope that caught his attention, as the return address was so unusual:

Chablis and the Terrorist
Who Resurrected the Spirit of Che Guevara

FROM:

The Spirit of Che Guevara
#1 Avenue of Redemption
Sitting Things Straight, USA

He looked at for awhile, holding it up in his hands in front of the desk lamp. He shouted to Harry Roberts, "Got something that might be big here I think Harry."

Harry walked over, looked down at Donald and said, "Open the damn thing boy and stop staring at it."

Donald gently picked up the letter opener and inserted it, tearing it neatly along the top seam. He took out a three page letter and Harry sat beside him. They both began to read:

THE CHE GUVEARA MANIFESTO

Let all men and women of America know that the spirit of Che Guevara has been resurrected and justice is about to be meted out to the 1% who have gorged at the table of plenty far too long while disregarding the plight of those at the bottom of the economic ladder. The people at the bottom have been ignored by an uncaring government and beaten down for so long that they have lost the will to fight and demand justice. They now accept their fate as the government serves the interests of those at the top while ignoring the people who beg for a crumb from the table of plenty. I, the risen spirit of

Chablis and the Terrorist
Who Resurrected the Spirit of Che Guevara

Che Guevara will rectify this by doing the following:

1. *Be warned tyrants of commerce who accumulate wealth without sharing it with those who toil in despair for you. Your ruthless disregard for decency and fairness has been duly noted. Your worship at the altar of greed will finally make you reap what you have sown. Your day of reckoning is at hand. You will not be safe in your luxuriously appointed office. You will not be secure in your splendorous mansion in a guarded and gated community. You will not be immune from my wrath, although you are protected by bodyguards. Wherever you go or whatever you do always look over your shoulder, because retribution and divine vengeance for your misdeeds are close behind you. When you least expect it, the angel of retribution will appear with the sharp sword of vengeance to cut out the heart of evil that beats within your breast. Be aware that I shall not halt the punishment for your misdeeds with just you, because like the Bolsheviks who slew the Tsar's family, I see the need to wipe out your evil seed; otherwise, your evil will be maintained in perpetuity through nepotism that assures your progeny will continue your despotic economic chicanery.*

2. *To those who treat employees with dignity, and share your bounty graciously, I say to*

you that no harm shall befall you from the Spirit of Che. You know who you are, and I wish you to sleep well knowing that you are doing the right thing and shall be justly rewarded with continued life for you and your loved ones. However, be it proclaimed that the day will come when all will equally share in the bounty of this nation, so be prepared to give up your luxury, too, because as long as one man hungers, no man is entitled to accumulate too much. Until all have shelter, sustenance, healthcare and any other necessity for a good and fruitful life no one should accumulate more than they need. You, too, must prepare for the day when all men and women in this nation will truly be free and equal. There will always be adequate room for the especially talented at the top, but you shall not be afforded exalted status, not allowed to store up excess at the expense of others.

3. *Now, for those elected representatives who use their positions to serve the privileged, be forewarned, though the captains of industry are to be brought before the bar of my justice first, you are also on my list. Start now to do what you were elected to do and you may escape my wrath. Continue to put money in the pockets of weapons makers to prosecute wars of conquest all across the globe while ignoring the hungry, the sick, the homeless and the persecuted in this nation, and you, too, shall reap what you sow. Put an end to*

your excessive salaries, lavish retirement and parsimonious benefits. Close the revolving door between government and business, pass tax laws that are equitable by making the rich pay their fair share and you may escape my wrath; otherwise, you, too, should always be looking over your shoulders for the avenging angel.

4. *To church leaders who support war and sanction the aggrandizement of greed, I say that you, too, must be vigilant. Do not use God to accumulate wealth for yourself and the hierarchy that runs religion. Use the money to lift up, not tear down. Avoid finger pointing as you remember what Jesus said, "Let he who is without sin cast the first stone." I shall give you time to make the necessary adjustments to rectify your drift into sanctifying the culture of greed and justifying poverty, war and a host of abominations that you perpetrate in the name of God. I have no religion, but that does not make me unholy. I see suffering and try to heal it. I see war and try to stop it, and I see evil and confront it. It is your duty, as sworn servants of the one you call "the Prince of Peace" to do the same. See that you do, or you will also face the wrath of the avenging angel of justice.*

5. *I regret that things have gotten to point that these actions must be taken, but a nation that decries torture while it practices torture, a*

Chablis and the Terrorist
Who Resurrected the Spirit of Che Guevara

nation that preaches equality while promoting inequality, A nation that calls itself god-fearing while committing acts of barbarity must be made to look within and see its own darkness. Hypocrisy was built into America from the start when its founders put in the phrase that all men were created equal while all but one of them were slaveholders. I say to all Americans that until you confront the hypocrisy and lies that enslave you this nation is doomed.

These are not idle threats that I am making, as by now you are aware of the execution of Thomas Kimberline. He is a relatively minor irritant in the grand scheme of things, but he is only the first of many who will fall. I am giving the C.E.O.'s of America two weeks to change things by asserting their intentions to do the right thing.

Be it further understood that I am exacting revenge for all the wrongs suffered by the downtrodden, those oppressed by a cruel, inhuman economic system that enslaves the many to the few. Revenge is an act of passion, and sometimes vengeance is the only avenue of justice available to the powerless. I am revenging injuries that have gone untreated for far too long. Be warned and be prepared, for the swift sword of justice is about to swing a mighty blow against oppression. Remember that justice cannot be for one side alone, but for all sides.

Sincerely, The Spirit of Che Guevara

Chablis and the Terrorist
Who Resurrected the Spirit of Che Guevara

By the time Donald and Harry had finished, others had gathered around the desk and were enthralled by what they were reading. A cub reportrer said, "Damn, this dude is taking no prisoners. You think he is serious?"

Not answering, all Harry Roberts said was, "Donald, run this upstairs. See if they want to go with it in the next edition?"

As he started to leave, his phone rang. "Hello, city desk section, can I help you?" A look of shock came over Donald's face. He covered the speaker part of the phone and whispered, "It's him. It's the guy calling himself the *Spirit of Che Guevara.*"

"Put it on speaker phone," barked Harry.

"To whom am I speaking, please?"

Harry signalled for Donald to talk to him. "I'm Donald Beckman."

"Ah, I read your piece attacking *Stop and Frisk* as nothing but racial profiling in disguise. Good work. I think you are the guy I want to do business with. I am sure you have higher-ups sitting and standing around your desk now, as I am on speaker-phone. It is OK for them to listen, but in the future we are going to be talking a lot – just you and me."

Harry nodded his head affirmatively, indicating Donald should do the talking. "Sure, we can talk no problem. So, your manifesto is pretty broad ranging, very comprehensive. You going to be a busy guy if you take on all those people."

"Well, I am like Che in Bolivia. I am hoping that others will join my cause, but we both know what happened to Che. After his death, the people there took over 40 years to finally throw off the yoke of oppression forced on them by U.S. capitalists and embrace socialism. Unfortunately, the brand of socialism they are embracing still has too many concessions to capitalists. Anyway, my focus is on this country, and Che is by my side day and night. His spirit is my guide, and I will not rest as long as there is one capitalist taking advantage of those who toil in the fields of despair, the offices of discontent or on the factory floors of anguish. It is time the rulers were brought to heel and made to realize that their fortunes are built on the backs of workers."

Nodding his head as if J.J. could see him, Donald said, "I can relate to that. No doubt the working man in this country could use a little European style capitalism where social amenities and wages are more lavish and more fairly distributed than in this nation."

"You don't have to agree with me Donald, debate is healthy. However, agree or disagree, the bottom line is that fairness should be a part of any economic system, and there is no fairness in corporate style capitalism like that practiced in the U.S.A. My manifesto will cause a correction in that, or those who perpetrate the inequity will pay a very high price."

Chablis and the Terrorist
Who Resurrected the Spirit of Che Guevara

"And what am I to do, sir," said an almost contrite sounding Donald.

"You are my conduit of hope who will spell out my demands. You will let those in power know that there is a course they can follow that will avoid bloodshed."

Donald, now feeling more comfortable with J.J., said, "Is it really necessary to kill people to accomplish these ends?"

In a very serious tone, J.J. said, "Switch on your cell-phone and record this Donald."

Donald reached down, turned on the recorder on his cell phone, placed it at the speaker and said, "It's on."

"OK, to those authorities who will be listening to this and all my other communications, I want to make it clear that you are wasting your time trying to trace my calls. My computer skills are way above the norm, and I am relaying my voice through several routers all across the globe that I have hacked into. Finding me will be as difficult as finding weapons of mass destruction in Iraq. Hey, maybe you can get that buffoon Bush off his ass down in Crawford and see if he can find me. My guess is that he will have as much luck as he did finding WMD in Iraq. As for that asshole Cheney, I can't wait for him to pop up on FOX talking about how I am just another one of those wild-eyed terrorists who needs to be brought to justice. There is about as much chance of me being brought to justice as that sanctimonious bastard being brought before the World Court to stand trial for war crimes. It just isn't going to happen. I may not kill the hundreds of thousands he and Bush did, but those I am going to kill are far more germane to the problems in this world than the innocent men, women and children those two bastards slaughtered."

Donald offered an observation. "Those are old crimes that people have forgotten. They have moved on. Isn't it time you faced reality and moved on. You can't change what happened years ago. It is over and done with. And what you are talking about doing won't change things either. The system has always been set up to protect the wealthy and privileged, and it will always be that way. One man isn't going to change things."

"Donald, one man found a vaccine to prevent small-pox. One man discovered a vaccine to stop polio. I am a one man vaccine. I am going to inoculate the populace against the infectious disease of greed that spreads like a cancer throughout this nation and destroys everything in its path. You just sit tight Donald, and await my next call. I will see how things go the next two weeks. If I see some movement toward justice, I may be able to corral the spirit of Che; otherwise, a reign of terror will befall the privileged of America like an ancient plague. I do not make idle threats. With the death of Thomas Kimberline, I have already proven my capabilities. Make no mistake, I am deadly serious about my mission. I embrace my role and accept my fate whatever it may be. Men are not prisoners of fate, but only prisoners of their own minds."

"You killed Kimberline?"

"I did, and there will be more if I don't see some immediate changes.

The phone went dead and all those around the area stared in disbelief. Those words seemed to reverberate and bounce about the room: *men are not prisoners of fate but only prisoners of their own minds.*

CHAPTER 4
IT GRINDS ALL

Love has its place, as does hate.
Peace has its place, as does war.
Mercy has its place, as do cruelty and revenge.

That day in the coffee shop, Chablis, who had usually gravitated toward white men since being in the U.S.A., found herself, after he left, very curious about Rodrigo, who was Puerto Rican. He was a charming man, and as she sat there sipping the last of her coffee, her mind wondered, as it usually did, toward sex. She wondered if he was cut. Probably not she thought, as in America you had to pay extra for that, and most Puerto Ricans were poor and would, by necessity, not have it done. That was the result of the health care for profit model that had saddled Americans with the poorest and costliest healthcare in the First World. She preferred cut, but had come up in a small village where all the men but a few were not cut, so as she liked to jokingly say, "I cut my teeth on uncut cock."

Well, if things worked out the way they usually did on a first date, Chablis would know by the end of the evening whether he was cut or not. She always said, "Hey, if you like the guy you will eventually have sex. So, why make him wait. Reward him on the first date."

Aaron strolled in and said, "I'm off to the Merchant's Council. Hey, they are a dying breed in this city – the hand full of entrepreneurs that have managed to survive the corporate takeover of Manhattan. They are the last of the real capitalists left. They don't get preferential treatment from the government and struggle to keep their heads above water while the big guys are gobbling up everything in sight. Come on, why not go with me and see what an extinct species looks like."

Rodrigo had already paid the bill and placed a generous tip on the table when he left. Chablis looked down at the 20 dollar bill and thought about how she used to cut corners by telling her date as they were leaving the restaurants, "Oh, I have to use the little girl's room." Then she would go back in and take part of the tip off the table. Survival was what is was called, and when she first got to Manhattan; her budget was so tight that she even considered prostitution a time or two. Then, Aaron Adams came to her rescue, as he always did. She took one last sip of coffee, and said "Let's go boss."

That night, Rodrigo picked her up for dinner, and they had a pleasant evening getting better acquainted. He said that he lived in Spanish Harlem, and that his place was a mess or he would invite her over. She said, "No problem," my place is on the eastside of lower Manhattan. Come on and I'll give you a nightcap."

Now, it should be stated categorically that Chablis was not at all timid about sex, and she liked to play the game of seductress. Perhaps it was being trans-gendered that made her enjoy using her feminine wiles so much, but with men who had never been with a trans-gendered woman, she was very careful to make certain they were comfortable with what a trans-gendered girl had between her legs. She sat down across from Rodrigo and crossed her legs seductively, purposely making sure he got a good glance at her luscious thighs.

Rodrigo couldn't take his eyes off her gorgeous legs. He said, "I know you hear it all the time Chablis, but you are the most beautiful woman I think I have ever seen."

"I do hear it on occasion, but I realize it is often said by horny men who just want to get in my pants. You wouldn't be one of those would you?"

Laughing slightly, Rodrigo replied, "Well. I will be honest. Of course I want to get in yours pants. What man wouldn't?"

"Well, you'd be surprised. There are many men who look at me as an abomination."

Rodrigo shifted his position, because it was obvious to Chablis that he was getting an erection. He, in an almost whisper, said "That is because they are idiots and have no comprehension of the malady from which you suffer. They are the same kind of fools who would make fun of a handicapped person. The Christians don't help matters by saying God doesn't make mistakes. I suppose they don't think Hitler was a mistake."

Chablis, smiling, chimed in, "Or George Bush."

Chablis and the Terrorist
Who Resurrected the Spirit of Che Guevara

They laughed uproariously as Chablis continued "or Dick Cheney."

Chablis got up, walked over and picked up his empty glass. "Ready for a refill?"

"No, one drink a night is fine for me. Hey, I had a glass of wine already at dinner. You might get me drunk and take advantage of me. "

Chablis placed the glass back down on the coffee table and sat beside him. She gently played with a napkin that she had placed on the able. She eased her finger through it, making a little hole.

Chablis swallowed hard as she squeezed her thighs together, feeling the first bit of wetness dribbling from the instrument of joy in her panties. Hormones kept her from getting hard, but she still had semen in her balls.

Rodrigo sighed and shifted position in a discreet attempt to adjust his pants to relieve the pressure from his growing erection. Chablis smiled and softly said, "You seem to have a problem there Rodrigo."

She eased over to him and they embraced. She placed her head on his shoulder for a few seconds, then looked up, tilted her head as she continued to rest it on his shoulder and their lips met in a fiery, passionate, lingering kiss as their tongues fought a darting, probing duel of delight that made them both sigh with unrestrained ecstasy.

Chablis and the Terrorist
Who Resurrected the Spirit of Che Guevara

Chablis very delicately said, "I don't want to shock you Rodrigo. Have you ever been intimate with someone like me before?"

"No Chablis, but I know you are a woman. I have no interest in what is between your legs, but I am not afraid of it. There are some things I am not able to do. You understand that?"

"Of course I do. Believe me; it will be no different than being with a genetic woman. You'll just use a different hole."

They laughed, got up and hand-in-hand strolled slowly to the bedroom as they gazed into each others eyes. They stood by the bed and kissed. Chablis' 5:2 frame melted passionately into his masculine 6:2 body that was not overly muscular, but still gave her a feeling of being safe in his arms. He had more than strength of body. He had strength of character. He had told her that he was between jobs and wanted to find something different from his job as a commodities trader, because he was tired of being part of a system that aggrandized greed. Yes, Rodrigo was a man with character, a man she could feel comfortable with.

She unzipped her skirt and watched it slide off her hips, immediately exposing her naked lower half to Rodrigo. She twisted around as she removed her panties and gave him a magnificent view of the most gorgeous ass he had ever laid eyes on. Chablis was actually pretty happy with her posterior. She hoped Rodrigo was also happy with it too. The way he was nearly salivating with delight indicated that he probably was. Chablis made sure that her genitals were neatly tucked between her legs, so that she looked like a normal woman with an extremely hairy snatch.

She quickly removed her blouse and unhooked her bra before tossing it in the far corner. Her nipples were erect and feeling extra sensitive. She guided his hands to them. They were small, as she did not have implants, but rather had natural 34B's from taking hormones. Rodrigo removed his shirt, as Chablis, in her usual skilful fashion, masterfully removed his pants and briefs in one swift motion as his shoes had been left at the front door when he came into the apartment. His shaft was at full-staff and Chablis was pleased to see he was cut. She glided him toward the bed, and they fell onto it in each others arms.

Slowly, but assuredly Rodrigo's left hand found its way on her firm, round ass and he could feel it quivering, gently imparting its pulsing vibrations to the opening that his index finger was gently massaging. She whispered, "Let's make it nice and ready for your attention." She reached down, pulled his hand from the crack and said, as she coaxed him from the bed, "come and shower with me."

They lingered in the shower for what seemed like hours, embracing, kissing, fondling and delicately washing each other in those private areas that were not so private when two people's passions flowed like a wild river raging through a gorge. The kisses were like a turbulent torrent of lust raining down from a storm of tempestuous desire with winds of hurricane force.

In bed, Chablis made sure her genitals were again tucked between her legs as she did not want to shock Rodrigo too much. Embracing with fomenting passion, kissing in lingering ecstasy, touching each other longingly in those places that are hotbeds of pleasure, the two floated off in the blissfulness of sexual excitement that was consuming them like a roaring fire in a blast furnace. They were so hot they could melt steel.

Chablis had learned at an early age how much men enjoyed her oral talents, and she was proud of her abilities. So much so that she probably derived more pleasure from the act than did the recipient of her attention. She worked her way very slowly down to Rodrigo's passion stick, kissing his body gently along the way. She was thrilled with his its size.

He was focused on her firm but not extremely muscular body and as she playfully stroked his passion stick with her long nails, he began to moan. He kept opening and closing his eyes, mesmerized by her skilful ability to stroke it so gently and send waves of ecstasy though his nerve endings. She was masterfully teasing him. She sidled down between his legs with her face, being careful not to let her lips touch it, as she artfully blew on it and gradually opened her mouth wider and wider. She only took a small portion of it in her mouth and held it there, gently swirling her tongue around the head. She licked under the head just past the ridge of the crown and drew a shudder from him as she ran her tongue back to the end and up his slit. He started thrusting gently into her mouth. Making a groove with her tongue she let him have his way for a few moments just ramming his joy stick a little farther into her mouth with each thrust forward. He was fully erect and ready for the pièce de résistance.

She gripped him around the hips and began to pull in him further and further until he was completely filling her mouth with his wonderful love tool and Chablis then took his hips in both hands and slowly leaned in taking him right down her throat until her nose was buried in his pubes and she could feel his large heavy balls against her chin. This brought a sigh from him and he started whispering, "Oh that is great." Wanting to make him experience the height of carnal pleasure, Chablis stopped for an instance and pulled back. He was breathing heavily now as she again slowly slid all the way down the length of his shaft, allowing him to push deep into her throat. Once he was buried to the hilt down her gullet she proceeded to do a swallowing reaction, and as the muscles in her throat contracted and moved around his thick, long shaft he groaned his appreciation.

Just then, while she was deliciously impaled on his member, she was rewarded with copious amounts of pre-cum as she alternated between sliding it right down her throat and pulling back to lick around the head and underside. He warned her that he was getting close to climaxing which made her suck all that much harder on him. Suddenly, he let loose with a burst of sexual energy and a low, long grunt as spasm after spasm overwhelmed him and spurt after spurt of thick joy juice slid down Chablis' throat. This was her time! Yes, when a man burst force with his load of passion, Chablis always felt a sense of exhilaration, as if she had climbed Mount Everest, won the lottery of love, soared to heaven to float in blissful rapture with the angels of lust.

She crawled up his mildly muscular taunt frame and they kissed passionately their tongues duelling with delight, as the touch of her now rock hard member did not seem to bother him. Miraculously, she felt his joy stick rising again. "Oh my," she whispered, "I think you are ready for entry into my chamber of delight, and it is quivering already with anticipation."

She reached down, took the throbbing member in her soft hand, got up on her knees straddling him, and easily glided it into her gapping opening that had been used so often over the years to bring pleasure to so many that it was like a serene, pastoral valley of passion bounded by two cantaloupe shaped mountains of soft, pliable flesh that beckoned for the pile-driver of pleasure to pound it into oblivion.

She rode him like he was a wild mustang and she was a wrangler trying to tame it. They both moaned with pleasure and so excited was Chablis that she squirted her passion seed all over Rodrigo's stomach, but never let up on her ride as she wanted to feel him explode deep inside her cavity, seeding her like he was a farmer planting a crop of pleasure.

He let out a mighty groan as he exploded in her cavity like the raging waters of a river overflowing its banks. He was gushing like an oil well that needed to be capped. Pulsation after pulsation brought waves of euphoria to Chablis who was moaning with pleasure. As he went soft, she gently rolled off him and lay there satiated, satisfied and contented.

She reached over and flipped on the television. Remember that this was the day they had met in the coffee shop, and that afternoon, Thomas Kimberline had been killed. She had inadvertently turned on Fox News, and as she started to change the channel, Rodrigo said, "No don't. I love listening to these right wing buffoons justify every capitalist indignity. Fox News is the best comedy show on television."

Snickering, Chablis replied, "Yeah, I equate it to Sunday morning religious shows. Short on depth, but loaded with finger-pointing emotion. Liberalism is always the culprit."

They shared a laugh as the news anchor deplored the violence that had destroyed another titan of finance in a nation that spent too much time overseeing the markets when it should let the market, as that Hollywood buffoon, President Ronald Reagan said, work its magic."

Chablis and the Terrorist
Who Resurrected the Spirit of Che Guevara

Chablis said, "I didn't know Kimberline, but I do know Myerson, and if he was anything like him, the world is better off without him. Mind you, I am not condoning murder, but if a social worker who does something truly worthwhile by helping people in the ghetto had been killed it would not be news, but when a rich person, a celebrity or politician dies or is killed, then it is news. The people who really count don't count."

"You are right about that Chablis. I quit my last job, because I got tired of doing nothing that made a difference. You and your friend Aaron Adams make a difference. You help the desperate. Hey, maybe I should take a detective course on line and join you two crusaders for justice."

Chablis cuddled up to him and whispered, "I am not sure how much good we do. It always seems like the unworthy come out on top, but we do bring down a few of the tyrants from time to time."

They slept for awhile, had sex again, and when Rodrigo left the next morning, he felt that he had been with a remarkable woman, not just for her sexual prowess, but for her depth of character. He was already in love with Chablis.

As the days passed, Donald Beckman was given the job of trying to get more information on Che Guevara so he could do a feature article on him and why the killer of Thomas Kimberline was trying to emulate Che. Meanwhile, the manifesto was published and the nation was abuzz with news about

Chablis and the Terrorist
Who Resurrected the Spirit of Che Guevara

what was being called the Che Guevara CEO killer.

The President even went on television and before an audience of millions said:

"We have battled terrorists since 2001, and we are not about to let a cold bloodied killer who thinks he is emulating Che Guevara put fear into the hearts and minds of the people of this great nation. Maybe some C.E.O.'s have been lax in the way they run their corporations, but that is no reason to resort to murder. We have a system of jurisprudence that will take care of those who break the law. The outcomes might not always be what one would hope for, but that is the great thing about democracy. Everyone gets a fair shake in this nation from the executives who make decisions in the board rooms of corporations to the janitors who sweep up the boardrooms after meetings. This so called manifesto that he sent to the New York Times is nothing but the rhetoric of a communist. Communism was defeated by this great nation that refused to bow before its tyranny. We will defeat this sadistic terrorist and stand triumphant as we always do when confronting terrorism."

J.J., as he sat and watched the President's address with his mom and sister, could not contain the indignity that was growing within him. He excused himself, went into the bedroom, lay on his bed staring at the ceiling and hearing a faint whisper looked to his right at the open window. It was foggy outside and the fog was slowly rolling in the window. There it was, the mist that always offered a precursor to an image that would gradually take shape. The whisper was more audible now; the image was saying, "Respond with the truth. In the end, the truth will trump the lies."

Thus, J.J., with the guidance of what he now knew was the *Spirit of Che Guevara*, composed a letter that he mailed to Donald Beckman and the next day, on page one was the following:

The Spirit of Che Responds to the President's Lies

I, the spirit of Che Guevara, must respond to the lies of the President, because Americans swallow lies as if they were coming from the fountain of truth. But the fact is, in America, lies are substituted for the truth and the populace willingly swallows them because they have been propagandized into believing America is exceptional. Lies are part and parcel of what keeps those in power from ever really answering to the people. The people are so engrained with fear that they are easily manipulated into thinking the entire world is out to get the U.S.A. The truth is the entire world just wants the U.S.A. to leave it alone. America has nothing most nations want. The freedom Americans enjoy is illusionary. How much freedom do you have when you can die because a cruel system based on greed that turns healthcare over to corporate executives who make decisions based upon the bottom line, not on compassion. Most civilized nations offer their citizens free and universal healthcare, but in a nation that aggrandizes greed, you are on your own when you get sick. The greatest disease in America is the disease of greed which afflicts every man, woman and child with its evil. How much freedom do you have when you can be locked up for checking out library books that the government deems subversive material? How much freedom do you have when the streets are filled with people carrying automatic weapons that can be bought easier than you can buy birth control pills? How much freedom do you have when corporations use your labour and then when you age dispose of you as a useless commodity and provide you with no decent pension for all you years of service? How much freedom do you have when due to the colour of your skin you are automatically assumed guilty and often executed on the spot by an overzealous police force that is there to protect the privileged class? How much freedom do you have when the sons and daughters of the poor are dispatched to fight wars of conquest while the sons and daughters of the privileged stay at home and enjoy their luxurious lifestyles in peace and splendour knowing they get all the benefits and never have to make any of the sacrifices? Americans actually live a well-orchestrated illusion.

Once again Mr. President, you have lied to the American people and they lap it up like someone who has gone without water for a week. They believe your lies, because inside they know the truth, and they do not want to face it. They do not want to face the reality of the shallowness of this nation when it comes to fair treatment. They live an illusion that is promulgated by a government that is

Chablis and the Terrorist
Who Resurrected the Spirit of Che Guevara

there to serve the interests of the few at the expense of the many. That is the truth!

I say to you, Mr. President that the reason I fight is that I have compassion for those who do not have the will to fight for themselves. Most people in this nation have given up on changing things. I do not blame them, because they have been weakened by years of watching all the good things flow to those at the top. The children of the rich are exalted and given a preferred place at the table of plenty, and vetted with doors that open wide for opportunity, while the government cuts funds for the poor to get educated while building more prisons than universities to house those who now are cash cows for the corporations that have taken over the incarceration business. This nation sees more corporate economic benefit to locking people up than educating them.

Your words define me as a terrorist, but rather, it is the corporation that is the true terrorist. It is the corporation, which is the holy grail of the wealthy, which brings people to their knees in supplication to the will of a monolithic monster. There is no core to this nation. Its heart has been ripped out and sacrificed at the altar of greed. There is no moral fibre left, as capitalism is even promoted as the preferred choice of Jesus, who, in reality, was the world's greatest socialist who told the rich man – give all you have to the poor. I, like he was, am a social reformer. I am taking up arms against the greatest oppressor of mankind – the corporation which represents the interests of the rich and keeps

J. Wayne Frye 93

Chablis and the Terrorist
Who Resurrected the Spirit of Che Guevara

my brothers and sisters chained in misery and ignominy. I take up arms in response to the oppressor, and if the people begin to free themselves from propaganda, they will join me in tumbling this hypocrisy that keeps them in chains. It is the thought of an aroused, fed-up public that you fear most. For once the people see what real freedom is like; there will be no stopping them. For he who has tasted true freedom has eaten the earth's most bountiful harvest.

Sincerely,

The Spirit of Che Guevara

The bodyguard business picked up appreciably over the two weeks J.J. gave corporate America to start initiating changes, but there was no movement on the part of C.E.O.'s to meet his demands for fairness; although, a few C.E.O.'s of company's did release statements about their fairness with employees. In fact, one hamburger chain in New York City that paid its employees $15 an hour, gave a yearly bonus based on profits and offered stock in the company to employees at a discount was touted by the employees themselves as a fair and decent company for which to work. Their union head spoke glowingly of how the company was willing to always work to makes things better for those it saw as the ones who made the company a success. This was an exception in America, a corporation with a heart. The union president was careful not to say anything derogatory about what J.J. was doing. All he said was, "This is a company that cares, and we urge you to not target any of those at the top of the corporate chain, who show personal restraint in their own salaries as well. These are good people."

J.J. took due note of all corporations in New York City that were fair with employees. He only intended to target the C.E.O.'s who were notorious union busters and those who were known for having disdain for the working man and women who were the real reasons for any company's success. He compiled a list and kept it under his mattress in his bedroom. The list started with people who had brazenly caused the financial crisis back in 2007, crashing the world economy while pocketing millions. One of those people was Bob Myerson. He was next on J.J.'s hit list. He had never been prosecuted as the government under Barrack Obama in 2009, when he assumed office with people having high hopes of bringing justice to those who thought they were above the law, saw him turn a blind eye to all the crimes of the Bush Administration from financial malfeasance to brazen torture while continuing many of his insane paranoid policies that had, like its endorsement of terror to fight terrorism, cast a pall of darkness over a nation that had simply lost its way. Yeah, Kimberline was just a "give-me" a "freebee" for his sister. Myerson was the real deal, and making him pay would be a pleasure.

While J.J. plotted his next kill, Chablis was still euphoric over her tryst with Rodrigo, and was looking forward to their next date which was Friday night. She and Aaron were sitting in his office talking when Myra walked in and said, "A Mr. Harrington to see either one of you about a problem he has. Which one of you wants to take it? He looks like he is loaded, by the way."

Aaron took a deep breath and said, "Send him in; we'll both talk to him."

Harrington was a man in his late 40's, maybe early 50's, whose thick solid white hair gave him a look of distinction. He was immaculately dressed, but not in an ostentatious manner. His open collar shirt was unbuttoned enough to show a slightly hairy, well-defined chest that indicated he was a man who worked out regularly. He introduced himself as Joe Harrington, as if they might recognize the name. Neither did. He was a writer of some renown who specialized in social commentary. One of the several books he mentioned, Chablis and Aaron were both familiar with. *The Free Market Bible* had been on the *New York Times* Best Seller list for a few weeks a couple of years ago.

Smiling he said, "See, if I keep mentioning enough books, eventually people have at least heard of one. Now, if you want to help me out with some royalties go out and buy one. You'll earn it back with the fee you are going to charge me."

Aaron said, as he motioned for him to take a seat on the sofa next to Chablis, "Well, we have a plethora of cases, but we may be able to fit you in. What can we do for you?"

Chablis and the Terrorist
Who Resurrected the Spirit of Che Guevara

"You my two Sherlock's can find the guy calling himself the *Spirit of Che Guevara*. I want to interview him, maybe write a book about what he is trying to accomplish. Just an over-the phone talk of moderate length might even be adequate. This has the makings of a great book. Disaffected socialist conjures up the spirit of Che and takes on corporate America. That is a mighty task. No one has done that since Teddy Roosevelt went after John D. Rockefeller, and now the Standard Oil Company that was broken up by the great trust buster is back in business just as it was back in the early 1900's, courtesy of the same Republican party that Teddy Roosevelt wouldn't recognize today. So, what do you say?"

Aaron eased back in his chair, looked at Chablis and asked, "What do you think Chablis? I'm jammed up. You want to take this on?"

Almost laughing, Chablis said, "Hey Mr. Harrington, I'm a capitalist. You got your chequebook?"

Harrington reached in his inside coat pocket and brought out a leather chequebook. "5000 do as a retainer?"

"Well, that is a bit light," said Chablis as she gave him a wink and continued, "our rate is 1500 a day and we usually get one week in advance."

Without hesitating, Harrington, took out his pen, leaned over and placed the chequebook on the coffee table and said, "So, let's make it a 15,000 retainer. That do it?"

Chablis said, "That will do it, and I'll even take you downstairs and buy you lunch. Not a fancy place but the food is good."

While they were having lunch, Chablis found her mind wandering to the day she had met Rodrigo. Strangely, she also found herself attracted to the distinguished and scholarly acting Joe Harrington. She was intrigued by him and remembered a book she had read as an assignment in a university class, and said, "So, I once read a book called *The Other America* by a man named Michael Harrington. Are you two related?

"No, but I know his work. He was the premiere socialist in this nation in the 50's and 60's, and the book was responsible for Presidents Kennedy and Johnson deciding to attack poverty. In fact, although he could not admit it, because he would have been branded a socialist, Lyndon Johnson made that book the centrepiece of his War on Poverty programme. There was a time when there was a concentrated effort to eradicate poverty in this nation and give everyone an equal opportunity. That all died when Ronald Reagan ushered in the era of get what you can for yourself and to hell with everyone else. Before Reagan, there was a 90% tax bracket for the upper income earners, and tackling poverty was more important than going all over the world to spread corporate democracy. Today, this nation blames those in poverty for being poor and points the finger of condemnation rather than extending the hand of compassion." For some reason though, his words seemed to lack sincerity.

"So, you have sympathy with this man calling himself the *Spirit of Che Guevara*. You see him as a sort of everyman character who is trying to write the ills of a society based on greed?"

"In a grudging sort of way, yes I have empathy with him. He sees the damage done by a nation that caters to those at the top of the economic order while ignoring the needs of the many. He is just attacking the symbol of greed which has taken hold of this nation and is destroying its soul. In a perverted sort of way, I admire his courage. Che Guevara said you don't change America by killing the President, you change it by killing the C.E.O.'s of the giant corporations which is where the real power lies."

"Ronald Reagan was the beginning of the end of compassion and a reasonable semblance of fairness, but George Bush was the culmination of our slide into fascism, which was only codified by the acquiescence of Obama to allow the continuation of the evil perpetrated by those who were enablers for the moneyed class. If we are going to be fascist, it is time to look in the mirror and use the right terminology. The beginning of wisdom is to call things by their right names. We seem, as a country, to be in denial as to the implications of what we have allowed to occur. Today, this nation is actually the antithesis of what the word freedom means. The propagandists continue to tell us how exceptional we are and how much freedom we have. Remember Hitler said that the bigger the lie the more likely people are to believe it. Americans believe this massive lie, and they are too complacent to stand against the status-quo and demand fairness and justness. The government keeps them in fear that there is some evil plot to end the freedom that they don't really have." Still, there seemed a lack of sincerity in what he was saying, almost as if it was rehearsed.

Intrigued, Chablis said, "So, you think some good will come out of this plot to assassinate the corporate leaders of America?"

"What harm can it do? The nation is already going down the road to fascism. In fact, it is here. It has been since 9/11 was used to institute oppression and make it acceptable to curtail freedom. Why 70% of the people enthusiastically said yes when asked after 9/11 if giving up some freedom to fight terrorism was acceptable. People are so stupid they line up for their own shackles and chains."

Still, there seemed be a hallow ring to what he was saying as there was a lack of conviction in his voice. Why was he faking sincerity thought Chablis.

Chablis, politically astute, interjected, "I agree, as we pass judgment on countries we consider un-free, while since 9/11 the laws and practices of this nation has comprehensively reduced civil liberties in the name of security."

Chablis and the Terrorist
Who Resurrected the Spirit of Che Guevara

Joe was impressed with Chablis depth of knowledge as he continued. President Obama, who was supposed to end the fascist drift, claimed, as President George W. Bush did before him, the right to order the killing of any citizen considered a terrorist or supporter of terrorism, and who defines a terrorist. Why, it is the President. The President now decides whether a person will receive a trial in the federal courts or in a military tribunal. Sounds pretty dictatorial to me."

Chablis was now fascinated and enthralled by the case that was dumped in her lap. "I have almost nothing to go on Joe, but I will find him if he can be found. I am as tenacious as a pit bull."

Joe smiled and replied, "I can see that Chablis. You are an incredible young woman, and I am relieved to know you are on the case. I have confidence in you. That is why I hired this firm."

Chablis gave him the methodical smile that slowly crept across her succulent, puffy, thick ruby red lips and said, "I don't always succeed, but it is never from lack of effort. Tell me, what type man would you guess him to be?"

"Like the man he is emulating, this guy is an idealist. He believes in a utopian ideal that says all things are possible if the hearts of men are purified. He sees the pursuit of money and the crass accumulation of material possessions as evil. He believes that an equitable distribution of wealth is a cure for poverty. Like Che, he believes that only

Chablis and the Terrorist
Who Resurrected the Spirit of Che Guevara

violent revolution is the way to change things, because the power structure will only bend to keep the masses at bay, never agree to what is necessary to introduce real fairness into the system. That is why they must be toppled, totally destroyed before real change can be implemented."

He leaned forward and looked directly into Chablis deep, alluring, twinkling dark brown eyes as he continued in fake earnest. "My guess is that he is highly educated as evidenced by his manifesto. He has given this great thought over the years. He probably comes from poverty and had to struggle to achieve his education while watching the students from the privileged class lead a life of carefree frivolity, knowing their spots in the hierarchy of the system that he abhors are assured. This is a man who simply sees the inherent evil of nepotism practiced by the elite and has decided he is the only one with the courage to make a stand on the principle of fairness and justness."

Chablis, showing intense, sincere interest said, "You should be a psychologist."

"In a way, I am Chablis. I write about people's thoughts and deeds; consequently, I need to know their motivations, their inner most thoughts and desires. Like, if you look at me right now, you can see my inner most thoughts and desires. Can you figure them out?"

Chablis smiled, and replied in a low, sensual voice, "Why Joe, you are embarrassing me. Of course I know what you are thinking. I am not an unattractive woman, and I have noticed your fascination with me as you speak. I am flattered, but I make it a policy to never get involved with clients." Then she gave him a wink. "However, when the case is over, we can perhaps scratch your itch."

Joe laughed. "Then solve this case in a hurry, because I am itching really badly."

They laughed, finished their meal and parted with a hug. Chablis genuinely wanted to like him, but there was something strange about him. He spoke eloquently about justice and fairness, but there was that seeming lack of sincerity in his voice. Everything he said seemed rehearsed.

Her thoughts shifted to the man calling himself the *Spirit of Che Guevara*. She tried to get a mental picture of what he looked like. She envisioned him as someone she would probably find attractive both physically and intellectually. He was likely a minority and intensely devoted to family.

She began to stroll upstairs and slowly go over ways to begin the search. This was like finding the proverbial needle in the haystack. She sat in her office, swivelled her chair around and just stared out the window at the Manhattan skyline. Offices and tiny cubicles in those buildings were filled with people who were slaves to the 9 to 5 routine. Many of whom thought they were living the good life with their daily commutes to drudgery so they could maintain that co-op in the city or picket fenced cottage in the suburbs, drive that nice SUV to take the kids to their soccer games on weekends, pop the cork on a nice bottle of Bordeaux, shop at the trendy shops and borrow money to take that expensive summer vacation every year. They all lived on the edge and were only a couple of paycheques from poverty, but were too wrapped up in the "American Dream" to realize just how precarious their lives were. Yeah, they were the very ones who swallowed the propaganda and served as the grease that kept the engines of capitalism humming along so the elite could enjoy their splendorous lifestyles. There was a violent anarchist out there, one lone man who was trying to expose the hypocrisy of a society based on greed. Who was he? Where was he? Who was he planning to kill next?

She remembered a poem she once read:

Though the mills of hope grind slowly:
They still grind ever so methodically.
Fate stands anticipatorily waiting,
As with exactness it grinds all.

Chablis and the Terrorist
Who Resurrected the Spirit of Che Guevara

CHAPTER 5
YOU'RE ALWAYS WELCOME DOWN HERE

I hunger for a dish of vengeance
With gravy made of the wealthy's blood.
I want a dessert of glorious retribution.
I long for a repast of sweet revenge
That is icy cold around the edges
And as hot as molten lead at the core.

Let me make medicine of great revenge
To cure this intense deadly grief that has
Been hoisted by those who sit in splendour
Dining on the fatted calf while the rest of us
Scramble for the crumbs that dribble from
The table of plenty in the hall of disregard.

I shall not depend on God to cure the ills
Of economic discontent that abound,
For he has done a less than credible job
In the proper dispensation of the wealth
That should be shared rather than hoarded.
Therefore, my gun is ready and the trigger cocked.

We live on an earth where the goddess of wealth
Is worshipped as if gold was in her hair.
Her smile lures those who long for riches.
People drink the very diamond of her air.
Her breath perfumed silver for awhile,
All sanctity and fairness do defile.

And wait for her the gifted line,
That wild and witchingly lay,
And swear all hearts are her shrine,

J. Wayne Frye   105

Chablis and the Terrorist
Who Resurrected the Spirit of Che Guevara

That only owns her greed induced sway.
I swear to seek revenge at last
Marked by that scornful cheek I turn.

Ay, now by all the bitter tears
That I have shed for the poor,
The racking doubts, the burning fears,
Avenged they well may be.
The days of endless woe
Caused by the rich who are the foe.

I wish to see these barons of greed laid
Within a dastardly cold tomb,
For they all humanity have betrayed,
And only brought on their own doom.
It is I who will provide fitting punishment and pain,
My sweet revenge for the afflicted who toil in vain.

Go thou and watch their lightest sigh,
And bark discontent beneath the greedy eye.
I shall not turn on thee who in poverty lie,
For I, the Spirit of Che, will deliver the blow
That will provide sweet retribution
And lay the evil of greed low.

Bob Myerson was on J.J.'s hit list, basically because he was an arrogant asshole. True, he had brazenly bragged about getting off with a 28 million dollar fine when he stole 100 million dollars, but that was only the tip of the iceberg. It was truly arrogance that was his death warrant, and he didn't even know it. In fact, when Kimberline was killed, it never occurred to Myerson that he might be on the hit list. He generally kept a low profile and the

Chablis and the Terrorist
Who Resurrected the Spirit of Che Guevara

guy calling himself the *Spirit of Che Guevara* was obviously threatening C.E.O.'s; consequently, Myerson never even entertained the thought of hiring a bodyguard as he was a stock manipulator, not a C.E.O. His lack of concern would cost him dearly.

J.J. watched him pull out of the parking garage in his brand new Mercedes and head uptown. He pulled right behind him in the Crown Victoria. He saw no need to be coy about following him, as Myerson was obviously oblivious to any perceived threat. Myerson pulled into the secure garage at his Manhattan co-op and got out to go up to relax in splendorous luxury in his 10 million dollar apartment.

Getting inside the apartment would be easy thought J.J. as he headed to his Lock and Leave storage unit where he meticulously applied the makeup that made him appear to be in his mid 40's. He went over to his array of props and removed a NYPD badge number 9348 and made his way uptown. He parked the Crown Victoria in Mid-town Manhattan Self-Park, where they no longer used an attendant to take the $10 an hour they charged for parking, as the 1200 spaces they had only took in $100,000 an hour and, of course, they did not want to pay some attendant $10 an hour to take the money. Such is the nature of greed that even an extra penny is coveted as the miserly want no one to share in the largesse they accumulate to enjoy the good life of the rich and famous. This was capitalism at its greedy best!

Chablis and the Terrorist
Who Resurrected the Spirit of Che Guevara

As he walked across the street toward the *Maison à Manhattan*, a place so fashionable it had to use the French language, because English was not exclusive enough, he looked to his left and by a bus bench at the far end of the street was a mist forming. In that mist was a barely discernable image of a man in a beret, army fatigues with a cigar in his mouth. The image moved every so assuredly toward him with a stride that reflected extreme confidence. J.J. assumed it was only an illusion caused by a furtive mind that was now in the complete mode of a revolutionary bent on retribution for the evils committed by those who saw no shame in stepping over those living in the streets on their way to luxurious penthouses in the sky. The mist moved beside him as he stood on the corner down from the entrance to *Maison à Manhattan*.

There was complete stillness in the air, almost as if everything around J.J. was silenced. The sound of the traffic was completely muted and there was an orange glow that seemed to pulsate all about as he heard in a very light whisper words that made his pulse quicken with the knowledge that he was about to deliver another blow for justice in a nation that had long ago forgotten the meaning of the word. "The true revolutionary is guided by a great feeling of love. His every action in the battle against the evils of greed is a cry to the masses to rally around him in the support of justice for the people forced to bow and scrape by those who want more and more and look upon the poor as a blight upon humanity. Whenever death may surprise us, let it be welcomed with the knowledge that our battle cry has reached some receptive ears and that another hand may take up the clarion call and that in our funeral dirge will be those with the staccato singing of the rhythmic machine guns and new battle cries that will lead to victory."

J.J. was ready. He took a deep breath and walked up to the doorman at *Maison à Manhattan*. Taking out his badge, he said, "NYPD, let me in please. I need to see Bob Myserson. There was no hesitation on the part of the doorman. He buzzed J.J. in and walked slightly inside and pointed at an elaborate Provincial 17th Century French desk where an immaculately dressed guard was sitting as if he were the overlord of admission to exclusivity.

The guard, not getting up, asked, "Mr. Myerson does not like to be disturbed after 10. I suggest you come back another time."

J.J. knew that the NYPD was always respectful of the rich, while showing complete disdain for the poor, so he tried to be very delicate. "I appreciate that very much, as I do not want to disturb him, but this is an urgent matter that requires his immediate attention, as we have received word of a security breech at his office building, and we are fearful that someone may have hacked into his computer system. We need to have him check his computer and make certain there was no breech of security. I am certain he would want us to contact him right away. I hope you understand, sir. I am just doing my job."

Chablis and the Terrorist
Who Resurrected the Spirit of Che Guevara

"Just a minute, I'll call up to ask if he will see you."

The arrogance of the rich, thought J.J., knows no bounds. If he was in a tenement in Harlem, he would just knock on the door and shout, "Open up asshole."

The guard explained things to Myerson and then said, "He says you can come up." He then pointed at an elevator with a gold encrusted door and continued, "just push the button and Charlene will take you up. Tell her the Presidential Penthouse."

Sure enough, the elevator had an attendant. It had come down from the 11th floor and let out an elderly lady wearing a sable coat and garish sparkling diamond earrings, who was fawned over by the guard who escorted her to the door where the equally obsequious doorman treated her like the Queen of England. After holding the door in a servile and referential manner for the lady, the mini-skirted attendant sat back on a stool that had an embroidered cover. She crossed her legs, smiled and said, "What floor please?"

J.J. remembered an old cartoon he had seen from the 1960's making fun of hippies. An elevator attendant was looking at a hippie waiting for him to give the floor number and all he said was "Blast off daddio." He thought it would be fun to tell her that, but perhaps a bit unwise under the circumstances. Anyway, she wouldn't get the joke, so he just said "Presidential Penthouse."

Chablis and the Terrorist
Who Resurrected the Spirit of Che Guevara

She nodded and gave him a little smile as she looked up and down his frame, obviously deducing that he was no associate of Mr. Myerson since he was not wearing a $3000 tailor made suit.

On the ride up he remembered something Che once said, "You must carry the war into every corner the enemy happens to inhibit – into his home, his business, where he gets his entertainment, even where he worships. It is necessary to prevent him from having a moment's peace. You must attack him wherever he may be, make him feel like he is a cornered beast wherever he might move."

The elevator did not come to an abrupt stop, as that would be inappropriate in such a place. Rather, it slowly coasted to a stop, gliding gently to that rarefied atmosphere where the air is purer, cleaner, crisper and smells like freshly minted 100 dollar bills. The door did not open quickly, but rather glissaded gently, opening into a splendorous hallway that glistened with thick walnut panelling that reflected the glitter from the gold inlaid ceiling. The attendant smiled and said, "Just use the knocker on the door, and you have a real nice evening, sir."

The door was opened by a Hispanic woman who said, "Good evening. Mr. Myerson is in his study. This way please."

How does one adequately describe obscene opulence? The entryway was almost as large as J.J.'s entire apartment and the walls were lined with thick Corinthian leather inlaid in a walnut panelling that had niches where high dollar vases sat with a light focused on them from overhead in the niche. As they proceeded down the hall, under J.J.'s feet was white Italian marble. At the end of the hallway, they turned right and walked into a round foyer that had a ceiling overhead sparkling with gold tailings that had been intricately placed to maximize the glittering effect created from the huge crystal chandelier that dangled 30 feet overhead. The maid said, "In here please," as she turned a gold doorknob on a thick, 10 foot door that was rounded at the top and opened like J.J. was about to enter a vault in Fort Knox.

Sitting behind a large circular French provincial desk was none other than the potentate of plenty himself, Bob Myerson. He motioned with his hand for J.J. to come forward and bow before the wizard of Wall Street manipulation as he said, "That will be all Effie. No need for tea or coffee as this gentleman will not be staying long."

As Effie curtsied and backed out showing worshipful respect to his highness, Mr. Asshole, he motioned with his hand for J.J. to come forward and worship at his altar of ostentatious arrogance. "So officer, what may I do for you? You say there is fear my security has been breeched. Well, I seriously doubt it."

J.J., as the door behind him closed, knew that the room was basically soundproof, and he would be able to kill Myerson with relative ease and the shot would probably not even be heard. Yet, he decided a bullet was not the best way to dispatch Myerson, as he wanted to enjoy the kill. "No, Myerson, there is no breech of security," said J.J. as he reached into his pocket and brought out a Beretta he had picked up at the Lock and Leave.

Myerson's facial expression showed intense terror as he said, "I know you. I know that voice. I talk to hundreds of people, I never forget a voice."

J.J., the gun levelled at Myerson's chest said, "Put your hands on the desk. You don't know me. I am just one of millions of voices crying in the wilderness of misery caused by your arrogant, self-serving greediness. I am here to rectify things tonight. I am the *Spirit of Che Guevara*."

With the words *Spirit of Che Guevara*, Myerson nearly passed out from fright, as he began to beg, "I-I-I have over a three million dollars in a safe right here. It's yours. It's yours – all of it. Just please don't do this. I have a family."

Looking at the safe behind him, J.J. motioned toward it with his gun. "O.K., I might consider it. Let me see the money."

With J.J. standing by his side, Myerson quickly spun the tumbler and within a few seconds the safe was open and there was a huge amount of money all bundled up, too much for J.J. to get into his pockets. He noticed a large briefcase sitting over on a chair. He backed over to it, not taking his eyes off Myerson, as he picked up the case and tossed it over to him. "Fill it up."

Myerson quickly filled the briefcase, but there was probably at least 100,000 that he couldn't get in it. "J.J. walked over and placed it in his coat pockets and pants. "Thanks, this will go to a good cause, I promise you."

"O.K., O.K., are we cool now?"

J.J. was hovering over him, and felt great exhilaration watching an asshole that made people squirm and crawl finally do some squirming and crawling himself. He reached down, nudged him up and motioned for him to go over to the window. With the gun, he motioned for him to raise it, and the two stood there, Myerson shaking with fear, as they looked out at the New York skyline. J.J. moved behind him and whispered, "spread your wings asshole, you are about to take Flight 666 to hell. I'll be sending some of your buddies to join you."

J.J. gave him a shove and Myerson screamed as he hurtled downward. J.J. headed toward the door with suitcase in hand. He walked into the hallway, down the corridor and as he got to the door the maid said, "Let me show you out sir."

J.J. thanked her as she walked him to the door. He waited a few seconds for the elevator and the nice attendant smiled at him and took him down to the lobby. As he got out, he reached in his pocket and gave her a hand full of $100 bills as a tip saying, "Nice ride lady. You're a good pilot."

Chablis and the Terrorist
Who Resurrected the Spirit of Che Guevara

Staring down at the bills, she, in shock, said, "Thank you sir. Thank you so much."

J.J. strolled out into the street as people were gathering around the splattered remains of Myerson. He never looked, just proceeded on down the street to the parking garage. He wondered what to do with the money as he drove up Park Avenue. He wouldn't give it to the church as they would probably blow it on fancy pews, candelabras, a trip for the priests to kiss the Pope's ring or some other useless endeavour. It never went to help the people who really needed it, but to help those who were part of the church hierarchy which made it another money-grubbing corporation. He'd try to find the name of the lawyers representing those who were ripped off by Myerson and give some to them, but they were also part of the problem and would rake their 40% contingency fee off the top. Giving it to a charity wouldn't do any good as the heads of the charities all got exorbitant salaries too. Charities had, for the most part, been turned into corporations that paid the executives far too much. Yes, charities, like churches, were just big business using God and good works as cover for greed. He would give a little bit of the money to his sister and mom, but only a little, as they might become suspicious if he gave them too much, but the rest would take some thought. He took it out of the briefcase and hid it under the mattress that night, and unlike many people who would have been lying on so much money, he was not filled with euphoria, rather he was filled with determination to make his next victim even more high profile than Myerson.

Chablis and the Terrorist
Who Resurrected the Spirit of Che Guevara

He drifted off to sleep dreaming of a utopian America where the wealth was distributed freely, and human want was a thing of the past as spending on bombs and bullets to kill, subdue and control people was replaced by spending on social welfare programs that lifted people up from the despair of a cruel economic system. Yes, J.J., influenced by the spirit of Che would open people's eyes and make them see that there was a better way. J.J. had come to realize that the ends you serve that are selfish will take you no further than yourself but the ends you serve that are for all, in common, will take you into eternity. There was a God, but not a monotheistic all powerful ruler of the universe, rather, God was an ideal. He was an ideal of hope that shined brightly in the hearts of those who embraced the love of his or her fellow man and reached out to lift up those trapped in poverty by the most evil economic system ever invented. J.J. was a one man revolution now, but as time moved forward, others would see that he was paving the way for a brighter future where all shared in the great wealth of the nation, rather than the chosen few. Why? Because the chosen few were about to lay wasted on the field of greed they had sowed for themselves. Truly, the selfish wealthy were about to reap what they had sowed!

J.J. suddenly awakened at 1:00 AM and realized that the *New York Times* late edition would go to press at 4:00 AM. He had to dash off a tryst explaining the death of Myerson, so that he could counter the negative that would, as usual, equate his actions to terrorism against the greatest economic system in the world. His letter was discreetly dropped into the night box outside the building, and, knowing that there were cameras around, he made certain to wear a turned up collar that hid his face. By 7:00 AM, his words were on the streets in the morning edition and the morning news shows were all discussing how *The Spirit of Che* had again struck down a man, who, though of questionable character, was only a slight aberration of those who were the titans of capitalism who supposedly made America great. J.J.'s letter:

To the Oppressed and Marginalized:

Colorful demonstrations and weekend marches are vital, but alone are not powerful enough to stop wars or to curtail the domination exercised by those who hold the economic power. Wars will be stopped only when soldiers refuse to fight, when workers refuse to load weapons onto ships and aircraft, when people boycott the economic arrogance of a nation that is predicated on the belief that it is superior. As this nation wages war after war on foreign soil, the real war is waged on the poor in this nation who are short-changed by a government that neglects the real needs of the people. Yesterday, I excised one of the cancers that spread the disease of greed. His shove out the window of his palatial penthouse built by the money he stole from people, who, themselves, were handing him money because of their own greed to procure riches, was just one small act of many that will make those who make personal gain from the misery of others too big a price to pay.

Chablis and the Terrorist
Who Resurrected the Spirit of Che Guevara

We are told that we live in a system that espouses merit, equality and a level playing field. However, that is a lie promulgated by the aristocracy of power and commerce that exalts those with wealth, power, and celebrity, however gained.

The second most buffoonish man to inhabit the White House invented trickle-down economics, which is supposed to make us all believe that we will one day be rich, too, as the wealthy let their money trickle down to us who are their slaves. Once you realize that trickle-down economics does not work, you will see the excessive tax cuts for the rich as what they are, a simple upward redistribution of income, rather than a way to make all of us richer, as we were told.

The truth is that America worships royalty, and what makes you royalty in America – money. While people live in cardboard boxes, under bridges and overpasses, in the squalor of tenements, the royalty dines on caviar in splendorous luxury. Yet, this is a nation that calls itself Christian. What would Jesus, the person who told the rich man to give all he had to the poor, think of this appalling situation?

Fear is the element the establishment uses to keep people from demanding justice. Constant fear keeps the masses from seeing that the evil they should be fighting is not the evil on foreign shores, but the evil manifested right here in America where economic justice is denied, where an unfair tax structure awards those at the top at the expense of those at the bottom. Evil in your backyard is what a person should fear, not the evil that abounds 10,000 kilometres away.

America, which was founded by revolution, fears revolution. The government uses fear to keep the populace in bondage. The government fears the people might wise-up and demand fairness and that is why there must be a scapegoat, whether it is a Muslim chopping someone's head off in a far-away nation or a person of colour living in the ghetto who wants a welfare check. America building more prisons than universities and allowing the barbarity of torture to fight terrorism is permissible and just. Welfare to corporations and the rich in the form of an unfair tax structure is just good economics according to the American government.

Those in power need to know that Paine, Marx, Engels, Jefferson, Lenin, Guevara were the results, not the causes. The causes are apparent for all to see who will open their eyes. For many years now, Americans have been victims of fear. The government, which represents the moneyed interests, uses fear to keep the populace in line. Fear that others will come in the dark of night and steal the precious freedom that is only an illusion keeps the populace on edge, ever mindful that some evil entity is out to get that which you do not even have.

Jesus is revered by Americans who think God is always on their side. Jesus was not just a good guy. Rather, his teachings and behaviour reflect an alternative social vision. Jesus was not talking

Chablis and the Terrorist
Who Resurrected the Spirit of Che Guevara

about how to be good and how to behave within the framework of a system of domination by moneyed interests. He was a critic of the domination system itself. He was a wild-eyed revolutionary. I say to those who love Jesus, join me in remembering he said he did not come to bring peace but a sword. True peace, my dear readers, can only come when the sword of righteousness is swiftly lowered to sever the evil of greed. Join me – kill a C.E.O. today.

Sincerely,

The Spirit of Che Guevara

There was much debate at the *Times* on whether that last sentence should be printed or not. When J.J. called Donald shortly after depositing the letter, Donald said, "We can't print that last sentence as it is irresponsible for us to let someone use our paper to advocate the murder of individuals. You have to understand that."

J.J., with deep emotion, replied, "It is the height of irresponsibility to hide the truth from the people. Does not your paper display the words on the front page: *All the news that is fit to print*? This is news of the most profound kind. I can cloud the words, but the meaning is the same. Bush and Cheney called torture legitimate repetitive use of force and somehow it was no longer torture because of semantics. Isn't it time we called things what they are and stopped being restrained by semantics? Tell your editors and the publisher that I will find another source that will print things exactly the way I write them. It is their choice."

When J.J. picked up the morning paper and saw the exact words there, he felt he had an ally in Donald Beckman. The television news shows were filled with the stories of how another C.E.O. took it on the chin for good old American free enterprise. J.J. had avoided television news as a source for his manifestos, because it was inhabited by pretty boys and girls who spent more time putting on makeup than researching stories. The days of real journalism had been sacrificed, like everything else in America, at the altar of greed when corporations took over the media and consolidated it into just another corporate empire. News shows were not intended to inform the public, but to titillate them with the latest news on what movie stars and singers were doing. Lady Ga Ga's latest antics were more important than how many people starved to death in a nation of plenty. News, like everything else in the media, had been dumbed down to the lowest common denominator.

J.J. sat at the breakfast table and Keita said, "J.J. what you think about this *Spirit of Che Guevara* guy? The cops were here yesterday asking about me being fired. Said that they were checking on anyone who might have had a grudge against him."

J.J., shaking his head, replied, "Tell them to go all the way back to elementary school then. My guess is he was as big an asshole at 6 as he was 40. They ask about me?"

Chablis and the Terrorist
Who Resurrected the Spirit of Che Guevara

"No, why would they ask about you J.J.," said a puzzled Keita.

"No reason, just curious. Always curious about what the local Gestapo is up to."

Keita looked at him with concern. "You watch your step J.J. You have been acting strange the last month or so."

J.J. smiled and, as he placed two hundred dollars on the table, said, "Take Mama out for lunch today. She needs a break from the routine around here. I'm looking at a place in Connecticut for us. We're getting out of this dump soon."

Keita, though older, had always felt like J.J. was the wiser one, and she looked up to him. "Be careful out there in the corporate world today J.J. This man calling himself the *Spirit of Che Guevara* is dangerous."

"I am in no danger. He is only killing the C.E.O.'s. I am never going to make it that far as I am a ghetto rat from Harlem. There are no spaces reserved for us in the boardrooms of America."

Keita looked at him and said, "There is always a place for you in my heart brother. You are the C.E.O. of respect around here. You could desert us, but you don't. You are a man of integrity which there are few left in this nation."

"Thanks sis."

Chablis and the Terrorist
Who Resurrected the Spirit of Che Guevara

"By the way, what was the firm's name you are working for now?"

J.J. glanced over at a wall calendar advertising Frye Shoes and said, "Frye and Shoe Investments. I'm off to work. Talk to you later."

She gave him a kiss and J.J. left for his next kill. This was going to be a big one.

While J.J. was preparing for his next execution, Chablis was trying to get a line on who the *Spirit of Che* was. She started off by investigating Thomas Kimberline. A visit to his home took her to where luxury prevailed and the wife seemed more worried about Chablis high heels marring her fine floor than the fact her husband was gone. Chablis had to remove her heels and walked into a large den where Mrs. Kimberline pointed to a chair and Chablis thought she acted more like it was a work of art rather than a place to sit your ass. She looked down at the small chair while Mrs. Kimberline, dressed in a long flowing robe with mink trim seemed to float onto a large white divan. Chablis slowly glided into the chair, crossed her gorgeous legs and said, "I am so sorry for your loss."

Mrs. Kimberline, almost brushing it off with little thought, said, "Thanks, what may I do for you?"

Lying, she said, "Well, it is just that I am trying to put a stop to these heinous murders. I have been hired by a public minded citizen, and I was wondering if there is anything at all that your husband might have done to an employee or a rival that might have created animosity and led to an act of retribution. Anything might be helpful."

Looking with obvious disdain for Chablis, whom she felt was beneath her, she said "No, no one in particular. Although, he did subcontract some work awhile ago to cut expenses and maximize profits. Some employees had been with him as long as 15 years and were let go."

"Any chance you would have a list of those employees?"

"She reached over to the end table by the sofa where a wireless intercom was. She leaned over slightly, her silicon breasts nearly falling out of her gown as she said with precise diction into the intercom, "Charlene, go to my husband's office and get his termination folder. It is in the top drawer of the filling cabinet I am sure. Bring it in here immediately."

Chablis heard Charlene utter "Yes ma'am."

She was silent for awhile as Mrs. Kimerline looked disapprovingly at her, obviously assuming Chablis was some low-life whore based upon her short skirt, spiked heels and alluring makeup. Chablis smiled, thinking to herself that Mrs. Kimerline was nothing but a high priced whore who had roped the fatted calf. She would inherit a bundle and was probably glad to be free of the son-of-a-bitch.

Chablis and the Terrorist
Who Resurrected the Spirit of Che Guevara

Mrs. Kimberline broke the silence. "So, what's it like to be a female private-eye? Guess you meet some pretty rough people."

"I do, on occasion, yes, but I can handle myself."

Charlene walked in, meekly went over to Mrs. Kimerbline in a semi-bow and handed her a leather-bound notebook. Lowering her head, she said, "Will that be all madam?"

"Yes, you may go."

Charlene obsequiously, almost cringing in a servile and slavish manner, backed out of the room in a partial bow. Chablis could not help but shake her head in bewilderment that in modern America that was founded partly because of distaste for royalty, people were expected to bow before those who, because of their station in life, thought they were better than others. She was almost ready to throw up from watching such a nauseating scene.

Mrs. Kimberline flipped thought the notebook and said, "The police have copied it, so if you want, you can just have it." She thrust it out toward Chablis, expecting her to get up and get it as she said, "I have no use for it." She extended it toward Chablis, holding it in front of her, waiting for Chablis to come and get it.

Chablis walked over, took the book from her hand and asked. "Would you know any of the people who were terminated?"

Chablis and the Terrorist
Who Resurrected the Spirit of Che Guevara

Acting offended as if it were an impertinent question, she replied, "Oh my goodness. Of course not – no, definitely not." She shrugged her shoulders as if the very thought of associating with low class poor riff raff was abhorrent."

Chablis was more lady than this bitch could ever be. She appreciated the common people who toiled in obscurity so rich assholes like her could feel superior. As Mrs. Kimberline rang for Charlene to show her out, Chablis could not resist as Charlene walked in, putting Mrs. Kimberline in her place. "Mrs. Kimberline, you are a rich bitch, but you have no class. You equate class with fine wines, fancy couture like that robe you have on, a night at the opera, luxurious furnishings in this ostentatious apartment that reeks of low class taste trying to pass as high class chic. I come from a poor village in Mexico and the village whore has more class than you." She then turned to Charlene, pointed at her and continued, "This is a woman with class, who is probably supporting her family the only way she knows how by taking a demeaning job like this. She kisses your ass, because she needs a job, but one day people like her are going to get fed up with arrogant snobs like you, rip out your hearts and dance on your corpses." Then she let out a broad smile as she said, "Remember what the guy calling himself the *Spirit of Che* said – he is going to kill the C.E.O.'s family too, to wipe out their seed for all time. Keep looking over your shoulder bitch."

As Mrs. Kimerline sat there shaking, Chablis looked at Charlene and said, "Show me out while this bitch pisses in her pants in disbelief that someone had the nerve to tell her like it is."

Charlene walked her to the door and as Chablis left, Charlene whispered very softly, "Thank you so much."

Chablis was wondering what she would do when she found the guy calling himself the *Spirit of Che*. Yeah, her job was not to bring him to justice. Her job was to simply find him so Joe Harrington could interview him. She had no obligation to the authorities.

She strolled onto 5th Avenue and began to walk slowly uptown. She got that old feeling she had so often as the hairs on the back of her neck bristled. There was a sensation that slowly overcame her, a certain warmth that made her body tingle. She moved into a doorway and waited. After a few seconds, she stepped out onto the sidewalk and looked back. No one was there, but she knew she was being followed. Instincts in her business were rarely wrong. He or she was there, but where, and why?

She was still instinctively aware that someone was following her, but whoever it was, the person was extremely good. Chablis was enjoying the game.

She went through the same routine several times, stepping in a doorway, waiting, then stepping out and looking back. Still, there was nobody there, but she knew she was being tailed.

Chablis and the Terrorist
Who Resurrected the Spirit of Che Guevara

It was almost noon, so she ducked in Hardy's Dine-a-Rama for a sandwich. She was sitting at a table, when suddenly she lit up with delight as through the door walked none other than Rodrigo. He spotted her right away, walked over and said, "What a pleasant surprise. Mind if I join you."

Pointing down at the seat opposite her, she said, "I would be insulted if you didn't."

"Well, I would never want to insult a lady," he said as he eased into the booth.

"What are you doing in uptown Manhattan," said Chablis curiously.

"Why, I am looking for beautiful women, and it looks like I have found what I am looking for."

Almost blushing, Chablis in a coy manner, replied, "Well, do you know what to do with one when you find her?"

"I don't know, you tell me. How has my performance been in the past when I was with you?"

Making an "O" her thumb and index finger, she held it up beside her right ear and flashed him a smile along with it, recalling the magnificent love-making they had shared.

Rodrigo gave her a wink. "Glad to know I am appreciated."

Chablis and the Terrorist
Who Resurrected the Spirit of Che Guevara

They laughed and had lunch together. Chablis, still worrying about being followed, kept glancing out the large picture window at the front of the restaurant and methodically surveyed the dining room trying to spot her tail. Apparently, the person following her had moved on. As they had coffee, Rodrigo, noticing her trepidation, asked her, "So, you on a case?"

"I am, just got back from talking to Bob Myerson's widow. You remember him from the coffee shop?"

"I do, and I also know he was a victim of the guy calling himself the *Spirit of Che Guevara*. Not a good time to be a C.E.O. in this country. If I was one, I'd be worried, and also be trying to mend my ways. This guy means business."

Chablis told him about being hired to find the man calling himself the *Spirit of Che Guevara*, but did not share information on her client, as she felt, even with an intimate partner, like Rodrigo, ethics prevented her from revealing her client's name. They agreed to meet for dinner and a movie that night and parted ways outside the restaurant. She watched him, with his confident stride and assured manner, fade from view. She felt a little tingle between her legs and she sensed her sphincter muscle relaxing as she had thoughts of how the evening would end in fornicating blissfulness. She shook it off and proceeded up town to Harlem, as she was going to call on the first name on the list – Keita Martinez.

Chablis and the Terrorist
Who Resurrected the Spirit of Che Guevara

Strolling through the tenement where Keita lived, many people would have been fearful, but Chablis had come from poverty, rose above it, but never forget that she was one of the lucky ones, so she had no fear of these people. It was she they now feared, because she represented the establishment, the people who were the oppressors. She was attracting a lot of attention as she strolled through the square that was surrounded by eight 30 story apartments.

There was a time when properties like these were owned by the city, but the drive to privatize everything had turned the buildings over to a corporate slum lord. The corporation simply billed the city for subsidized rents, and a few were getting rich off the poor. It wound up costing the city more, as the money went into the pockets of people who decried the poor as leeches living off welfare when their empires were built off billing the taxpayers for maintaining the slums the poor were forced to live in. Now who was really living off welfare? Ironically, the public rarely thought of the welfare the rich got, only the welfare the poor received. As always, the rich were entitled.

A group of three teenagers whistled at Chablis as she walked toward Keita's building. They came over by her side and one of them said, "So, you looking for a big one to suck on baby?" He patted his crotch and continued, "Right here it is doll."

Chablis turned her head toward him and winked as she never broke stride, her heels clicking a sweet stiletto symphony. "Baby, when you grow up I might take some of that monster and transport you to heaven, but I only suck and fuck men, not boys."

He swallowed deeply and his chest puffed out as he began to reach for her. She stopped, faced him and made sure the other two were to her right and left. "You don't want to do that big boy. You might wind up with nothing but a stub where your hand used to be. Don't fuck with me. It will be a big mistake."

"Listen bitch, you in the wrong place at the wrong time." He reached for his switchblade, but before he could put his hand in his pocket, Chablis raised her knee into his crotch and he grumbled to pavement, grabbing the only jewels he'd ever have in his life. Simultaneously, she reached out with her left and right hands, fingers curled to project only knuckles and rammed the other two hard in the throats and they fell too, gasping for breath.

She continued walking, her heels clicking a sweet melody of self-assuredness as she glanced back over her right shoulder and said. "I'll be out in a few minutes. We'll play some more once you get your breaths back and pick your balls up off the pavement. I'll have a friend along though, so get ready to share me."

Chablis had done it, not out of anger, but out of concern. She wanted them to know that there were simply some people you did not mess with, some people who were not representative of authority, some people whom you showed respect until you found out they didn't deserve it. She was not the police who were always harassing them, but rather, she was one of them, a child of poverty. They just didn't know it. It was important to realize that there were those in suits, ties and fashionable dresses who did not look down on them, but rather had empathy for them. That old saying don't judge a book by its cover was certainly apropos. Not all people on the outside were evil. There were many people who genuinely cared, and they had to learn to tell the difference.

Chablis and Keita seemed to develop an instant simpatico, and Mama Martinez was a gracious host offering tea and cookies. Chablis asked about Keita being fired, and she said, "I guess I am what Americans hate. I am on unemployment, because I am making almost as much not working as I did working."

"No need to apologize. You paid into it. You earned it. Why shouldn't draw it? It's yours. Until they raise the minimum wage to a living wage, nobody should work for the peanuts they want to pay you. The barons of greed you work for spend the afternoons on the golf course, take a two hour lunch and deduct it all from their already too low taxes. Yet, the easily manipulated public, most of whom will one day be unemployed just like you, blames you rather than the greedy bustards that run things."

Keita laughed and said, "You should meet my brother J.J., you two think alike."

Chablis and the Terrorist
Who Resurrected the Spirit of Che Guevara

"Is he cute?"

"Well, he is my brother, but yes he is cute. He works up in Connecticut. As soon as he pays off all his student loans, we are moving from here."

"Smart guy I bet."

Projecting a sense if pride in her voice, Keita said, "Yes, very smart. He has a Ph.D."

"Impressive," replied Chablis.

"Well, he worked really hard. It wasn't easy."

"No," replied a thoughtful Chablis, "it never is easy for those of us who come from poverty. We get all the heartaches of struggling for an education while the rich kids act like school is just one big party."

"You are from Mexico, I assume," said Keita with a note of respect to her voice.

"I am, from a small village. Believe me, I know poverty's pinch."

Mrs. Martinez chirped in, "Don't we all?"

They had a few laughs and then Chablis asked Keita about her termination. Keita sighed and said, "I was there for 12 years and it meant nothing to Myerson. Hey, maybe I should be sorry about his murder, but frankly, I'm not. People like him are despicable human beings who are self-absorbed beyond redemption."

Nodding in agreement, Chablis eased back in the faded red chair that had been around almost as long as the tenement itself. "So, you know of no one who had a grudge against him, or maybe I should rephrase that – no one who had a big enough grudge against him to commit murder. You don't think this *Spirit of Che* fellow might be among some of the disgruntled people he let go?"

"No, no way anyone there would have done that. They just aren't the types. We are all too meek."

Smiling, Chablis said, "Well, remember what the Bible says, the meek will inherit the earth."

Keita interjected, "Well, my brother often says that the meek will inherit absolutely nothing. Being meek gets you a kick in the ass. If you don't fight for your piece of the earth the rich will just cobble it all up."

"You're brother sounds like my kind of guy. He's got his finger on the pulse of what it takes to get justice in this country. I am looking forward to meeting him."

Chablis made her way to the door, after saying goodbye to Mama Martinez, she then said to Keita, "Good luck. You seem like a nice family. I hope you do get out of here. I hope to meet your brother someday."

Chablis and the Terrorist
Who Resurrected the Spirit of Che Guevara

"He would like you Chablis. He loves short women with an attitude, and I since you got attitude."

Laughing, Chablis said, "If you only knew. Bye Keita."

Attitude was something she had since she realized as a precocious child she had been born with the wrong body. Walking into the courtyard, she noticed the three boys she had tangled with over by the water fountain that had been dry for years since the owner decided to save a few pennies on his water bill. Unafraid, chest stuck out, a swagger to her stride; she strolled unhesitatingly their way, with no fear or any trepidation and that was what was a source of frustration for them, as they were used to people cowering in fear before them, especially demure, tiny women like Chablis. They had to prove their manhood, so they defiantly and arrogantly approached her. The one she had kicked in the balls said, "Listen bitch, we gonna kick your ass. We may even ram one dick up your cunt, one up your ass and one down your throat. How'd you like that?"

Standing in front of the three, she smiled and said, "Well, if you boys washed those puny little things between your legs, I might like it, but I don't do unwashed sex. Go home and let mommy give you a bath. Then, come back and talk to me about an orgy. I don't usually do guys with dicks the size of my index finger, but I might make an exception for you boys."

Chablis and the Terrorist
Who Resurrected the Spirit of Che Guevara

You could see the veins pulsating in the boys necks as they were boiling with fury. Chablis was actually enjoying herself and very casually reached down under her short skirt for the blackjack she carried in a garter on her thigh. She pulled it out quickly and swiped it viciously across the leader's face, knocking him into the guy on his right and they both tumbled to the ground. The other guy, figuring discretion was the better part of valour, went running off like someone had scalded him with hot water. As the two on the ground struggled to get up, Chablis said, "I told you I had my friend with me. Fuck with me anymore and you'll spend the rest if the night picking your teeth up off the concrete. You boys should find something else to do besides intimating people. You ain't that tough."

As the leader reached in his back pocket, obviously for a gun, she said, "Don't do it asshole. Big mistake! I'll shove that rod up your ass." She pulled back her jacket and there on her hip was a big bastard of a 45, dangling by her side. She did not even touch it. She just said, "mines a lot bigger than yours, and I know how to use it. I eat boys like you for breakfast. I am not a broad you want to mess with, believe me."

He untangled himself from his buddy as, still laying on the ground looking up at Chablis, he put both hands up in front of his chest and said, "You win bitch. You win."

"Get a job punk. You aren't going to make it as a gangster. Not when you let a puny broad like me best you. You're a nice looking kid. Clean yourself up, get a job and you'll get more ass than a toilet seat."

Breaking out in laughter, he said, "Name's Tony Mercante, maybe you right woman. What's your name? You are one alright broad."

Chablis Louise Chavez – pleased to make your acquaintance."

Sitting up, he asked very politely "O.K. if I get up."

She nodded yes and Tony rose to his feet as did his pal. He looked directly at Chablis and said, "You are one tough bit----, I mean broad."

"Where I come from Tony, you are either tough or you get eaten alive."

"You ain't Puerto Rican, You a Mexican."

"Well, I am a Mexican-American. By the way, you know the Martinez family?

"Sure, they are a righteous bunch. The son, name's J.J., he is always talking about we need to form a tenants' committee and make some demands on the landlord and report him to the city for code violations, but people around here too scared to do anything. They afraid they'll get kicked out. Hey, we get inspectors down here all the time and J.J. says its cheaper for the landlord to pay a fine than to fix things."

"Yeah, he is probably right," said Chablis as she began to walk away.

Tony hollered at her as she was leaving, "Anything I can ever do for you Chablis let me know. You're always welcome down here."

Chablis and the Terrorist
Who Resurrected the Spirit of Che Guevara

CHAPTER 6
A MIGHTY BLOW FOR JUSTICE

*If a free society cannot help the many
who languish in poverty amidst plenty,
it cannot save the few who live in splendour
from the wrath of those living in squalor.*

Donald Beckman opened the letter from the nom de plum *Spirit of Che Guevara* with great anticipation, as even though the murder of people was abhorrent, he had developed an intense respect for J.J.'s intellectual acumen when it came to analyzing the sad state of things in a country that was run by and for the wealthy. This letter was intended as a precursor to what would be a dramatic act to make the nation and the C.E.O.'s who ran it realize that J.J. was not just a fringe revolutionary, but a man who was going to lift the curtain on the evils of a system that rewarded the 1% while ignoring the 99% who begged for a crumb from the table of plenty.

TO: C.E.O.'s Who Live a Life of Excess on the Backs of Those Who Toil in Obscurity

FROM: The Spirit of Che Guevara

To the C.E.O.'s who support the evolving fascist state with police who are not here to protect the poor but to protect the wealthy from the wrath of the oppressed, be advised that there are far more of the oppressed than there are of you. You compensate the police well and provide them with

Chablis and the Terrorist
Who Resurrected the Spirit of Che Guevara

lavish benefits because they are the last line of defence between the haves and have-nots.

I assure you that these fascists will not be able to protect you from the coming storm, because it is not just I who will rain down my vengeance upon you, but I shall soon be joined by others who have had enough of your greed. You will not be safe at your place of work. You will not be safe in your limousine as you motor to your palatial estate in the suburbs. You will not be safe in your gated, luxurious, opulent home guarded by your private gendarmes. You will not be safe on your yacht out on the high seas. You will be eternally looking over your shoulder for fear the Spirit of Che is stalking you, about ready to deliver a blow against the misery you promulgate. And be aware that I will soon be joined by others who will rise up against the tyranny of the 1% and the government that represents them.

Sincerely,

The Spirit of Che Guevara

The mayor and the police commissioner had pleaded with the *Times* not to publish anymore of the manifestos, but so far Donald's bosses, even though part of the corporate structure themselves, as newspapers had long ago ceased being an independent voice of the people, were determined to continue proper coverage of the story. That afternoon, even the President projected himself into the fray as he appeared before cameras to say:

Chablis and the Terrorist
Who Resurrected the Spirit of Che Guevara

"I have called this press conference to address the two recent murders of C.E.O.'s and to make it plain that all Americans, rich and poor, will be protected by this government. We do not play favourites. We are here to serve all Americans, and any threat against any American is a threat against us all. Although there is some disparity in income in this nation, this administration is dedicated to making sure everyone shares in the benefits of our glorious free enterprise system that is the envy of the world."

"To this terrorist who thinks he can change things single-handedly, we say we will not flinch in our devotion to free enterprise. This nation is great because of the economic system we embrace and love."

"This terrorist thinks evoking the name of Che Guevara will rally people to his cause, but the truth is we all know that Che failed, because he was on the wrong side of history. This nation won the Cold War, because capitalism is the greatest economic system on the face of the earth, and it is a system we will defend to the death. It makes it possible for the lowest to attain heights unimaginable in other economic systems."

"Che Guevara died a lonely and violent death. This terrorist will suffer the same fate."

"I am instructing the F.B.I. to coordinate efforts with New York City Police, since that is where this terrorist apparently has his base of operations."

J. Wayne Frye   141

Chablis and the Terrorist
Who Resurrected the Spirit of Che Guevara

"These people he is targeting are important to this nation, as they are the captains of industries that fuel our economy. Without these people, our economic well-being will be affected. Join me my fellow Americans in stamping out this evil so that this great nation can continue to keep its economic engine humming unrestrained. Be eternally vigilant and report any suspicious activity at all. We will never bend to terrorism, because we are a great beacon of freedom in the world."

"Now, I will take a few questions."

J.J. was watching the President's performance and considered it to be just what he expected. He came down on the side of the wealthy, as he and every other President had always done. He was trying to rally the poor and the middle class to stand against a man who was killing their bosses. Most citizens would stand with him, because they foolishly fell for that old adage "anyone can make it in America." They were too stupid to understand that for every 1 out of 1000 who made it out of the ghetto, 1000 out of 1000 made it out of Beverly Hills, because in Beverly Hills, daddy owned the company. People had been swallowing that propaganda for far too long. J.J. was about to deliver a blow that would shake the very foundations of a society based on greed. So far, not a single C.E.O. had offered to make amends and change the corporate culture toward a more equitable distribution of wealth and to share the profits with those who were responsible for them. After today, people would know that the *Spirit of Che Guevara* meant business.

Chablis and the Terrorist
Who Resurrected the Spirit of Che Guevara

Later, J.J. called Donald Beckman, and told him that he wanted to let him know that by 5:00 PM that afternoon, people would be comparing that day with 9/11, because he was about to strike a blow for the poor. He asked Donald to record his words, so that they would be available for him to transcribe and to give to any network news he deemed appropriate. The following are his words verbatim:

"Americans believe many things that are obviously untrue. They are propagandized into believing that it is easy for any American to make money. They will not acknowledge how, in fact, money is not easy to make, and, therefore, those who have no money blame themselves. This blame plays upon the psychology of the poor, as they begin to genuinely believe it is their own fault they are poor. In America, less is done for the poor than in any other country. That is because the government refuses to fairly tax the rich, rather, relying on the middle class to provide lavish welfare for the rich and a pittance of welfare for the poor. The poor are made villains in America. Conservatives say if you don't give the rich more money, they will lose their incentive to invest. As for the poor, they say they have lost all incentive because they are given too much money. This kind of convoluted thinking was pushed by idiots like Ronald Reagan who invented the story of the woman on welfare driving a Cadillac and collecting six welfare checks. It was a lie, and even if it was the truth, for every woman like her, there are 100 rich barons of greed milking the government of revenue through nefarious schemes to avoid taxes."

Chablis and the Terrorist
Who Resurrected the Spirit of Che Guevara

"The poor are poor not because they are untrained or illiterate, but because they are not fairly rewarded for their labour. They have no control over capital, and it is the ability to control capital that gives people the power to rise out of poverty. Capital is passed down from one generation to the other by the wealthy, and, therefore, it is always used to further the solidification of the privileged class. George Bush was never successful at anything, including being President, but he started out at the top because of his name. He decried welfare, but used it himself to have the taxpayers bail out his failing baseball team. He railed against affirmative action, but used it to get into Yale as the son of an alumnus. Affirmative action for the wealthy keeps them assured a spot at the table of plenty."

"The problem with the poor is poverty. The problem with the rich is their complete uselessness. They serve no worthwhile purpose whatsoever. Today, some of the most useless of the rich will finally serve a purpose. They will be used as an example of what is going to happen if things don't change. The wealthy are headed for a rude awakening courtesy of the Spirit of Che Guevara."

The phone was immediately hung up by J.J., and by that time, many people had gathered around Donald's desk, and they all stood there silent, dumbfounded by the intense perceptiveness of the man calling himself the *Spirit of Che Guevara*. They all knew that everything he had said was correct. In fact, there was much empathy with him.

Chablis and the Terrorist
Who Resurrected the Spirit of Che Guevara

Harry Roberts stood there just staring at the phone. He looked over at Donald and said, "What the hell is this guy going to do? Get this out on the wire immediately, get it to the networks and get it ready for a special edition. Damn, what is he up to?"

J.J., sitting in his Crown Victoria, where he had used the computer for the call, simply opened the door and placed the computer on the sidewalk. No need to throw it away he thought, someone could use it. He drove away and headed for Wall Street where he was about to unleash hell.

While J.J. was headed toward Wall Street to unleash his fury, Chablis was working through the names of people who had been laid off by Kimberline. As she took the Metro-North subway to uptown Harlem where former Kimberline employee, Louise Fleck lived, she reflected on Keita Martinez and how she seemed content with her life, despite the poverty. She did have a brother who seemed to be doing all he could to get her and his mom out of the ghetto, so maybe she was content knowing that there was light at the end of the tunnel. Of course, Chablis remembered once reading that the light at the end of the tunnel for the poor was often a freight train heading their way.

As she got off the subway and made her way up the stairs to the street, she was attracting the usual attention from both men and women. Part of being a sexy, alluring woman is adjusting to the attention you attract. Chablis was used to it, and had actually grown to crave it, especially from men, as it gave her validation as a woman, something she had to seek all her life, because of her unique condition. Her tough, determined, swaggering exterior self-confidence was not just an act she had perfected as a result of years of being persecuted, as it was genuine, but beneath the surface there was still that self-doubt that was planted there by a society that refused to embrace her wholeheartedly with acceptance. It was better in New York than Mexico, but America was a society engrained with religion, and that meant judgmental arrogance from those who were always pointing the finger of disapproval at anyone who deviated from the norm.

She was slowly moving north of 100th Street where the neighbourhoods were a sporadic mixture of bad and very bad. Burned out buildings dotted the streets as slum lords often just collected the insurance from fires they set themselves or arranged to have set and left the remains for the city to clean up as they used shell corporations to insulate themselves from liabilities. Just another example of how the system was set-up to provide minimal welfare for the poor and lavish welfare for those who preyed upon them.

Wretched apartments with broken windows patched with rags and paper: every place let out to two or even three or four or five families at astronomical rents, often subsidized by the city that got out of public housing and handed the money over to entrepreneurs who made a living off human misery. This was business American style – rant and rave against the welfare state, but make millions off it. Taxpayers railed against those who lived in the squalor of poverty, but they conveniently overlooked the real welfare recipients who laughed all the way to the bank – the rich.

Wretched apartment buildings lined the streets, with broken windows patched with rags and paper: every room let out to a different family, and in many instances to two or even three, four, five or six as the exorbitant rents charged by the slum lords nictitated communal living. Filth was everywhere as basic sanitation measures were ignored by the landlords who wanted to maximize profit at the cost of human decency. Clothes were dangling from fire escapes as the tenants could not afford the electricity it took to run a clothes dryer. Children were walking about barefooted, while others somehow managed to walk about in Air Jordan's. Parents splurged to satisfy the whims of children who fell for the advertising hype that said you were somebody if you had expensive sneakers. How ironic thought Chablis, the poor buy high priced sneakers that were made by slave labour in China so American corporations can get rich by producing nothing in America. They handed a basketball player millions, whose only accomplishment in life was being able to put a ball through a hoop, which lifted him from poverty by selling himself to a group of billionaire white men who ran a monopoly called the NBA. Yeah, it was the American way, and those ball players who made millions did not realize that though they enjoyed the good life, they were still slaves to the owners of the plantation that was called the NBA. Nothing had changed, only like Bush and Cheney calling torture "legitimate use of repetitive force" the name had just been altered to mask the truth. The workers, in this case the players, still provided the labour while the owners did nothing but sit in their expensive luxurious private suites and count their money.

This was all an affront to common decency in a nation filled with excess. While there was always money for bombs and bullets to subdue others, there was never money for things that mattered. She found the address and walked into a filthy vestibule with human feces piled in one corner.

Here was where the lowest forms outside the leeches of Wall Street and the environs of the politicians, lived. Various classes of thieves common to large cities were banded together because they we relatively safe here where they easily blended in with the poor. The low-rent thief was harboured among those whose only crime was poverty, and these appalling conditions prevailed because a nation simply didn't care. A nation had simply lost its way, or never really found it. Ironically, those who professed religious conviction were among the most vociferous in blaming the poor for being poor. How easy it is to say, "Get an education." However, no consideration is given to those who simply don't have the mental capacity to get an education. We are not all born equally economically, nor are we all born with the gifts of a superior intellect. Chablis was one of the lucky ones, but she had used sex to get her education; or otherwise, she would have been stuck in poverty like these people. Her good looks and brains offered her a way out, but if it had not been for her good looks, even her brains would not have been adequate.

She looked at the row of mailboxes and found number 418, the Fleck family. She moved up the stairs cautiously, as they were made of wood and some of the planks were obviously rotten. As she got to the 3rd floor landing, there, smiling down at her was a rotten toothed gangster who said, "Hey baby, you a nice looking broad. Wanna go to work for me and make a few bucks?"

"No thanks. I have a job."

"Hey baby, what kind of job you got," he said as he put his hands on her shoulder and began to massage it.

"Why my job is amputating the hands of men who think they have a right to touch me without being asked. I cut them off at the wrist and fix it where they can't even jack-off anymore. Now, I am sure you do a lot of jacking-off, because not many women are going to fuck a low-life gangster like you who obviously hasn't had a bath in a week, so move your ass out of my way, before I toss you over the railing and laugh while you lay on the lobby floor looking up at me with a broken neck."

He could not believe a demure woman like Chablis could talk to him like that. He stared at her in disbelief. "Damn bitch! You talk tough for a little broad. You messing with Randy Ramirez, and that ain't smart."

"Randy, you are the one who isn't smart. Don't fuck with Chablis Louise Chavez."

His jaw dropped and he stuttered, "You that transsexual P.I. brought down the cop for killing an unarmed dude over on Lenox Avenue and muzzling in on his drug territory."

"I am, but he got released on appeal. There isn't any justice when it comes to rogue cops. They are all protected, because they are the last line of defence against the rich and the poor."

Smiling, he said, "You are righteous dame. Yeah, you are."

"Thanks, I need to go to the 4th floor," Chablis said as she pointed upward.

Steeping to his right and standing against the wall, Randy said, "Do your thing Chablis."

She gave him a seductive wink and said, "I always do Randy."

He watched her go upstairs and thought about that old timey song, "The way you wiggle when you walk would make a hound dog talk. He grabbed his crotch to adjust his instrument of pleasure as she had caused an erection.

Chablis and the Terrorist
Who Resurrected the Spirit of Che Guevara

No matter how hard people who are forced to live in appalling conditions try, they cannot make a slum apartment look like they were living on Park Avenue. Obviously, the Flecks made an effort as the door, unlike all those around it was freshly painted and the entryway was clear of debris, unlike the other 12 doors up and down the corridor. A gentle knock and from behind the door came in Spanish, "yes, who is it?"

Answering in Spanish, Chablis said, "I am Chablis Louise Chavez, and I am interested in talking to you about Mr. Kimberline. I am not police, just a person trying to locate someone, and I thought Mrs. Fleck might be of some help."

Now speaking in English, the voice said, as Chablis heard the door chain being loosened and the door unbolted, "just a minute."

Standing in the doorway was a woman of maybe 30, who looked 50 because of hard work. Her shoulders were stooped, her eyes were deep set and her forehead was furrowed with premature wrinkles. She sighed as she said, "come in please."

The living room was exceeding small, maybe 8 X 6 but clean despite being unpainted and having unmatched floor tiles that were obviously remnants the landlord had picked up on the cheap. So small and confined was the room that you could smell the gathering scent of humans living in cramped quarters. The ceiling was peeling and paint flecks had dropped onto the floor and furniture.

Chablis and the Terrorist
Who Resurrected the Spirit of Che Guevara

Every repulsive lineament of poverty, every loathsome indication of lost hope abounded in this monument to man's humanity to man. This was the result of unrestrained capitalism that allowed poverty to be used to furl the engine of exploitation. Chablis glanced into the adjoining kitchen where there was no stove; only a hotplate used to prepare meals, and off to the left of the counter top, door closed, was obviously a bathroom right in the kitchen area, so money could be saved on plumbing costs when the place was being built. The poor had to defecate where they ate. On the right side of the kitchen Chablis saw an old metal washtub, as obviously the washing was done by hand, and on the fire escape, hanging up to catch all the polluted air were clothes. And this was called the greatest nation on earth, the hope of mankind. If this was hope, then there was no reason to expect a nation to ever rise from the despair of disparity? Where were the Bible thumpers who always talked about lending a helping hand? How could men and women of faith turn a blind eye to a nation of plenty that allowed this cancer to fester and grow? Did they not realize that without hope these people had no power to absorb the wrong and walk in love? These conditions brought about a lack of respect for self and a loathing for humanity that forced these conditions upon those who had done nothing wrong but be born into poverty.

Poverty was more than a physical condition. The mind was also bound by poverty and imprisoned in hopelessness. An economic system based on greed kept people in bondage both physically and psychologically. Chablis broke the silence as Louise Fleck pointed to a dilapidated chair in the corner, indicating Chablis should have a seat. Easing into the chair, Chablis said, "I am trying to get a line on anyone who might be even remotely involved in the murder of Mr. Kimberline. I am not here to accuse, but only to see if you might shed some light on any particular enemies who might have had reason to kill him. I know that the man calling himself the *Spirit of Che* is taking credit for the murder, but I thought that perhaps the *Spirit of Che* might be someone who was fired."

"Lady, everyone hated Kimberline. There was probably a celebration by most of his employees when they got word of his death."

Managing a little smile, Chablis added, "Yeah, I think even his wife was pleased about his demise. "

Louise laughed and offered an astute observation. "Hey, sometimes murder isn't all that bad if it is the right person killed. I can't say I don't have some sympathies with this person calling himself the *Spirit of Che*." She then looked around at her surroundings and continued, "I certainly don't have anything to fear from him."

Chablis smiled courteously and said with emphasis, "Me either."

They shared a laugh and Chablis continued. "Actually, my client is a journalist and wants to talk to him. My guess is that he will not degrade him but

Chablis and the Terrorist
Who Resurrected the Spirit of Che Guevara

shine a light of understanding on him. Sometimes, criminals are good people who just wind up doing bad things."

"Tell me about it. My husband is doing a dime at Sing-Sing for robbing a 7-11. We once went a week without food and he just could not stand to see our three children going hungry any longer."

"Welcome to America that builds more prisons than universities, because they need to incarcerate those who rock-the-boat or commit a petty crime. You rob a 7-11 of a few dollars and you are in the slammer doing a dime like your husband. Ten years for a petty crime to feed a hungry family in a nation where the rich pay no taxes and dine on caviar every night. Rob people of their pensions and they fine you 25 million dollars when you stole 100 million. That is justice American style. Why wouldn't people reared in poverty be resentful of authority?"

Chablis continued passionately, as Ms. Fleck listened intently. "If poverty is ever eliminated, we'll need to build museums to display its horrors to future generations. They'll wonder why poverty continued so long in human society - how a few people could live in luxury while billions dwelt in misery, deprivation and despair."

Smiling, Louise said, "You are really smart."

"Not so smart, just astute when it comes to what the problems are in this nation. Anyway, anybody at all you can think of who might have been motivated to carry a grudge against Kimberline all the way to murder?

"Not that I can think of. You know Keita Martinez was always trying to organize us workers, but we were too stupid to realize that in numbers there is power. She isn't the type to commit murder though."

"I've already talked to her. Nice lady," said Chablis.

"Yes she is nice. You want to meet a really nice person, talk to her brother, J.J. He came down to pick her up at work a few times. He tried to talk us into organizing. He was always quoting Marx about how the capitalists controlled the means of production and thereby controlled us. He worked for the city, but I heard he had quit, got fed up with the incompetence and self-serving that led to nothing worthwhile ever being done."

Chablis took out her notebook and went over all the names in it with Louise. None of them seemed to offer any hope for an individual who would adopt the name *Spirit of Che* and go on a murder spree. Yet, Chablis could not help but think somehow Kimberline was the key. He was a crook alright and a financial manipulator, but in a day and age when people and corporations stole billions, he was relatively small potatoes. Still, her instincts just wouldn't let it go. She knew there was something there, something she was missing.

Chablis and the Terrorist
Who Resurrected the Spirit of Che Guevara

It was noon, and J.J. was preparing for the day of atonement for some of Wall Street's greatest financial wizards who were still raking in billions after nearly collapsing the entire economy on 2007. While petty criminals were prosecuted and locked away for years, these financial manipulators, who had used other people's money to bring down the world's biggest economy, continued their chicanery unabated as their crimes were ignored by a new administration that bailed out big business while letting the little guy go under. While all this was happening, the man who was at the helm of the ship when he sank it through malfeasance, George Bush, was down on his farm drawing a huge taxpayer funded pension as a reward for his incompetence. Welcome to politics, where the first rule of the game is to take care of yourself, and ironically, there were people who still idolized the biggest buffoon to ever inherit the White House. Well, today, J.J. was about to strike a blow for the common man, and it might not rival 9/11 in its overall carnage, but it would surpass it in effect, because he was not taking down the secretaries, the janitors, the window washers or the stock boys. He was going to bring down some of America's tycoons of tyranny.

For weeks, J.J. had gone over a list of Wall Street manipulators who had been at the helm when the economy was crashed to satisfy their greed. His list was long and inclusive:

1. Delbert Manley of Manley and Associates, net worth 3.4 billion dollars

2. Anderson Belmont, Belmont, Inc., net worth 3.2 billion dollars
3. Harold Lepperstein, Hatfield and McDonald, net worth 3.2 billion dollars
4. Martin Attronsky, Darwin Fund, net worth 3.2 billion dollars

In addition, there were 32 other names, bringing the total he planned to kill to 36 and their total net worth to more than 85 billion dollars. Now, to get all 36 of these arrogant, self-serving men in one place would be difficult, but what one factor would motivate them all to risk life and limb to show up at the same place at the same time? What else but money?

It appears that an anonymous Middle Eastern Sheik wanted to meet with them all to arrange a giant consortium that would corner the world's gold market and make them all rich beyond any of their wildest dreams. The greatest motivating factor in the world for these titans of capitalism was the thought of getting even more money than they already had accumulated. For them there would never be enough.

A sheik showed up with $50,000 in cash to rent a conference room at 39 Wall Street Towers. (The one million J.J. got from Kimberline was actually going to contribute to bringing down some of his fellow manipulators.) How ironic thought J.J. as he appeared in darkened skin, long flowing robes and a kuffiya on his head that he would be using ill gotten money to lure the barons of greed to their doom.

Chablis and the Terrorist
Who Resurrected the Spirit of Che Guevara

The meeting place was across the street from the Trump Building which at one time belonged to former Philippines President, Ferdinand Marcos, who, though termed a dictator by the USA, was not deposed until he threatened to nationalize some industries that were vital to U.S. interests, and in that building J.J. had rented a suite on the 24th floor so he could observe the people going into the 39 Wall Street Building, where his meeting with the potentates of finance was supposed to occur.

After 9/11, paranoia set in as a result of America's inability to tend to its own business. For some reason, every blip on the radar that involved a militant group, especially in the Middle East, was interpreted as a signal to Americans that someone wanted to do them harm. Americans have lived in paranoia since the Cold War, because keeping them in constant fear of something or somebody allows the government to exert maximum control over a populace that is easily manipulated when it comes to so-called patriotism. Unfortunately, Americans are too naïve to realize nobody cares about them, and very few people want to be like them. How many countries want for-profit healthcare where citizens don't get free coverage for illnesses? How many countries want their tax dollars wasted on bombs and bullets rather than social amenities? All the world wants is to be left alone to sort out its own problems free from interference from a nation that thinks it is somehow superior to all others. What America has to offer is not wanted by most of the world, because they see it as a society ruled by greed, religion and arrogance.

Chablis and the Terrorist
Who Resurrected the Spirit of Che Guevara

Well, that greed was about to end the lives of 36 of its wealthiest citizens. J.J. was actually very proud of himself for how he had set it up. The day before, in order to get three bombs and a cache of weapons past the metal detector and guards, he had devised a very unique diversion. He rented a van under an assumed name and fake driver's licence. He put a plastic sign on the side of the van that read *Denman Window Washing*. That was the company that had the contract to clean the windows. He was amazed at how easy it was to first of all, build three bombs that he was going to strategically place in the building's inner structure that would collapse it in one well-timed implosion. He had gotten the architect's drawings from the city archives and through meticulous study of engineering concepts found the exact stress points that would easily collapse the building. He simply placed the scaffold on the side of the building and began to slowly pull it up as if he were preparing for work. In the three buckets that were supposed to contain the cleaning mixture he delicately placed the bombs. In a huge work case, he placed three Uzi machine guns. As he pulled the scaffold up the side of the building, he noticed a guard walk below him and look up, but he made no attempt to do anything as he obviously assumed J.J. was performing a legally assigned task. Outside the window on the 12th floor was a small ledge that had bronze metal trim. J. J. had attached magnets to the buckets and the metal case with the Uzis. He simply activated the electronic magnets and the buckets and case were secured against the ledge. Fortunately, this was an old building, and it had windows that opened. He lowered the scaffold and got off, packed it up and drove around the corner where he got in the back and put on his sheik disguise. Upon telling the guards who he was, they passed him through the metal detector, and of course, since he appeared to be of Middle Eastern origin, thoroughly searched him.

He went up to the 12th floor of the building, opened the window and simply walked down the hall in three trips and put the buckets and Uzis in the conference room he had rented. He spent the night there, and at 4:00 AM, when the last of the cleaning crews had left, he went into the elevator shaft and placed the bombs on the pillars that should easily bring the building down into a pile of rubble. He waited until 10:00 AM, went home, showered and got cleaned up and went back to the Trump Building across the street from 39 Wall Street where he used binoculars at 5:00 PM to make sure all the men showed up.

They all finally had assembled in the conference room at 6:00 PM. J.J., in his sheik's clothing walked across the street and was easily passed through the metal detector. What follows is a verbatim account of what happened that day which would be called by the United States President another day of infamy, but was, in fact, a day of divine retribution against those who accumulated fortunes by abusing and using others to satisfy their greed.

The conference room was abuzz with conversation about how this person seemed to have his hand on the pulse of matters related to gold, and that they were all going to realize huge profits.

J.J. walked in, and without introducing himself, walked over to a huge wall cabinet that he had put a lock on. He unlocked it and removed one of the Uzis and all there were overwhelmed with fright as J.J. said, "All have a seat and put your cell-phones on the table. Anyone makes a move without my permission is dead."

J.J. had them slide the cell-phones to the end of the table and he raked all but one onto the floor. He picked up the phone and dialled 911. "There is a bomb in the 39 Wall Street Building. You'd better evacuate it quick."

The flamboyant flim flam artists of Wall Street all sighed in disbelief. J.J. smiled as he slowly removed with one hand, while holding the Uzi with the other, his sheik outfit and picked up a wet towellette and rubbed off his makeup. The men who controlled the lives of thousands and acted like royalty were now in mortal fear of what was going to happen.

J.J. took a seat and began to talk as there was mass confusion and in the outside hallway, people were pounding on the door, but J.J. warned the financial wizards of Wall Street that any cry out would lead to his finger touching the hair trigger of the Uzi and all of them would be dead in an instant. Soon, the commotion had died down and J.J. said, "You all came here in hopes of gaining more wealth. Well, I am going to give you a wealth of information about yourselves. All of you are to human dignity, sanity, integrity and character what cat piss is to fine wine."

J.J dialled Donald Beckman's number. Donald answered and with a very low "hello."

When J.J. put the phone on speaker and said "this is the *Spirit of Che Guevara*," all those sitting at the conference tabled let out sighs of fear.

J.J. said, "Those are the sighs of fear from people who have no remorse for all the chicanery they have practiced over the years to accumulate fortunes on the backs of the downtrodden. I am about to have a serious discussion with 36 men who have lied, cheated and stolen for years with impunity in a nation that has no heart and no soul when it comes to giving a hand up to the least of us.'

Donald pleaded with him, "Don't be rash. Please let me help air your grievances and maybe people will begin to understand that things in this nation must change."

"Oh, people will listen, but they only listen when acts of violence make them listen; otherwise, they sit around complacently and allow this obscenity to go on and on unabated."

So frightened were these captains of industry that you could almost cut the trepidation with a knife. One of them said, "There's only one of you and 36 of us. We'll subdue you with minimum casualties."

Chablis and the Terrorist
Who Resurrected the Spirit of Che Guevara

J.J. reached in his pocket and brought out a grenade, pulling the pin, and holding it, he said, "Made by the good old USA to do maximum damage. You will be dead before you can get up. It is a percussion grenade – and throws out ball bearings in all directions. Of course, America wouldn't call that a terror weapon, only a legitimate dispensation of justice weapon."

Thus began J.J.'s oration to these cretins of cash, masters of money mayhem, deceivers for dollars: "The few own the many in this nation because the few possess the means of livelihood of all. The country is governed for the richest, for the corporations, the bankers, the land speculators, and for the exploiters of labour. The majority of mankind are working people. So long as their fair demands, the ownership and control of their livelihoods is denied them, there are no workers rights. The majority are ground down by economic and political repression in order for the few to enjoy lives of grandeur and splendour. This is an abomination."

"America is the wealthiest nation on earth, but its people are mainly poor, and poor Americans are told it is there fault they are poor. No industrialized nation of Europe allows this kind of poverty to exist in the midst of plenty. There, a safety net is provided that lifts up the lowest, and a hand of compassion is offered to assist those who need it. In America, the wealthy are glorified and even the poor worship them as if they were royalty, when in fact, they are nothing but leeches.

Chablis and the Terrorist
Who Resurrected the Spirit of Che Guevara

America's poor mock themselves and glorify those they assume are their betters. These men here should not be exalted, because there only accomplishment is the accumulation of money. They offer no concrete benefit to mankind. They pile up wealth while people who really work, the man who serves you your meal in McDonald's, the woman who toils cleaning office buildings, the young man who weaves through traffic delivering that UPS package, the maid who scrubs your toilet bowls is chastised and ridiculed for not getting an education so they can be among the elite, when the truth is, even the educated today, if they are not from wealth, are servants to the royalty of commerce and the inheritors of position based upon, not what they did, but what their parents did. This nepotism is at the core of what perpetuates inequity."

"Ironically, it is the poor who often are the most vociferous in their flag waving and love of Jesus. They are propagandized into believing they live in a nation of equals, and they are told by the three thousand dollar suit wearing pompadoured preachers of pie-in-the-sky, who, themselves, live the high life, that the poor will get their reward in the sweet by and by. They cling to the false belief that they have opportunity when the only opportunity they have is the opportunity to be fodder for the machine of capitalism that will grind them up. They cling to religion, because their only real hope is that in the end they will somehow be rewarded for all their pain on this earth. Religion is an invention of the rich to keep the poor at bay by giving them hope for riches in the afterlife. Does the pope not live in splendour? How many ministers do you see living in poverty? Do they not drive fancy cars, receive lavish salaries and live in abodes of abundance while telling the flock Jesus will give them all riches in an afterlife while they enjoy riches in this life? Hypocrisy is at the very core of this giant, blood-sucking Jesus corporation that is like every other corporation. People go to the mall to buy happiness. With a dollar in the collection plate, they believe they are buying happiness in the afterlife."

The richest among those gathered, Delbert Manley, interrupted. "Don't disparage Jesus. I am a believer. I gave my church over one million dollars last year. If you kill me today, I'll be in glory with my saviour."

J. J. let out a subdued, muffled laugh. "Hear that Donald? Mr. Benevolent here, who stole 100 million, gave his church one million." Then J.J.'s eyes nearly burned a hole in Manley as he penetrated his heartless soul. "You gave nothing; the people you stole from gave it, and if you tithed as your beloved Bible says you should, you would have given the church 10 million which is 10% of what you stole." Then he pointed the Uzi directly at him and continued, "Tell Jesus hello when you get to glory, asshole."

He pulled the trigger and pumped a bevy of bullets into a man who was already spiritually dead. Now his body had just caught up with his soul. The others were now redoubled in fear. They knew J.J. meant business and they were all beginning to beg for their lives, the only way they knew how. They were all offering him money, as Donald, his phone on speaker, was surrounded by the shocked workers who had all heard the rat-a-tat-tat of retribution that spit out from that which Americans loved almost as much as money and Jesus – a gun.

Donald pleaded with J.J. "Please no more deaths. We can work to get your point across without violence."

J.J. then said, "America proves it time and time again. Power comes from the barrel of a gun. I am only doing what America does, using violence to accomplish that which I desire. You reap what you sow, and America has sowed the seeds of violence that will be its own doom. I am the grim reaper of retribution for all the ills that this nation has left unchecked. Tell your readers that blood will flow. I, the *Spirit of Che Guevara*, am a one man revolution, but they can join me. They can refuse to bow before these barons of greed. They can band together and demand fairness. If every worker at McDonald's, Burger King, Wendy's and KFC refused to go to work today, within a few days they would begin paying fair wages. If every worker at GM, Chrysler, Ford, American Toyota walked off the job until the wages of those at the top are cut and that the workers share in the profits they generate for the company, the stockholders, who would see their investment diminish in value would demand that the company do the right thing. The people fail to realize that there are more of us than there are of them. There are not enough bullets to slay all of us if we just make a stand against the tyranny that robs us of our dignity."

Then J.J., looking to his left, noticed a fine mist forming outside the window as a slight drizzle began to fall. There, in the mist was an image, and for the first time, others saw the image. All there, except J.J. began to cringe in fear. It was a ghost-like figure forming at the window. It wore a beret, puffed on a cigar and had loose fitting army fatigues on. They were all aghast. J.J. simply said, "Yes," and he pulled the trigger mowing down in mass the evil that sat at the table before him. As this went on, Donald and those in the editorial office bowed their heads and stood in silence.

J.J. could be heard saying with great conviction, "Yes, this is only the beginning of what will be a new hope."

He removed the rest of his Sheik outfit, as underneath he had a suit and tie. He carefully removed his false nose, thick eyebrows and mole he had put on his left cheek. He used a moist towellette and washed away the darkener from his skin. He shouted out for Donald to hear, "Be sure that no one goes into this building. It will be a pile of rubble that can serve as a reminder to all that the wages of greed shall be dealt with harshly by the *Spirit of Che*. The clock is ticking and change had better come soon or every visage of exploitation will lie in ruins along with the corpses of the exploiters."

Chablis and the Terrorist
Who Resurrected the Spirit of Che Guevara

Donald heard the door to the conference room slam and shouted. "Call the police department instantly and tell them no one should go into that building, even in a rescue effort, as it is obviously going to be blown up."

J.J. walked calmly down the stairs until he arrived at the lobby, where the last few people were frantically scurrying out the door. He strolled out into the street, where the police were hurriedly forcing people to move away from the periphery of the building. He wondered how many of these policemen and firemen would be declared heroes by government officials and the media. Yes, they would be heroes for doing the job for which they were paid. What convoluted thinking thought J.J.? Meanwhile, the real heroes, people who went about their jobs every day so they could put food on the table for their families were ignored. The true heroes were those who led lives of quiet desperation oiling the machinery of capitalism with their labour.

Soon, the patriotic dribble would flow like a raging river through a gorge as it would be used to unite the people in an unjust cause. The glorification of American superiority, the invocation of God as being appalled at how a nation of good Christians could be so dishonoured would be used to rally the people so that the status-quo could be protected. The glorification of those poor titans of industry who had suffered at the hands of a deranged individual would begin, because their deaths were more important than the deaths of the janitor who cleaned their toilets, or the maid who served them their dinners or the chauffeur who drove them to their country club.

In the crowd that day was Joe Harrington, who had fortuitously been on his way uptown to see Chablis. He did not know it but he was actually standing only three feet from the man he had hired Chablis to find. As the building was finally free of all people, J.J. noticed a tall, well-built, distinguished looking gentleman walk up to a captain of police, who was obviously in charge of the evacuation of the building and whisper something. The man was Joe Harrington. He wondered what a civilian would be whispering to the police captain. The captain was obviously intimidated by the man's presence as he began to, in an animated way, move with him to the control centre where they met with another plain clothes policeman and the three engaged in a heated discussion. They were pointing at the building, and the captain kept nodding his head up and down in agreement with something that was being said by Joe Harrington. Eventually, Harrington moved away from them and headed down the street, away from the building. J.J. watched as he got to the corner, where he met with another well-dressed man. They talked for awhile. Harrington rounded the corner and disappeared from view as the other man walked to the control centre where he engaged in a conversation with the two others. What was the connection thought J.J.?

J.J. stood a few hundred feet away from the building and contemplated what he saw, but suddenly his chain of thought was broken when he watched gleefully as a mighty explosion ripped through the 12th floor. The monument to greed imploded on itself and within a few seconds nothing but a pile of rubble lay where once a mighty tribute to exploitation stood. And above the building, as people in the crowd began to gasp and point, the giant outline of a man in a beret and army fatigues formed out of the dust that soared toward the heavens. Some people had seen the face of Jesus in the 9/11 smoke while others claimed to have seen the devil's outline. Of course, the Reverend Jerry "Silent Majority" Falwell attributed the carnage to homosexuality. J.J. wondered what people would say about the faint image in the dust that formed above the rubble from 39 Wall Street. He smiled, turned and walked away, confident in the knowledge that no innocents had died while he had delivered a mighty blow for justice.

Chablis and the Terrorist
Who Resurrected the Spirit of Che Guevara

CHAPTER 7
THE PICKIGNS WERE PLENTIFUL

Ginsbergian metaphors float on a crimsoned sky,
where dreams float about awhile and then die.

What hammer of iron bashed open their skulls and
ate up their brains and imagination?
Filth! Ugliness! Ashcans of unobtainable dollars!
Children screaming under the stairways!
The poor in armies of discontent weep in their misery.
Incomprehensible prisons built to house those
who dare question the economic order of things.
The system causes a congress of sorrows.
The God these people are to worship is green.
Money is the cannibal that devours all.
Skyscrapers erected to greed stand like sphinxes
over the streets that are but smoking tombs.
The air belches fogs of greed from those
who cannot see anything but dollar signs.
Poverty dances among the spectre of genius.
Light streaming out of the smog filled sky!
Robot apartments! Invisible suburbs!
Skeleton treasuries! Blind capitalists!
Demonic industries! Spectral nations! A madhouse!
Build monstrous bombs to subdue
while ignoring hunger in the midst.
They break their backs lifting caches of money for
those who rain like royalty over all.
Malls, movies and televisions to occupy time
so that rebellion will be stayed.
Orwellian slavery is the destiny of all.
Visions! Omens! Hallucinations! Miracles! Ecstasies!

Chablis and the Terrorist
Who Resurrected the Spirit of Che Guevara

Gone down the river of no return.
Dreams! Adorations! Illuminations! Hope!
Awaits in the arms of Jesus who
is used by the wealthy to placate
those will get their money in heaven.
Wait! Wait! Wait! Wait!
The hereafter will reward you with some gold.
They see it all, but are given none.
Capitalism blots out the hopeful sun.

Ginsbergian metaphors float on a crimsoned sky,
where dreams float about awhile and then die.

As crowds gathered in dismay, many lamenting another act of evil against a great nation, vendors seemed to appear out of nowhere on the streets near the collapsed building selling miniature American flags made in China for people to wave as patriotic symbols of a nation that had once again suffered the wrath of some evil terrorist. Yes, it was the height of evil to kill 36 blood-sucking leeches and bring down into rubble a building that housed the maliciousness of greed.

Instant news flooded the airwaves as talks of terrorism abounded everywhere, but J.J. very calmly walked to a phone booth, one of the few left in Manhattan, as greed made a cell-phone a necessity, even for the poor, as companies no longer wanted to provide a cheap way for making a call. Even bums on the street were expected to have a cell-phone. He dialled Donald Beckman and said, "I am in a hurry. Listen carefully. Do you have your recorder on?"

Chablis and the Terrorist
Who Resurrected the Spirit of Che Guevara

Donald replied, "Yes, Go ahead."

"I am sure by now that the networks are trying to rally the poor patriotic rabble to stand in unison against terrorism, but I hope you will continue to publish the truth. I killed no innocent person. I only brought justice to those who thought they were above the law. Tell the people that regardless of patriotic dibble poured forth by the flag-waving morons at FOX I try to avoid collateral damage against the innocent workers who are nothing but pawns in a system of economic slavery. This is a day of infamy alright. It is a day of infamy that will be recorded as a mighty blow against the barons of greed. I await two things: Number one, the reforming of the system so that workers will benefit from their labour. C.E.O.'s who begin that process immediately will be spared. Number two: I await compatriots who will begin to rise up against the unjustness of the marketplace. If they join me in this fight they shall be free of the chains that have for far too long bound them in economic servitude. The *Spirit of Che Guevara* shall free us all!"

He hung up and proceeded to walk toward home, secure in the knowledge that he had planted a seed that would grow into a mighty tree with many branches. This would be the beginning of the end for a system based on greed. He felt someone by his side. He looked, but there was no one there. He walked on, moving briskly along the sidewalk, but he could still feel the presence. Someone was beside him, someone was there. He took a deep breath and looked to his right. The faint smell of a cigar was in the air. J.J. smiled and proceeded onward, because he knew who was by his side. Yes, his companion was the resurrected *Spirit of Che Guevara*.

Now, Chablis had gone through every name on the list of discharged employees, and none of them seemed capable of the in-depth knowledge it would take to accomplish what the *Spirit of Che* had. The building destruction three days before required a man of great intelligence, and frankly, not one of those discharged impressed Chablis as being intelligent enough to pull that off.

She made her way home, as she had a date with Rodrigo that night, and she was looking forward to an evening of companionship with a man whom she had grown very fond of over the past weeks. This night he had promised to take her tot he *21 Club* for dancing. They had talked every night on the phone and she was growing very accustomed to having him in her life.

Chablis' place was not in an affluent neighbourhood, but it was certainly a bit above middle class, and though she had not been to his place, she felt Rodrigo was a man of culture and refinement as evidenced by his demeanour and the general way he presented himself. In fact, he surprised her by saying, "I know we were going dancing, but I managed to get to tickets to the opera. What do you think?"

Chablis, who was dressed for dancing, but preferred the opera said, "I love it but I can't afford it. Give me 5 minutes to change."

"Great, I can't afford it either, but I actually got the tickets from a friend who couldn't go tonight. Lucky us, uh?"

The truth was, he had bought them himself, but splurging felt right to him when it came to this woman. However, he saw her as someone who would not want him to spend lavishly on her; therefore, he felt it better that he tell her a lie, so that she would not think that she was taking advantage of him."

The opera is something almost everyone should enjoy at least once in their lives, but at $200 a ticket for sky seats and $750 for orchestra seats, not many people can afford it, so in Manhattan, it was a refuge of the rich. Rodrigo apologized for being in the sky seats, but Chablis said, "I am thrilled to be here, no matter where the seats are, and the man I am with makes it even better."

Rodrigo had fallen in love with her the very first day when they sat in the coffee shop, and each date, each conversation with her just solidified his belief that this was the most exceptional woman he had ever met. What she had between her legs did not matter to him. He had never touched a man down there, but when he inadvertently brushed against it when making love to her he was not repulsed by it, because she was not a man. It was simply a birth defect, and he was intelligent enough to know that, unlike so many who could only condemn what they were incapable of understanding. Too many people were confined by the narrow-mined religious structure that made them prisoners of that which they were taught to abhor by those with no compassion, no tolerance and even less intelligence.

Chablis, as they sat enthralled by the opera, holding hands, looked over at him, and wondered what he was thinking. She was falling in love, but knew she must be cautious, because she had already been burned twice, once because of infidelity, and once because of circumstances. She squeezed his hand, leaned over and whispered, "thank you so much." He smiled at her and lightly squeezed her hand in return.

There are magical nights in all our lives, and this was one of those nights for Chablis and Rodrigo. He asked if she wanted a drink, but as the strolled arm-in-arm down the sidewalk, she said, "No, I want to take you home Rodrigo and make love. This is one of the most incredible nights of my life. It has been a magical evening filled with the splendour of magnificent music and more importantly, filled with the companionship of a wonderfully kind, generous and gentle man."

She leaned her head on his shoulder, and Rodrigo sighed as he said, "You know I love you. I loved you from that very first moment Chablis – the very first moment I laid eyes on you. I knew there was something special about you."

She giggled a bit. "You are right about that."

Chablis and the Terrorist
Who Resurrected the Spirit of Che Guevara

"No, Chablis, don't joke about being a transsexual. Don't ever make fun of yourself. You are a woman, 100% woman."

She smiled and felt that she had a man who was enough of a man to be comfortable with her. Some men were more concerned about what others thought than about what the person they were supposed to love thought. Rodrigo was a man of supreme confidence, and she saw him as a rock – a rock upon which she could lean.

The love making that night was not as intense as it had been before, but it was more rarefied and esoteric. There was a depth to it that was not there before. As Rodrigo prepared to go home at 1:00 AM, Chablis said, "Don't go. I want to lie in your arms all night." Then she giggled and said, "And suck your cock when I wake up."

He eased back in bed, and they laughed together as Chablis wrapped herself in his arms. She felt safe. She was a woman capable of taking care of herself like few other women could, but this man made her want to depend on him, to allow him to be her protector. They drifted off to sleep, and the next morning, just as she had promised, she eased down between his muscular legs to work her magic with the mouth that melted men's joy sticks in it like the noonday sun melted butter. Rodrigo lay in ecstasy, staring at the ceiling for what seemed hours, unable to move, unable to speak, unable to even lift his arms as he had just had an angel ascend from on high and wrap him in the rapture.

Chablis and the Terrorist
Who Resurrected the Spirit of Che Guevara

He asked Chablis if he shouldn't do something to bring her pleasure and she replied, "You brought me more pleasure last night than I could have ever imagined, and I am not talking about sex. Sex is the icing on the cake, the salt on the meat. It only enhances flavour. It does not provide the real nourishment. You nourished me last night with the depth of your love for me. I am satisfied as I have never been satisfied in my life. The pleasure of your words far exceeds the pleasures of the flesh."

They sat at the table, enjoying a leisurely breakfast together. Chablis was topless, but had on a pair of men's boxer shorts. Rodrigo was wearing a towel around his waist. On instinct, Rodrigo got up, went over and gently kissed Chablis as she looked up at him, blinking her dark eyes seductively. He said, "Thanks for letting me kiss those gorgeous puffy lips."

Freshly showered, she was ready for sex. She stood up, feeling miniature standing there in her bare feet, measuring only 5:2. She reached to where his towel was knotted, pulled it lose and it dropped to the floor. He was at half-staff as she whispered "Now, I am going to kiss you."

She lowered herself to her knees and gently kissed his member on the head, lovingly blowing on it periodically and sliding her tongue rhythmically up and down the shaft from underneath. He sighed long and deep as he tilted his head down watching her finally gorge herself on its full length, her little head moving agilely and skilfully back and forth.

J. Wayne Frye   178

Chablis and the Terrorist
Who Resurrected the Spirit of Che Guevara

A few adroit, long, gliding gulps made Rodrigo think he had just hooked up his member to the nozzle of a powerful commercial vacuum cleaner that sucked up everything in sight, and he exploded like a volcano blowing off its top. He pumped load after load of joy juice so violently that it slammed against the back of Chablis throat with the force of a tsunami roaring ashore. She gobbled every last drop and moaned in ecstasy, as this was the supreme sex act for her, the crème de la crème of coupling. It gave her a sense of tremendous power, as men were mere putty in her hands when she had them in her mouth. She was the salacious, wanton vixen of the suck, and she was proud of it. She got up, looked at his chest heaving in and out, reached over on the table and put two fingers into the soft margarine tub and removed a small portion of the slippery stuff. She said, "It is very clean, as I look after it with meticulous care," as she slowly turned around and jutted out her gorgeous ass while rubbing the butter on the cute brown gapping hole that was actually pulsating with anticipation of coming pleasure. She placed both hands on the table and begin to enticingly wiggle and squirm as Rodrigo stood in awe of what was, without a doubt, the most alluring mountain of flesh he had ever had the pleasure to gaze upon. He dropped to his knees and began to kiss the glorious cheeks of frolicking flesh as he gently separated them and began to lick the butter and lovingly suck on the hole that was now the grand canyon of delight.

What gives people pleasure is an anomaly of the mind. One man's perversion is another man's fun.

Chablis and the Terrorist
Who Resurrected the Spirit of Che Guevara

Chablis was the most completely uninhibited woman Rodrigo had ever met, and what he was doing simply made sense, because his sole purpose in life was to bring her pleasure at that moment in time. Chablis moaned with delight as she felt whole and complete as a woman. Waves of ecstasy rolled over her. She was using her body as it was meant to be used. She was an instrument of pleasure that brought waves of euphoria to a man who was now at the very centre of her universe.

He got up from his feast of carnal pleasure, his member now throbbing violently with desire, and Chablis, looking back over her right shoulder said, "Give it to me hard, baby. Ride it like a wild stallion you were taming. He bent forward and their mouths met in a long, lingering kiss as she tasted the saltiness of the butter while their tongues were duelling one another like two snakes hissing in the desert sun.

So open was she that Rodrigo slid his huge member in with ease and immediately went all the way up into her with a mighty thrust that sent waves of delight all through her body. He began to pump furiously as she met every thrust with a backward movement and a guttural moan that got him so excited he pumped harder and harder as if he wanted to put not just his tool of pleasure deep inside her, but his soul.

The sound of flesh banging flesh bounced off the ceiling and the table began to rock as it slammed against the wall. Chablis and Rodrigo had the perfect rhythm now and the motion was smooth and steady with a cadence that was building to a grand and glorious crescendo of passion.

Around front, Chablis had a tremendous erection and she could feel the joy juice inside the heavy laden balls start to work its way up her shaft. She was going to have a mighty cum, but she fought to hold it so she could explode at the same time as Rodrigo. Suddenly she felt the pulsating of his member and his fountain of festive fertilizer began to seed her just as she exploded with so much force the juice of joy nearly tore a hole in the floor. They let out screams of delight. Chablis collapsed onto the table, and Rodrigo leaned over her, feeling like he might pass out as his member slowly went limp and squirmed its way out of Chablis love canal.

They just relaxed for awhile, breathing heavily until Chablis whispered. "Shower anyone?"

Rodrigo said, "as long as you promise to keep your hands to yourself. Another session like that and you will have to call 911."

After Rodrigo kissed her in the shower, he said "I have been looking for a long time. I didn't know for what. I didn't know her name or where she lived or what she did. I found a new job which gave my life purpose. I walk into a second-rate coffee shop and find a first rate woman in the booth across from me. I have found what I was looking for. My life was in turmoil as I was a depressed person who had really decided that my life was the pits."

Chablis and the Terrorist
Who Resurrected the Spirit of Che Guevara

They dried off, got dressed and by then it was time for lunch. They went over to the same café where they had met and ordered two grilled cheese sandwiches with fries. As they sat there eating, Chablis shared a few details about her case with him. It was then that she began to realize the depth of compassion this man had, and that he was just as concerned with justice as she was. He munched on a French fry, put the uneaten half down on his plate and said, "So, you sure this Harrington guy is who he says he is?"

"I think so, yes. I see no reason to doubt him. Why?"

"Frankly, I have great empathy with this guy calling himself the *Spirit of Che Guevara*. I wish I had the courage to act on my convictions. So far, he has harmed no innocents, as I see these leeches just as he does, a blight on humanity. Chablis, I am going to tell you something about myself, because I think our relationship is getting serious. I know it is on my part."

She reached across the table and took his hand in hers. "It is on my part, too, Rodrigo."

"Then, I think you need to know I have a problem. Now, I am not a pedophile, so don't get nervous," he said as he continued, "You ever see the movie, *The Woodsman*, with Kevin Bacon? It makes you actually feel sorry for a pedophile. They have a sickness, and in that film he battles this sickness, but he keeps looking at children and you know what his thoughts are, and you find yourself feeling sorrow for him, because he is trying so hard to fight against this corruption that is spreading inside him. "

Chablis, a woman of intelligence and compassion said, "I know it is a sickness. I can understand the desire as long as it does not include murder or the actual acting out of the desire to have sex. It is a disease. I am smart enough to understand that, maybe because of my condition. We are born the way we are, and despite what people say about God not making mistakes, it isn't true. If there is a God, he makes mistakes all the time. I am living proof of that."

Rodrigo smiled and seemed to be in contemplative thought for a second as he said, "You are God's perfect creation."

"I have a feeling you don't believe in God either, so it wasn't God who created me, but I appreciate the compliment."

"Anyway, you could actually feel sorry for a pedophile and the agony he goes through every day. Fortunately, I am not a pedophile, but I am a very sick person, who must fight every day to find a reason to continue as the smallest things often overwhelm me. I never realized the depth of my sickness until recently. You see, I suffer from severe depression on occasion. Some days are worse than others. Today is one of those really good days for obvious reasons."

Chablis and the Terrorist
Who Resurrected the Spirit of Che Guevara

"Depression is an insidious disease you think you have defeated, but then one occurrence starts the cascading of pain that overwhelms you. Just when I think the pain is beginning to stop hurting so bad, it starts all over again. When I see that there appears to be another irrevocable movement toward the complete end of things, I look at a morning as cloudy and dark as the evenings, as if the sun had never decided to rise. There is no wind, like the world is holding its breath along with me, waiting for something positive to happen. I had been holding my breath so long now that I realize I was slowly dying from the lack of oxygen provided by love. I was only alive, barely alive in body, but my spirit had passed on when you suddenly appeared on the horizon. I was a man without a core, so alone in a city of millions. I was devoid of any hope as I was empty inside, so lost that it is as if the warmth of a bright sun was covered by a cloud of despair that simply would not recede."

She looked long and compassionately into his eyes. "I am here for you now, and we will fight whatever problem you have together, because I love you. There, I said it. I love you."

Smiling broadly, tears formed in Rodrigo's eyes as he simply reached out and held her hand. They needed no words between them. Outside it began to drizzle rain and Chablis said, "I need to get to work, but I hope we can repeat what we did this morning soon."

Rodrigo winked. "How about every day the rest of

our lives."

Rodrigo said goodbye and walked out into the drizzle. He pulled the collar of his topcoat up around his neck and slowly strolled toward the subway. Fortuitously, the drizzle was a precursor of the heavy rain that was about to fall across the country as the clarion call to action against economic injustice was about to be heeded by many."

Chablis found Joe Harrington waiting in her office. He was still the handsome older man, but she had no urge to act upon her earlier inclination to make love to him. She had found the man to fill not only her voracious sexual appetite, but to satisfy her longing for love. She greeted him and took a seat behind her desk.

"So, how goes your search? The rumour is you and Mr. Adams are the very best. I hope you are going to prove the rumours correct."

"Rumours are more exciting than the truth. The truth is we fail many times, and so far I have failed to turn up anything positive, but certain ideas are beginning to germinate, and I am sure that there is something I have overlooked, something that might just turn on that little light in the darkness and shine on something small, something infinitesimal that I have somehow overlooked.

Then, Harrington said something that bothered her and squirmed in his chair as he shifted positions in a manner that indicated a defensive posture. His chest puffed out and then he crossed his legs. "I was at the 39 Wall Street collapse. If he continues this unabated charade of indignity against capitalism, this nation is going to descend into chaos."

That did not sound like a man committed to nothing more than just interviewing an anarchist for a proposed book or article. She swirled her tongue across her lower lip and said, "So, why the chastisement all of a sudden. I thought you admired his chutzpah."

"Oh, I do! I do! Yes, in so many ways his commitment to justice is admirable, although violence is never the answer. I am just a bit frustrated. That's all. I am under a deadline?"

Why, thought Chablis, would he be under a deadline? A few weeks ago, no one even knew the *Spirit of Che* existed. There was something about Joe Harrington now that she did not like. Something was not kosher about him. He was not what he appeared to be. Still, she and Aaron had taken the case, and that meant they had certain obligations. Things about this case were leading her to question whether she should proceed or not. Myerson's death was also questionable. She had a connection with him, and suddenly he is on Che's hit list. Was she more involved than she realized? She brushed her long hair back off her shoulders and said, "Mr. Harrington, if you think you can do better than Adams and Chavez, go ahead and hire someone else."

Chablis and the Terrorist
Who Resurrected the Spirit of Che Guevara

Putting both his hands in front of his chest, indicating a stopping motion, he adamantly retorted, "No, no not at all. You and Mr. Adams are definitely the best. We know that,"

That was where he slipped up. He used the word we. Chablis jumped on it immediately. "What do you mean, we?"

"Oh, did I say we? No, I. Yes, I."

She stared directly into his eyes. "Clients who keep things from us are not very reliable. We can only do our job if we are confident in our clients."

"You can be confident in me. I am a man of my word."

"O.K., said a perplexed Chablis, "but I have a question for you."

Now, Chablis was beginning to suspect that she and Aaron were perhaps pawns in a sinister set-up. "Do you know, or maybe I should say, did you know Bob Myerson?"

"No, nothing other than the fact he was the *Spirit of Che's* second victim. Nothing more than that."

He was obviously becoming uncomfortable. "So, you never met Myerson before?"

"Hey, who are you investigating, the *Spirit of Che* or me?"

Chablis and the Terrorist
Who Resurrected the Spirit of Che Guevara

"I'm a good P.I., I cover all my bases."

"That's what I want – a good P.I. I want you to find this guy before the police do. I want to interrogate him before they get hold of him. Once they have him, I am afraid he may be turned over to the F.B.I., as this is now a federal case. He is a terrorist and the power of Washington will come down on him hard, real hard."

Chablis eased back in her chair and with extreme confidence said, "Make no mistake about it Mr. Harrington. I am loyal to my clients, but if I find out they are lying to me, that loyalty ends. I actually respect this man calling himself the *Spirit of Che*, because I see the result of greed every day in this city. He might be going about it in the wrong way, but he is identifying a problem that no one is willing to tackle – the disparity between the rich and the poor. No one sides with the underdog anymore, even the heroes in the nation are billionaires. We worship wealth and lose sight of compassion, fairness and economic justice. I have read Marx. I have read Engels. I have studied Debs, Lenin, Orwell and Mandela. They all saw the flaws in a system that perpetuates wealth from one generation to the other and aggrandizes greed. I was even called by one writer *the avenging angel for the forgotten in the city of lost hope*. I learned to side with the underdog from the greatest champion the underdog ever had, Aaron Adams. He has championed the downtrodden his whole life, and I am proud to call him my friend. If you are sincere about finding this man to air his grievances, I will

J. Wayne Frye   188

find him for you. I have failed before, but it has never been because of lack of effort."

A contrite Joe Harrington shook her hand and left, but Chablis went in to talk to Aaron and shared with him what happened. After a bit of thought he said, "Cut him loose if you want. We don't need the money."

"No, I'll stick with it for awhile, but there is something about him that just isn't right, just doesn't make sense."

"Be careful, Chablis."

"Always am boss."

Aaron sighed and said, "So, any leads at all. How about the discharged employees? Anything there?"

"I don't know. There is one person that might provide a link. It's more hunch than anything else. Keita Martinez has a brother whom I have not met. Supposed to be a smart guy, and according to some of those I talked with, he was a bit on the radical side. Pretty far fetched I know, but it is all I have."

"Run it down woman. Hey, we are on Harrington's dollar, right?"

"Yeah, for now, anyway. I'm going to run a check on him, too. OK.?"

"It's your case."

Chablis and the Terrorist
Who Resurrected the Spirit of Che Guevara

"O.K. then, I'm checking him out for sure. I just know something is not right about him."

She walked toward the door, and Aaron could not help but admire the provocative sway of her gorgeous ass. Chablis stopped at the door, looked over her right shoulder and said, "It is nice isn't it? You know, it is my best asset, and I really put it to good use this morning. "

"Chablis, get that gorgeous ass out of here and go to work."

She smiled and left. She went back to her office took a seat and looked out at the Manhattan skyline wondering where the *Spirit of Che* was going to strike next. There were a lot of buildings filled with a lot of greedy bastards. In this city the pickings were plentiful.

CHAPTER 8
VIOLENCE! VIOLENCE! VIOLENCE!

The temper of the public mind
thirsts for a happier condition
of moral and political virtue.
Among the few who control the economy,
the tempests which shake the age
are but minor irritants of hostility
from the rabble who serve their interests.
Within the breasts of those who are in chains
must be stirred the enthusiasm for
violent upheaval that will begin the dawn
of a new age. For those who keep us
all in chains understand only one thing.
Violence! Violence! Violence!

Jose Juan Martinez was mesmerized as he watched the morning news and heard about what was going on all across the USA, where small uprisings of the disenfranchised were beginning. The news was being delivered by the typical pretty faced broadcaster who got her job on looks not talent. She looked into a camera, which was tilted down to get maximum exposure for her cleavage, and said, "In Chicago, apparently the terrorist calling himself the *Spirit of Che Guevara* has had a profound effect on the South Side. A group of citizens have banded together and will no longer be shopping at places that do not pay their employees at least $15 an hour and have profit sharing arrangements and retirement benefits. They are issuing a list of these companies and already have 50,000 members who have pledged to shop only at

Chablis and the Terrorist
Who Resurrected the Spirit of Che Guevara

approved   establishments.   Their   unofficial
spokesperson, Martin Balborman had this to say
when   interviewed   by   WSC   reporter   Diane
Festerman. "We are not condoning the violence of
this person calling himself the *Spirit of Che
Guevara*, but we do sympathize with the workers he
is concerned about. For too long this nation has
ignored the problem of the growing income gap.
While a few people pile up great wealth, others
scrimp by from paycheque to paycheque. It is an
abomination in a nation this rich for anyone to live
in the streets, go without healthcare or go to bed
hungry at night. This is a small step, but we hope
this movement will spread across the nation, and
that the C.E.O.'s of truly socially responsible
corporations will make the appropriate changes to
assure that all workers are treated fairly."

The newsperson, displaying her silicon breasts, as
all newscasters needed large breasts, continued,
"Similar movements are reported in Indianapolis,
St. Louis, New Orleans, Houston, Dallas and
Phoenix."

Jose Juan got up and switched off the television,
walked to the kitchen and poured a cup of coffee,
firm in the knowledge that those efforts were not
going to succeed without the one component that
the powerful understood – violence. He was the
catalyst for what was happening. He was glad he
had motivated those people, but as Che said, you
cut off the tail of the snake, the head is still
dangerous. He was going to cut off some heads that
were still dangerous.

Chablis and the Terrorist
Who Resurrected the Spirit of Che Guevara

The Comstock brothers were well known for supporting conservative causes. Their devotion to the Republican party was predicated on the simple belief that it was the party most responsive to the rich, and the Comstock brothers, who had inherited a 20 billion dollar fortune from their father were extremely rich. Like most of the rich, they had never put in a truly honest day's work in their lives as they were made vice-presidents immediately upon graduation from Yale. Now, they shared the helm of an empire that included oil refineries in New Jersey, where the Republican governor passed bills explicitly to benefit them tax-wise, a giant paper mill on the Hudson River in Tenafly where they also kept their fleet of helicopters at a nearby airport, and their own New York/New Jersey grocery store chain appropriately called *The Mother Lode*. They were also heads of an organization that was supposedly dedicated to preserving the American way of life, called *America First*. They bought politicians like most people bought gas at their local station. They came cheap, because politicians are after C.E.O.'s, the lowest life form on earth. There is nothing they won't do to stay in office, and staying in office means, not serving your constituents, but the rich people who bankroll your campaigns.

The Comstock brothers had padded their fortune with the war on crime. They were smart enough to recognize that a police state is big business. It needs criminals to survive. They were the chief proponents of privatizing prisons as they saw it as a growth industry in a police state, which American rapidly became after 9/11. In fact, Harold Comstock, in a board meeting, once said, "9/11 was a God-sent. It opened up great opportunities in security as keeping the public afraid guarantees more prisons, more firearms sales and more security guards. What this nation needs is more rules and bigger penalties for breaking them."

Thus, the Comstock brothers never missed an opportunity to use fear and patriotism to enhance their bottom line. They were the ones behind three strikes laws, as they wanted to make certain when you are deemed a law breaker, there are literally no more limits to what the authorities may do to you. Mounting a defence costs money, making deals costs money, none of which the poor have, so they will be locked up in one of the Comstock Brothers privatized prisons they owned in three states. The so-called justice system is the biggest racket in the police state - cops, judges, lawyers, politicians, prison guards, drug testing labs, many of which were part of the Comstock Empire, depended on crime to make money.

The Comstock empire was about to take a big hit. First on the list was the paper mill, and it would involve some intricate manoeuvring. J.J. cruised by the place in the Crown Victoria and watched as it belched smoke into the sky, spreading its toxins that were ignored by a New Jersey government that had been bought by the Comstock brothers. The previous democratic administration had tried to force them to put in a scrubber or close the mill. Big mistake for the democratic governor, as with an election coming up, the Comstock brothers simply poured massive amounts of money into the Republican candidate's campaign, courtesy of the Republican majority U.S. Supreme Court which gleefully made it possible for the rich to buy elections. At least it was official now. In America, it was legal to buy politicians.

J. J. let a sinister smile purse his lips as he rode to a hilltop and parked. He removed a canister from the trunk, and laughed about how easy it was to procure radio active material if you had a little money. Yeah, Myerson's money had certainly coming in handy. He had spent $200,000 to get a radioactive isotope on the black market. Once the plant was contaminated with radioactivity, it would have to close. No explosion this time, just a quiet little procedure to contaminate the contaminated.

Getting into the complex was relatively easy for a person as skilled at disguises as J.J. was. He instantly became a stack pipe technician and strolled into the complex almost unimpeded. When asked by a guard for an ID, he produced one from the Apex Scrubbing Corporation and was passed through with the isotope in his toolbox. He proceeded to the stack where he placed the isotope and started the timer on the small bomb in the toolbox. As he walked out the guard asked, "Where's the toolbox?"

"Left it by the smoke stack, have to go back to the plant and get a Bormann accelerator. Be back in an hour."

Chablis and the Terrorist
Who Resurrected the Spirit of Che Guevara

The guard joyfully said, "See you soon, then."

J.J. nodded affirmatively and simply strolled out of the building, down the street and got in the Crown Victoria and headed for the G.W. Bridge and Manhattan. Once across the bridge, he called Donald and said, "The first blow against the Comstock brothers is about to be struck. Call the Hudson River paper Mill in Tenafly and have it evacuated immediately. Also, tell them they will need a hazardous materials team there after the explosion, as the place is going to be radioactive for about another 300 years. Nice talking to you Donald. Talk again soon."

Donald did as told, and J.J. headed home. As he did so, the Crown Victoria passed Chablis on Fulton Street headed to his apartment building. The two of them would cross paths again soon.

Tony Mercante, the resident gangster at J.J.'s complex, greeted him as he walked by. "Hey, J.J., where you been dude. Ain't seen you lately."

"New job up in Connecticut. Takes up a lot of my time. See you later, Tony."

Tony noticed that there was a piece of paper on J.J.'s shoe that came off as he proceeded up the square into the building. Curiosity got the better of him, so he walked over and picked it up. It was a small piece of paper, maybe the size of a business card, probably a bit smaller. He looked at it curiously. It was frayed around the edges and discoloured, but he could make out a partial word: *Huds*. For some reason, rather than tossing it aside, he put it in his pocket and went back to the square where he sat down on his throne – the circular concrete abutment that was supposed to keep the water in the fountain that had been turned off for years to save the owner money.

J.J. went inside and turned on the television. There was the scantily glad newscaster frantic with excitement: "A giant explosion ripped through the Hudson Paper Mill in Tenafly less than 30 minutes ago. The giant smoke stack was brought down and it is rumoured that the explosion emitted radioactive particles into the air. No one was killed, and according to *New York Times* reporter, Donald Beckman, the man calling himself the *Spirit of Che Guevara* is claiming responsibility. The facility is own by the billionaire Comstock brothers. WTNT reporter Erica Holstein is on the scene. We join Erica for details."

J.J. turned off the television and wondered where his mom and Keita were. He took a quick shower and got dressed. As he was dressing, Chablis was walking toward the building when Tony leaped off his throne and ran over to her. "Hey, pretty lady. How ya' doing?"

"O.K. Tony. O.K."

He held his hands up in front of his chest, palms out and said, "No hassles from me lady. I ain't tangling with you again."

Chablis and the Terrorist
Who Resurrected the Spirit of Che Guevara

She smiled at him and said, "Going up to see the Martinez family."

"Sure Chablis, I know 'um. Keita and Mamma Martinez just left to go to the grocery."

"J.J., he's up there. Just went in awhile ago."

"Actually, that's who I want to see." She said, as she turned, look back over her right shoulder and continued as she was walking away, "Talk to you later."

"Yeah, and hopefully not while I'm laying on the ground this time."

Chablis laughed and continued into the building. As one might expect, the elevator wasn't working. There was a stairwell on the left and one on the right. She took the right one. Irony would have it that J.J., who was just going down as she was going up, took the left stairwell.

Outside, J.J., as he walked passed Tony, waved at him, but Tony jumped to his feet and said, "Hey man, they's a lady just went up to see ya."

"Lady, who?

"The best looking broad you ever seen man. You don't want to miss her. She got more curves than a mountain road and an ass that just makes you know she takes it up the Hersey Highway. I mean this broad's ass wiggles better than a dog's tail."

Chablis and the Terrorist
Who Resurrected the Spirit of Che Guevara

"Know her name?"

"Chablis Louise Chavez. That's her name. Classy ain't it?"

J.J. very quickly began to walk away as Tony was shouting, "Wait man. Wait. She'll be down here in a minute."

"Not tonight," said a troubled J.J. as he scurried away, never looking back.

Chablis strolled out into the courtyard only a few seconds behind the fleeing J.J. Tony was still standing there bewildered by J.J.'s quick exit. Chablis noticed a look of consternation on his face and asked, "What's wrong Tony?"

He pointed to the fleeing J.J. about 300 metres in the distance and said, "That's J.J., don't know why he didn't want to talk to ya."

Chablis did not hesitate one second; she immediately started running toward J.J. shouting, "Mr. Martinez! Mr. Martinez!"

J.J. never looked back. He started running, moving quickly toward the subway. Chablis wondered why a man she didn't even know would be running away from her. Something weird was going on. Cases were often like this, just when you least expected it, things start to fall in place. Was this the man calling himself the *Spirit of Che Guevara?*

Chablis and the Terrorist
Who Resurrected the Spirit of Che Guevara

J.J. made it to the subway entrance and was frantically moving toward the car, trying to make it in before the door closed. He just managed to squeeze in as Chablis, the sound of her high heels clicking on the concrete stairs reverberating against the tile walls of the station, made it down the last step and nearly stumbled as she tried to make it into the last car where she saw J.J., his back turned to her, moving frantically forward through the cars. She ran along side the train as it pulled away from the station, trying desperately to get a glimpse of J.J. She was breathing heavily as she finally stopped and stood, exhausted, just staring at the train as it went into the darkness of the tunnel. People were staring at her as she bent over placing her hands on her knees, gasping for air. An old man walked up to her and said, "You O.K. lady? No big deal, there's another train in 3 minutes."

Chablis, panting for breath, said, "Where is the next stop?"

"Lenox and 135th Street, about 10 blocks. "

She turned and quickly ascended the stairs, shouting "thanks" to the old man. On the street, she frantically walked toward 135th Street looking for a cab. Finally, one came along, and actually stopped, most likely because of her looks, because cabs refused to pick up people in that neighbourhood. The good people there, like most ghetto neighbourhoods, had to suffer, not because they were bad, but because they had the misfortunate of living in a poor neighbourhood.

Chablis and the Terrorist
Who Resurrected the Spirit of Che Guevara

Chablis, still breathing heavily, shouted, "135th Street and fast."

The driver, floored it and said, "Fast costs a nice tip, lady."

"I'll give you 20. Hurry."

"Damn right, I'll hurry," he said as he ran a red light and within a minute, slammed on his brakes and came to a stop at 135th Street and Lenox Avenue. Chablis reached in her tight fitting slacks and came out with a $20. "Thanks," she said as she climbed out and walked over to the subway entrance.

A few people were meandering up the stairs slowly and she stopped a woman, obviously Hispanic, and asked in Spanish, "This train just get in?"

The lady, very nonchalantly, replied, "About a minute ago. I'm too old to run up the stairs."

Chablis scanned the area, looking for a man in a light blue shirt and navy pants. She looked right, left, spun around and in the far distance, she saw a man that she knew was J.J. walking briskly around the corner. She hurriedly began to run after him, thinking to herself, "Why am I chasing this guy? He hasn't done anything that I know of, but then again, why is he running from me?"

She shouted loudly, "Mr. Martinez!"

Chablis and the Terrorist
Who Resurrected the Spirit of Che Guevara

Upon hearing her, J.J. broke into a frantic run, never looking back, but moving quickly toward the place where the Crown Victoria was parked. He had to shake this broad, and shake her fast.

J.J. ran quickly past a group of men standing by a barrel passing around a bottle in a brown wrapper. They looked stunned at a man running away from a woman, especially one that small. As Chablis came into view, one of them said, "Goddamn, check out that broad. That bitch is hotter than a firecracker on the 4th of July. Let's nail that bitch. I feel like dropping a load."

The four men moved in front of Chablis, and she was forced to stop. J.J. also stopped and looked back. The guy with the big load said, "We gonna nail you bitch. All four of us is horny as hell."

Chablis had no time for chatter, and the situation demanded immediate action. She quickly extended her right foot as she balanced herself on her left foot, landing a well placed rhythmic kick to the guy's crotch, while using her right elbow to land a blow to the guy on her left's stomach. The two guys on her right were too far away, so she pivoted toward them, but one pulled a gun and said, "Hold it bitch. Hold it right there."

Out of the corner of her left eye, she saw that J.J. had stopped running and turned around. He was very slowly and deliberately moving toward her. She could not make out his face, but his large, muscular frame made her feel safe for some reason.

Chablis and the Terrorist
Who Resurrected the Spirit of Che Guevara

The guy with the gun told her to move against the nearby wall. As his two buddies lay writhing in pain on the ground. J.J. moved quietly behind the two who were facing Chablis. One of them begin to unzip his pants, and pulled out the rod that shot more than bullets. He said, "Turn around bitch and face the wall. Drop those pants and let me see that ass. I am going to ram my cock so far up it I'll tickle your belly button."

J.J. rammed his knee into the back of the guy with the gun. As he collapsed toward the pavement, J.J. lowered the butt of his own gun on the back of his head so hard it opened up like a ripe watermelon dropped from a 10 story building. He was dead before he hit the pavement. The guy with his dick in his hand turned and J.J. fired one bullet into his head. The horny dude never let go of his cock, even in death. Chablis slowly turned, and as she did, she saw J.J.'s back as he stepped over the two guys Chablis had put on the pavement. His gun spit out a bullet that pierced one guy's skull, causing brains to spill out like water poured from a pitcher. In one smooth motion, he pointed the gun to his left continuing his slow jog forward just as the guy who had his balls rearranged by Chablis was trying to get up. A bullet between the eyes made sure he stayed down. J.J. then broke into a fast run, never looking back as Chablis shouted, "Wait, wait! I'm not a cop."

J.J. raised his right hand as if to say, "O.K.," but continued his run, and Chablis, exhausted from the ordeal was too spent to chase him anymore.

Chablis and the Terrorist
Who Resurrected the Spirit of Che Guevara

Chablis, wanting to avoid any confrontation with police, quickly hurried back to the subway station. Anyway, deaths in the ghetto were not that big a concern to the police. Their attitude was let them kill themselves and it saves us bullets. She boarded the train back to J.J.'s neighbourhood and as she passed Tony, who, as always, was surveying his domain, he leaped up and said, "You catch him?"

"No. Any idea why he would be running from me?"

Tony, shaking his head, replied, "Chablis, you got me. If you ever chase me, I promise to stop immediately. I'm all yours."

Chablis smiled and very seductively, just to give him a bit of pleasure, said, "Big boy, I am sure you catch plenty of women."

Swelling with pride, puffing out his chest, he bellowed, "Yeah, yeah I do."

For some reason, he reached in his pocket and came out with the piece of paper J.J. had on the bottom of his shoe and said, "J.J. had this on his shoe."

She looked at it and knew that you didn't have to be much of a detective to know what the torn business card with *Hud* showing meant. J.J. had a connection to the paper mill explosion. She needed to talk to Mamma Martinez and Keita to get a line on J.J.

Chablis and the Terrorist
Who Resurrected the Spirit of Che Guevara

She gave Tony a wink and asked, "Mamma and Keita back, yet?"

"Yeah, they just went up a few minutes ago."

She said thanks and went back into the building. Keita seemed pleased to see her, but when she told her that J.J, had run away from her, purposefully leaving out details of him killing four men, she was perplexed. She poured Chablis some tea and Mamma joined them.

"So," said Chablis as she sipped on her tea, "can you tell me about J.J.? I do want to meet him."

Mamma Martinez and Keita spent nearly 30 minutes talking about the attributes of J.J. Finally, Chablis said, "So, do you have any pictures of him? I adore looking at handsome men."

Keita said, as she got up, "Let me go into my bedroom. I have a pic on my dresser."

She came back in a few seconds later and with a puzzled look on her face, said, "It's gone."

Mamma said. "Get mine, darling."

She went into her mom's room, came back with the same puzzled look and said, "It's gone too."

They even went through some picture albums in Mamma's room and all of J.J.'s pictures, even the ones taken with other family members, were gone."

Chablis and the Terrorist
Who Resurrected the Spirit of Che Guevara

"Where did he work?" asked Chablis.

Keita, still puzzled said, "Department of Urban Affairs, Harlem division."

Just then, Keita's cell phone rang. "Hello. Yes, she is right here in the living room. J.J., where are all your pictures? What's going on?" As she continued to plead for an explanation, she handed the cell-phone to Chablis and said, "He wants to talk to you, Chablis."

"Hello. This is Chablis. Thanks for the help tonight J.J., but why all the mystery? I am not after you. I just want to talk."

"I know about you and the man you work for, Aaron Adams. You are two people who stand for justice and integrity. I am going to tell you something in confidence."

Chablis, experienced investigator that she was, knew J.J. was speaking with a handkerchief over the phone. Why, she thought, would he need to disguise his voice while talking to her? It did not make sense. She was curious, but also cautious. "J.J., I need a retainer from you to make our relationship professional. I get a retainer, then you are my client and what you tell me is confidential. $1 is fine, just something to make it official and I will sign a receipt."

"Put Keita on the phone. I'll give you $5000 as a retainer."

Chablis and the Terrorist
Who Resurrected the Spirit of Che Guevara

Wondering where $5000 was coming from in a dump like the Martinez home, Chablis handed the phone to Keita. She said, "J.J. what is going on. I don't understand."

"It will be clear to all of you soon, but Keita, put your trust in this woman. Hear me. Put your trust in her."

"O.K., J.J."

J.J. said, "I love you and Mama. Always remember that. Let me talk to Chablis now."

Handing the phone to Chablis, Keita sighed, bewildered by what was happening.

"Listen Chablis; go with my sister into my bedroom. There is 425,000 dollars under the mattress. Originally, there was almost three million, but I am putting it to good use. Get my mom and sister out of the city. It is for their own good. I know you can get them hooked up with assumed names. Use whatever amount of that money you need. In a few days, my identity is going to be revealed and my face will be plastered all over the news. There are elements in this country capable of unimaginable evil. After 9/11, government officials proved just how low they would sink with torture sanctioned by the President. There are a small group of people in this nation with no heart, no conscience and a firm belief that they are above the law. Well, they are above the laws of this nation, but they are not above my law."

Chablis and the Terrorist
Who Resurrected the Spirit of Che Guevara

Chablis looked over at Mama and at Keita, because what she was about to say would shock them, but she had to say it. "You are *the Spirit of Che*."

"I am the spirit of justice and fairness in a land that knows none of it. I am the mighty sword of retribution that will fall on those who have lived a life of luxurious splendour on the backs of the common man for far too long. The day of reckoning is at hand for all who do not heed my call for justice in the land of hypocrisy."

"J.J., there is a better way, a non-violent way to foster change."

Chablis could sense him smiling, "No, you know better than that. That has been tried before, and it is for suckers. Change is made for awhile, but the sinister elements are lurking beneath the surface, ready to bribe and cajole the activists and make them part of the rich class. Look at those who lead the civil rights movements, look at those who led the anti-war movements, look at those who led the anti-poverty movements, look at those who head charities. They are all rich, rich off the work of fathers and grandfathers who made it possible for things to change, but the new generation wants the luxuries that only come from money. They talk a good game, but in the end, check their bank accounts and see that they are part of the establishment that they are railing against. No one in this nation is immune from the greed syndrome. Ho Chi Minh led Vietnam to freedom, and he died without a dime in his pocket and his children and grandchildren lived as everyone else did, as nepotism was forbidden. Che Guevara died penniless, and left nothing but a legacy of compassion for his children who all today work for pennies to lift up those trapped by capitalist exploitation. His spirit has led me to see the light, and it is that spirit that guides me toward retribution against those who defile the human race with their avaricious greediness."

J.J. hung up without another word, and Chablis stood there just holding Keita's cell phone. All of them stared at each other in silence, in total disbelief.

After a few seconds, Chablis said, "Quick, we all have to get out of here. The authorities will be here before long. Do as I say and you will be O.K."

After the initial shock of seeing over $400,000, Chablis explained she needed a retainer. She did not take the $5000 J.J. suggested, but $100. She signed a receipt, gave it to Keita and explained to her that no matter what happened, she knew nothing, and that in order for her to be truthful, she would not reveal to her any of the details J.J. had shared with her. They left, money in a suitcase, and a few belongings in two other suitcases. On the way out, a perplexed Tony pressed for an explanation.

Chablis, was in a hurry, but stopped for a few seconds to give a cursory explanation. "J.J. is in big trouble. This place will be surrounded by cops,

Chablis and the Terrorist
Who Resurrected the Spirit of Che Guevara

F.B.I., N.S.A., pick any acronym you want. Tony, Mama and Keita are also targets of a government that is relentless in pursuit of anybody it considers a threat. Stall them for us if you can, but I don't expect you to endure torture. Just give us as much time as you can."

Tony, thrilled that he might be able to help Chablis, said, "You got it Chablis. I'll stall the bastards good."

She planted a kiss on his lips, and he fawned with a swooning motion and nearly collapsed. Such was the effect of one kiss from Chablis. He just stood there in ecstasy.

As they sped past the area where the four men had been shot by J.J., flashing lights, ambulances and a crowd of curious onlookers were milling about. Chablis knew it would not be long before the cops would get her description, connect her to the tenement where J.J. lived and start putting things together. She had little respect for those whose job it was to keep the poor in line to protect the rich, but there were those among them with a degree of intelligence and they knew how to put two and two together and come up with four.

On the way to Connecticut, she called Aaron and explained to him what happened. He said, "Well, we would have an ethical problem, as our client was Joe Harrington, but I sent him word today we resigned from the case, so there is no conflict of interest."

Chablis and the Terrorist
Who Resurrected the Spirit of Che Guevara

Surprised, Chablis said, "Why did we resign from the case."

"Found out he is C.I.A., and I told him this firm doesn't work for torturers and assassins."

"C.I.A., I knew there was something about him I didn't like," and then she made sure Mama and Keita couldn't hear as she whispered, "but I am not so sure about us not working for assassins. I just got a retainer from a man named J.J. Martinez, and he is the *Spirit of Che Guevara.*"

"Hey, so far he has only killed rich assholes. I'll take him over the C.I.A. any day."

"Aaron, I got two people I have to set up with a fake identity."

"Don't discuss it on the phone girl, nothing in this country is sacred anymore. There is no such thing as privacy since 9/11. Go to you know who at you know where. He is the man who can handle it. I'll expect to see you in the morning, and we'll map out strategy. Take care of yourself."

"Will do. See you tomorrow."

While Chablis was taking care of mama and Keita, J.J. was unperturbed about what had happened and he was determined to carry out his mission to bring down the Comstock brothers. He pulled the Crown Victoria up at a pay phone off the Jersey Pike and called the Mother Lode corporate headquarters where a perky young voice said, "Mother Load Holdings. How may I direct your call?"

"I need to talk to either Harold or Spencer Comstock."

"Oh sir, that would be impossible. They are too busy to take calls, but I can direct you to the right person I am sure. What is your concern?"

Aaron, very calmly said, "It is not my concern. It is theirs. This is the *Spirit of Che Guevara* calling."

She actually seemed pleased based on the infliction in her reply, "Oh, it will be my pleasure to get you Harold Comstock. Just a second, please."

After a few minutes, and no doubt a trace set-up, a gruff voice bellowed, "Harold Comstock here, and my brother Spencer is here with me. Is this really the man calling himself the *Spirit of Che*?"

"I'll prove it is Harold. Look across the street at the roof of your building there where you house all your records."

J.J. pushed a button on the pocket computer that sent a signal to the cell-phone on the roof. The phone was strapped to a water cistern and there was an explosive charge that went off. Water started cascading down the sides of the building. A few pedestrians got wet and started running. J.J. very calmly said, "Better send word to evacuate the building, it will implode in 30 minutes. Like your toxic producing paper mill in Jersey, that building is history."

Harold motioned for Spencer to get the people out of the building with a phone call. As Spencer was dialling, Harold said to J.J., "You goddamn commie bastard. You're fucking with the wrong people. "

J.J. very calmly said, "No Harold, I'm fucking with the right people. Think about making some big changes in your organization; otherwise, this is only the beginning of your troubles. We'll talk again soon."

"You mother.........." Before Harold could finish, J.J. hung up. Thirty minutes latter, the building empty, imploded in a pile of rubble.

Again, the news lambasted J.J. as a terrorist, but people all across America were beginning to see that this was not an act against the American people, but an act against the oppressors of the American people. Some liberal news outlets were actually, though not praising J.J., explaining how the American economic model was skewed in favour of the rich, which led to frustrations.

J.J. got into the Crown Victoria, drove a few kilometres and stopped at another phone booth where he called Donald Beckman.

Donald, beginning to empathize with J.J. more and more, said, "You are going after two of the most important men in America. They will fight, and they have the Republicans behind them, and even most Democrats who are fearful they will be branded socialists if they do not take determined stands against terrorizing the wealthy into doing the right thing. You can't win. You know that?"

"Donald, a small stone thrown in the ocean can cause ripples thousand of kilometres away. I am a small stone, and my ripples are beginning to be felt. The day will come when those small ripples will become a tsunami of towering waves that will flood everything in its wake."

Donald, man of peace, but a man who understood that sometimes the only answer to tyranny was violence, said, "Why are you doing this?"

"I came to the inevitable conclusion that the revolutionary is a social reformer. That he takes up arms only as a last resort when all else fails, when there is no compassion for the downtrodden left in a society that has allowed the cancer of greed to grow and fester. I am taking up arms against the oppressors, and I fight in order to change the social system that keeps so many people in bondage."

Taken with his words, Beckman said, "I shall publish your words, exactly as you have said them."

"Thank you Donald. I shall, in all likelihood die in the end, but I die knowing that I made the effort to effectuate change in the only way the establishment understands – violence, violence, violence."

CHAPTER 9
LIKE YOU CRUSHED THE CRUSHER

The privileged will never give up power willingly.
They will cling to it with tenacity.
The grip can only be broken with a mighty sword
swung by the oppressed who demand freedom!

The arrogance of the Comstock brothers had been apparent for years. They once said, "If you know how much you are worth, then you aren't worth very much," as there fortune increased daily. Typical of the immensely wealthy, they never really worked a day in their lives, starting out life by inheriting rather working.

However, their arrogance had taken a big hit as a result of J.J.'s actions, but he was not through. There were 44 Mother Lode supermarkets in New Jersey, and he was about to bring that part of the empire down too. The Crown Victoria had been parked under the G.W. Bridge and the van he rented under an assumed name had been cruising down the New Jersey Turnpike for almost an hour, as he was going to work his way back from the last exit to the first by the G.W. Bridge, blowing up supermarkets along the way. The stores were closed now, and J.J.'s first stop was the biggest store in the chain. It was right off Exit 41. He had the back of the van filled with plastic bombs he had made at the Lock and Leave facility. Each one was filled with enough plastic explosive to bring down a building within seconds. This would be a night of terror for the Comstock Empire courtesy of the *Spirit of Che*

Chablis and the Terrorist
Who Resurrected the Spirit of Che Guevara

Guevara. J.J. was dressed in old jeans, had put on his thick eyebrows, a plastic nose that gave him a Middle Eastern appearance and darkened his skin just as he had when he killed the billionaires. He knew that within a short time the authorities would know his identity and be swarming over his apartment in Harlem but it was O.K. now, because he knew Chablis would do all she could to protect his family.

He pulled into the parking lot of the first Mother Lode and walked to the entrance. A security guard came to the glass door and signalled they were closed. J.J. reached behind his back and brought out a pump action shot gun. The guard made no effort to go for his gun. He put his hands up and J.J, signalled for him to open the door, which he did quickly.

J.J. was direct and to the point as he reached into the guard's holster, removed his gun and gave it a toss down an aisle. "Anybody else in here?

"No, just me. Cleaning crew doesn't come in until midnight."

"Then run like hell for the street. I'm blowing this monument to greed up. You can tell the authorities that the *Spirit of Che Guevara* struck another blow for the little guy."

The security guard smiled and said, "I'll give you 15 minutes to get away. You doing some damn good work fellow. Keep it up."

Chablis and the Terrorist
Who Resurrected the Spirit of Che Guevara

Each stop off the turnpike, J.J. encountered security guards who actually seemed delighted to see him. They offered no resistance and made sure he had time to get away. Every few minutes along the turnpike, a brilliant explosion would light up the clear blue starless sky, turning it crimson as the stores all burned gloriously as a tribute to the ingenuity and dedication of one lone revolutionary who had simply decided he had enough.

Pulling under the George Washington Bridge to abandon the van, J.J. got in the Crown Victoria and cruised up the access road. He flipped the exact change in the fast-track toll booth and made his way across the bridge along with the other 7:00 AM rush hour commuters and listened to the reports of massive explosions at Mother Lode Supermarkets. He had hit 23 of them in six hours. That was almost 4 an hour. Pretty damn good thought J.J. Pretty damn good.

J.J. had rented a hotel room at The Marcus Garvey Hotel on Lenox Avenue and 188th, as he knew that rescuing Chablis was the end of his cover. It made no difference, because he was just one of 8 million people in the city. It would take a massive manhunt to locate him. He lay in his bed feeling great exhilaration and satisfaction as he had genuinely struck a massive blow against the empire of greed.

As J.J. drifted off to sleep, a massive array of armed police officers, F.B.I. agents and N.S.A. personnel descended on his apartment complex. Of course, Tony was sitting on his throne when they all arrived. Unperturbed, he jumped up and said, "Hey dudes, what's shaking?"

Joe Harrington, walked over and said, "What's up fucker is we are going level this place if necessary to turn up a terrorist. You know a Jose Juan Martinez?"

Tony, looking puzzled, said "Man. you know how many people in this neighbourhood are called Jose, Juan and how many people have the last name Martinez. You in Spanish Harlem dude."

"A guy standing beside Harrington grabbed Tony by the shirt and said, "Listen asshole, if you know this fellow and are holding out on us we'll ship your ass to Gitmo and hook you up to a car battery and light you up like a Christmas tree."

A man came running down from the building where J.J.'s apartment was shouting "Gone. Looks like they all packed up and skedaddled!"

Harrington very calmly motioned for two uniformed policemen to come over. "Take this asshole to the command van. I'll be there to interrogate him shortly." He then looked at Tony with piercing eyes. "Get your story straight asshole. I already got a line on you before we showed up in this shithole. You are Tony Mercante, resident neighbourhood thug. We aren't fucking around here."

Tony said, "Yeah, I got ya' man. I dig."

Chablis and the Terrorist
Who Resurrected the Spirit of Che Guevara

"You keep acting cute and you'll dig alright – dig your own grave. The New Jersey swamplands are full of assholes that made the mistake of thinking they could stand up to the U.S. government." Then he pointed to the command van and said again to the two officers. "Now, get his ass over there."

Everyone in the complex was being rounded up by the police, as these people had no rights in a country where being poor was a crime. Since 9/11, even the middle class had no rights when it came to national security, and, of course, almost anything could be branded a matter of national security. Fascism had not only taken hold during the Bush Administration, but when citizens had been asked if they were willing to give up some of their freedoms to fight terrorism, they enthusiastically said, "yes." People were so patriotically naïve that they lined up for their own chains.

Chablis had safely ensconced Mama Martinez and Keita in a backwoods cabin near Canaan Mountain, a small town in Connecticut so remote that it was often called the most isolated place in the state. With the $400,000 safely buried under the cabin, they would have the finances to, if necessary, live out their lives there as there was a general store within walking distance and the 44 people who lived in the area were fiercely independent and valued their privacy and the privacy of others. As she headed back to the city, she felt the urge to call Rodrigo. When he answered the phone his first words after hello was, "I love the hell out of you Chablis. When can I see you?"

Chablis and the Terrorist
Who Resurrected the Spirit of Che Guevara

Coyly, she replied, "You sure it isn't my ass you love?"

"Yeah, I love that, too. Guilty as charged."

She explained to him what had occurred the past 24 hours and said, "So, if I'm not in jail, I'll see you at 8 tonight, O.K.?"

"Sounds like a plan, see you tonight either at yore place, or at the city lock-up."

They laughed together and hung up. Chablis reflected on just how little she knew about Rodrigo, but what she knew, she liked. He was a man of integrity, kindness and compassion. Above all, he saw her as a complete woman, and accepted her as she was. That made him a man of character, too. She sighed as she also thought to herself – and what is between his legs isn't bad either. She felt a surge of excitement through her body, sighed again and thought about the great sex she was going to have that night in the arms of a man who had not only captured her body, but her soul. She was in love!

She and Aaron spent the day, first trying to figure out why they had dropped a client who was paying and, since they now knew he was paying with taxpayer dollars would, no doubt, have paid exorbitant amounts. They laughed as they said, "Yeah, having integrity can be costly." After a good laugh, they reflected on just what they could do for the Martinez family to kept their secret and how they were going to convince the man calling himself

Chablis and the Terrorist
Who Resurrected the Spirit of Che Guevara

the *Spirit of Che Guevara* to give up his fool hearted attempt to change things in a country that equated change with anarchy. They sympathized with him, and despite the fact that he had killed 36 billionaires, they looked at that act as nothing but retribution for all the wrongs those people had perpetrated over the years. This was a man with a social conscious who had actually aroused some of the citizenry to take a stand against the greedy bastards who had been in control for far too long.

Then something strange happened. Myrna walked in carrying a large envelope from FedEx. She was a bit tepid with it as she handed it to Aaron, saying, "With this Che fellow on the loose, packages of any size are suspect."

As Aaron nonchalantly opened the envelope, he said, "Don't fret Myrna until we all become greedy billionaires. Then we might be on his hit list."

Myrna's jaw dropped and Chablis eased forward in her seat as Aaron removed a batch of $100 bills from the envelope along with a folded 8 ½ X 11 note, which he opened and began to read:

Dear Mr. Adams:

This $50,000 is for your services in helping my family escape the wrath of the U.S. government. I am sure Chablis Louise Chavez has shared all she knows with you, and I know that you and she are people of integrity with reputations for always fighting injustice.

Chablis and the Terrorist
Who Resurrected the Spirit of Che Guevara

Please be assured that it has and will never be my intention to harm innocent people, although the people I am targeting never seem concerned with the collateral damage they do to innocents as they disregard environmental laws, labour laws and common decency in the pursuit of profits. Additionally, the U.S. government targets innocent people with regularity and complete impunity. I am not asking you to believe in my cause, but to believe in fairness and justice. Please convey my kind regards to Ms. Chavez, and tell her I am sorry I made her have to run so fast in her attempt to catch me.

Since you are people of integrity and astute investigators, I am certain you have discovered that Mr. Joe Harrington, although a writer with great socialist credentials to his credit, is, in reality, an undercover C.I.A. operative. I further am sure you are aware that the C.I.A. is forbidden by law to be involved in domestic spying, which is a law they and the President have allowed to be blatantly ignored since 9/11. I know the reputation you both have for supporting social justice, so I am certain you have probably already terminated your relationship with Mr. Harrington.

This money is to assure the continued assistance to my mother and sister, and any other legal request that I might make. I realize you must be careful as any direct connection to me might be ascribed as abating terrorism by a nation that is so invasive it even monitors what books you check out from the library.

Chablis and the Terrorist
Who Resurrected the Spirit of Che Guevara

Be assured that I shall keep a proper distance from you in regards to my activities against the oligarchs who rule America. I suggest you might share this letter with Donald Beckman at the New York Times as he is my conduit to the public.

Sincerely,

The Spirit of Che Guevara

Aaron eased back in his chair and said, "Damn, if I wasn't such a pussy, I'd be out there with this guy."

Chablis got up, walked over to the window. As she looked out at the street below, she let out a little sigh and said "I agree. For too long good people have just shrugged their shoulders and given up on effectuating change. Hell, I have given up. I know there are too many powerful interests arrayed against fairness and justice. Doesn't this guy know what happened to Che? He died in the Bolivian jungle waiting for the common people to rise up and join the revolution. While the C.I.A. was putting a bullet in his head those people he wanted to help were begging the rich for crumbs and accepting their fate, thinking that when they died they would walk the streets of gold in a heaven that is nothing but a myth created to keep the poor in line. People complain about their plight, but they aren't willing, at least in this country, to demand justice. Che died for people who just didn't care enough to stand up to authority. People in this country are even more complacent."

Chablis and the Terrorist
Who Resurrected the Spirit of Che Guevara

Aaron fondled the $50,000 and said, "Yeah, if the poor would walk into the corporate owned grocery stores that charge far too much for sustenance and start taking food off the shelves, there wouldn't be enough manpower and bullets to stop them. Fear is the problem in this country, fear of government, fear of outside forces that want to do us harm, fear of God and fear of everything that stands in the way of progress. 99% of the people in this country live in fear that is promoted by government and business to make people toe-the-line and not rock the boat. I'm on this fellow's side, and I say we help anyway we can. I say we do something worthwhile with this money, but no charity where the head of it is paid a lavish salary or the money is used to prosthelytize. As my old friend Reverend Blue used to say, "This country has enough religion, what it needs more of is money for the common man."

Chablis laughed and confidently said, "So, we can expect Joe Harrington anytime I would guess. He is probably tossing J.J.'s apartment right now and scaring the residents into spilling all they know about J.J."

Aaron placed the money in his top drawer and said, "Let's not wait. Let's go up to Spanish Harlem. I'm getting a handle on J.J. I want to get in his head, see what we can find out and maybe find him, and convince him that this is a fruitless exercise that will only lead to jail or death for him. Maybe we can help get him out of the country to safety. Did you get a good look at him? I have never even seen a picture on T.V. Does anyone know what he looks like?"

"I only saw him from the back, in profile and in dark shadows, but he is about 6:2, 190 and has a real confident stride when he walks. You can sense this is a guy who is really sure of himself." She stood there for a few seconds as in deep thought.

Aaron said, "What you thinking?"

"Nothing, nothing. It isn't important."

Actually, it was important, but Chablis was not certain of what she was considering, so she wanted to wait before sharing it with Aaron. She grabbed her purse and said "subamos al Español Harlem (let's go up to Spanish Harlem.)

Aaron replied, Vamos a Rocka nd roll (Let's rock and roll.)

Tony had withstood threats and some mild pushing and shoving. However, as he sat in the command van in a swivel chair, Joe Harrington leaned down and said, "We got an expert in interrogation coming Tony. You'll like him. He has experience at Abu Ghraib and Gitmo. He honed his talents on Muslim hoodlums who think they can take on the U.S. government. The ones who didn't come though with what we wanted are kicking up daisies now. His talents are lovingly called the Cheney Crush, as when the resistance is fierce he gets out the old water board. You heard of that?"

Chablis and the Terrorist
Who Resurrected the Spirit of Che Guevara

Tony took a deep breath, as he knew you did not stand up to "the man" and get away with it if you lived in the ghetto. He squirmed a bit, but tried to put up a brave front. "Yeah, I heard about all the torture you dudes done. Hey, we get plenty of torture from the man down here, too."

"You ain't never had torture like this, Tony. We love torturing you anti-American commie bastards. Hey, it is kind of fun when you assholes don't want to cooperate."

Art Dominic Deluca was as military as you can get. Close cropped hair that hugged his huge head that looked like chiselled stone, a forehead that appeared as if it could withstand a torrent of physical blows, a nose that protruded outward but was slightly flattened as it took up a good part of the middle of his face, almost non-existent lips that were tightly pursed and a chin that looked like it could absorb a blow from a sledge hammer. His broad shoulders were massive hunks that looked like they were made of steel and his barrel chest seemed to be looking for something to bump. His arms were huge like tree trunks and his hands were so big they looked like he could crush coconuts in them. This bulk of humanity was a walking, talking machine of destruction and he had Tony in his sights.

Joe Harrington greeted him cordially. "How nice to see you, Art. Let me introduce you to Mr. Tony Mercante, resident tough guy around here. Tony, meet Art. We just call him Crusher."

Chablis and the Terrorist
Who Resurrected the Spirit of Che Guevara

Tony was no marshmallow, but he felt like he was over a hot fire melting when he looked up at Crusher, who did not say a word. He just looked down at Tony and grunted.

"Now," said a smiling Joe Harrington, "let's get some answers to a few questions. I know you want to be cooperative. Don't you?"

Tony nodded his head as Crusher stood towering over him. Outside, Aaron and Chablis were walking into the complex and were stopped by a police officer. "Sorry, off limits right now."

Aaron feeling a bit miffed that the entire complex was shut down said, "What's wrong poverty become a crime now? You arresting everyone in the city who is poor?"

"Listen asshole, get the fuck outta here or I'll run you in for obstruction."

Just then, Captain Faraday from the 23rd Precinct spotted Aaron and walked over. "Hey Aaron, we are looking for your partner here," he said as he nodded a greeting to Chablis.

"Well, here she is. You guys taken on poverty now? Maybe you can arrest it."

Smiling, Faraday said, "Well, one guy thinks he can arrest it. Calls himself the *Spirit of Che*, and we think Ms. Chavez here might have a line on him. What about it Chablis?"

Chablis and the Terrorist
Who Resurrected the Spirit of Che Guevara

Chablis actually liked Faraday, as he was an exception to the usual arrogance of cops. "I'll help anyway I can, sure."

"Well, the man in charge is over there," Faraday said as he pointed to the command van. "Let's stroll over and meet Mr. Harrington."

Aaron said, "We already know him, and what the hell is the C.I.A. doing getting involved in domestic affairs? That's against the law."

Faraday, not sarcastically but dismissively said, "You'll have to take that up with your Congressman, if he isn't too busy playing golf or dining with billionaires."

"Hey, my Congressman is like half the police force – on the take."

Shaking his head, Faraday said, "I wouldn't suggest you be too flippant with these guys Aaron. They aren't as congenial as I am."

As Faraday knocked on the door to the command van, Aaron offered a bit of laconic praise. "Faraday, ain't nobody as congenial as you."

Chablis chimed in, "Or as good looking."

Smiling, Faraday winked at Chablis. "You got that right girl. I'm better looking than Brad Pitt."

Chablis winked back. "And more modest."

Chablis and the Terrorist
Who Resurrected the Spirit of Che Guevara

They opened the door just as Crusher was giving Tony a backhand across his left cheek. Aaron looked at Crusher and said, "Run out of Muslims to torture?"

Just as Crusher started for Aaron, Joe Harrington stuck out his left arm to stop him. "No, not yet Crusher. Not yet."

Aaron looked up at Crusher and said, "But soon Crusher, real soon."

Joe Harrington motioned for them to come inside. "So, you two still on the case, event though you dumped me as a client?"

Chablis said, "No case. We are just interested citizens wondering why the C.I.A. is involved in domestic affairs."

"There are no domestic affairs when terrorism is afoot. I hear you had a run in with Jose Juan Martinez, Chablis."

"I did, but never formally met him. Truth is, he saved my ass when four hoods tried to rape me."

Joe was not the man Chablis had met a few weeks before. Now he had lost his charm. He proved it when he said with a smirk, "Well, they would have had a big surprise when they pulled off you panties."

Aaron moved closer to Harrington and looked him

directly in the eyes. "You can insult me Harrington, but don't insult this woman."

Crusher started to move toward Aaron, and Aaron turned toward him. "And that goes for you too, big boy. I suggest you stop right there or you'll spend the rest of the night picking up your teeth." Aaron then turned back to Harrington. "Tell him Joe. He doesn't want to mess with me."

"Cool it Crusher. Mr. Adams and Ms. Chavez are going to be cooperative. Aren't you?"

"We may be, or we might tell you to go fuck yourself, because you have no jurisdiction in the USA. Now, this boy here is unaware that you have no right to question him in America, but being poor, he has no rights. Of course, you tarantula's of torture have been known to spirit people out of the country to violate human rights. You assholes think using terror to fight terror is O.K., but when someone like the *Spirit of Che* fights the terror of unfettered capitalism with terror that is a different story. Terror on our side of course is just legitimate use of repetitive force. I know what it is, you know what it is, but the American people prefer to bury their heads in the sand while acts of inhumanity are committed with impunity in their name. Now, ask me and Chablis whatever you want, but do it nicely, and tell this baboon of butchery to back off us and back off this kid here."

Harrington looked at Crusher and said, "Outside for awhile."

Chablis and the Terrorist
Who Resurrected the Spirit of Che Guevara

Crusher gave Aaron the death stare and Aaron winked at him, puckered his lips and made a kissing sound.

Meantime, Faraday stood observing, without saying a word, because he knew Aaron and Chablis were not the types you intimidated.

Harrington motioned for Chablis and Aaron to take a seat as he pulled out a chair and sat down. They obliged, and as Chablis crossed her legs, exposing a generous amount of upper thigh and rocked her muscular right calf back and forth, all the men sitting around a bank of video cameras that were scanning the area cut their eyes in her directions. She uncrossed her legs purposefully, making sure she exposed lots of inner thigh for their viewing pleasure. She loved playing with men, even government assholes who, if they knew what was between her legs, were probably too homophobic to make a play for her. Men, she thought, all a bunch of ninnies.

Joe Harrington flashed a scowl over at the men and they immediately turned their eyes away. "So, Chablis, you were looking for the *Spirit of Che*, and you wind up here. You talk to his mother and sister?"

"No, they were gone when I got here." She looked over at Tony, as she sensed he would go along with anything she said.

"What about you Tony? When you last see J.J.?"

Chablis and the Terrorist
Who Resurrected the Spirit of Che Guevara

"Well, right before Chablis showed up. I just said hi to him, that's all. She asks me about the family, and I tell her J.J. is in the apartment. They must have missed each other on the way up and down. J.J. comes by me in the courtyard and I tell him that there is this classy broad," then he looked over at Chablis, and continued, "I mean woman went up to see him. He looks real concerned and starts high tailing it out of there. Chablis comes down, and I point him out to her. He looks back over his shoulder and starts running and she does the same. That's it. That's all I seen. Them two run outta my sight and that was it."

Harrington looked at Chablis quizzically and she said, "Happened exactly as he said. That's it. I chase him to the subway, but just miss him. Catch a cab to the next stop. Just miss him again. Then, I catch a glimpse of him around the corner. I gave chase, get attacked by 4 hoods and he rescues me. Didn't see him up close though, as he was always in the shadows. Never been close enough to see him, and when I was up earlier to visit his mom and sister, he had removed all his pictures." She looked quizzically at Harrington and the bank of video cameras and asked, "What about it. You got some pics. I'd like to know what the guy I have been chasing looks like."

Shaking his head, Harrington said, "Funny thing, we checked his personnel file where he works, went back to his university, even his high school, and it seems he must have gotten in and removed them all somehow. In high school, the principal said that he never had a photo made and never showed up for make-up picture day either. We only have photos of him in elementary school. He never had a legitimate driver's licence. My guess is he has used fake ID's for years in preparation for these acts of terrorism. He may be part of a sleeper cell."

Chablis and Aaron burst out laughing. Aaron shook his head and said, "Sleeper cell, bullshit. You government boys have been playing that game since 9/11. Those 9/11 hijackers were in plain sight, but that buffoon Bush was too busy playing Mr. President, inflating his ego, to know what was happening next to him, much less in Boston, Miami or Minneapolis. It was bad enough the election was stolen and he was appointed President by a Supreme Court that has dismantled every protection for the poor against corporations, but the idiot Americans gave him a second term so he could prove how incompetent he really was. Then we wind up with fascists like you running all over the country trying to protect us from those evil Muslims. When I was a kid it was the commies, now it is Muslims. You people would be out of a job if you didn't manufacture somebody for us to fear. I know who to fear, and it is not some Muslim 10,000 kilometres away or some Che Guevara wanna-be bumping off tycoons and blowing up their monuments to greed. It is assholes like you who keep waving the flag and trying to get us to believe we are superior to everyone else. Fuck you, Harrington."

Tony sat mesmerized and dumfounded that Aaron would talk that way to a government man. If he did that, he'd be beat up, locked up and be in need of getting sewed up.

Harrington took it, because he knew that Aaron was not intimated like most people and neither was Chablis. The men at the bank of cameras sat in awe of Aaron and Chablis, because they were used to people fearing them.

Harrington, perturbed, but calm, said, "So, Chablis, where are Mama and Keita?"

"You got me. I haven't seen them in two days. Maybe they were scared of you guys and skedaddled. Can't say that I blame them. In this country today, you are guilty by association."

"So, you telling me that you didn't see them after J.J. helped you out?"

"Nope."

He looked over at Tony. "So, you didn't see her go up to the apartment after J.J. left? She never came back afterwards?"

Feeling a bit more confident, Tony replied, "Didn't see her afterward at all. Not till tonight, right here."

"O.K., you three can go, but don't plan on leaving town."

Tony, now almost cocky, said, "Got no money to

go nowhere dude. This here is the ghetto."

Aaron smiled, Chablis winked at Tony, and Tony, now feeling really cocky, got up and said, "Later, dude," as he walked out with Chablis, Aaron and the still quiet Faraday.

Crusher was waiting at the door, and he looked at Chablis and said, "I heard about you bitch. I catch you alone and I'll make you a real woman. I'm gonna rip your dick off and fuck you in the hole that's left with my monster cock."

Chablis, without a second's hesitation, as Harrington was about to plead with Crusher to shut up, rammed her right knee into his groin. As he crumbled over in pain, Aaron slammed his right foot with all the force he had down on Crusher's left shoe and he could hear the bones crack. Crusher collapsed in a heap on the pavement. Tony was laughing as Aaron took Chablis by the arm, looked over his left shoulder at Harrington and said, "Looks like Crusher just got crushed."

The cops standing by starting running toward the three, but Faraday waved them off. He looked at Harrington an said, "I wouldn't mess with these two if I were you Harrington. These two got juice in this town."

Harrington did not reply, only motioned for two officers to assist Crusher as Aaron, Chablis, Tony and Faraday walked toward the square. Aaron put his arm around Tony's shoulder.

Chablis and the Terrorist
Who Resurrected the Spirit of Che Guevara

Tony felt proud to have found some new friends who seemed to appreciate him. Aaron reached in his pocket and took out three $100 bills, making sure no one noticed. He put it in Tony's hand and said, "Take your girl out for a nice evening on me and Chablis."

Chablis and Aaron asked Faraday if he had the authority to let them look around the apartment. Faraday, actually having enjoyed watching the two of them fence with the Fed, replied, "Let's see. Hey, if I don't get you in, I hope you won't crush me like you crushed the crusher!"

CHAPTER 10
GRANDEST SYMBOL OF GREED

The way to fight injustice is with sabotage.
It cannot be planned recklessly,
nor for love of violence.
It requires calm and sober assessment
of the situation that has arisen
after years of humble pleading
for a just end to
tyranny, exploitation and oppression.

They found nothing of substance in the apartment, as it had been gone over thoroughly by the Feds and the local police. Chablis took a seat in a chair. Aaron and Faraday sit on the sofa. Chablis looked down at the coffee table and saw a piece of paper, probably torn from a small spiral flip pad notebook as it had frayed edges at one end where it had been pulled from the notepad, but the paper had been folded into a triangle. She looked down at it contemplatively, trying to wonder where she had seen something like that before. △

She stood up, as they prepared to leave the apartment, but could not take her eyes off the small piece of paper on the coffee table that was folded into a triangle. As they walked to the door, she kept looking back at it lying there on the table. What was its significance she kept asking herself? They walked into the courtyard, said goodbye to Faraday, and waved goodbye to Tony, sitting on his throne, and Chablis said, "Hey, I'm heading home. Got a hot date tonight."

Chablis and the Terrorist
Who Resurrected the Spirit of Che Guevara

Aaron said as he headed the opposite direction, "Be sure and use a condom. Wouldn't want you to get pregnant."

Chablis laughed, but didn't reply. She was still thinking about that piece of paper folded in a triangle on the coffee table. Why could she not put it out of her mind? All the way home, she kept reflecting back on it.

When Rodrigo showed up for their date, Chablis greeted him at the door with that mischievous, slow smile that gradually spread across her thick, succulent, ruby red lips. He took a deep breath and stood in awe as he gazed upon her. She looked as if the light around her was ghost-like, condensed as if she were a lithe gazelle slanting with precision ready to leap across the plain. She was a sleek racing yacht sailing upon the deep blue waters of lust, and she exuded peace and serenity that would soothe any man lucky enough to find himself in her arms. She was the bright North Star that was the beacon of navigation leading to sanguine peacefulness. She was the sunlight that came up on the morning horizon, the soft cool breeze that floated gently across the undulating waves and made them ripple with anticipatory delight at her carnal collaborations. The foam of her sweet, soft voice flew like flaky snow before the wintry tempest of temptation. The brightness of her sparkling eyes set her lover's course towards tranquility in a calm sea that radiated with her golden haze. This was not just a woman. This was a Goddess!

Chablis and the Terrorist
Who Resurrected the Spirit of Che Guevara

There seemed to be something deeply troubling Rodrigo that night, as Chablis sensed trepidation in his voice and manner. After they arrived at her apartment and she poured him a drink, she eased on the sofa beside him and said, "Something is bothering you Rodrigo. What is it?"

"Chablis, I'm in love?"

"That is what is bothering you? Well, if you are in love with me, there's no problem, but if it is with someone else, I may kick your ass."

He laughed and said, "Of course it is with you. That is why I am perturbed. You see, I am going to be really busy the next couple of days. I have clients from Boston to Philadelphia I have to see. I'll miss you."

"And I you, but remember that separation makes the heart grow fonder."

He was so pleased that she loved him. He took her in his arms and they kissed passionately. Before long they were on the carpet, discarding clothes and frantically fondling one another. She could not resist his passionate kisses as her mouth opened with delight to welcome his darting tongue as she moaned in ecstasy, anticipating the placement of his hands on her tight opening to paradise. She began to caress his muscular thighs with both hands, using her long nails to tantalize him, arouse his libido and get his gorgeously erect joy stick ready for the delightful plunge into paradise.

Chablis and the Terrorist
Who Resurrected the Spirit of Che Guevara

She eased down between his legs and blew on his pubic hair and nestled his huge balls with her nose and mouth before very adroitly, in one smooth motion, taking his joy stick into her mouth, devouring it as she was starving for lack of nourishment. He moaned and bucked upward to meet her downward motion. She let the hardness pop out and she began to make a small squiggly trail along the side of his stiffness. Before she reached the mouth watering head again, she looked up at him and smiled, letting him anticipate what was next. In a moment her mouth again found the base of his shaft. After a few approaches toward the head, he began to squirm and buck his hips. He grabbed her behind the neck forcing his stiffness deeper and deeper into her mouth.

She sucked him slowly and deliciously, never letting him get enough of himself into her mouth to fully enjoy what he wanted, always taking him back out, observing him, smiling deviously as if she were deliberately antagonizing him. She kept blowing on the shaft and the tip. She pressed it up against her cheek and jerked the base with her hand while her mouth worked on the rest of him. As she gave him wave after wave of ecstasy, he slid his hand between her magnificent ass cheeks, finding that opening that was pulsating with anticipation.

He spread her apart as they manoeuvred to a 69 position and she willingly relaxed her sphincter muscle, making it easy for him to enter her with his fingers. Having performed anal sex since she was a teenager, she needed no lubricant, but still she

Chablis and the Terrorist
Who Resurrected the Spirit of Che Guevara

reached over for the lubricant on the coffee table and skilfully opened it with one hand and put the lubricant around his fingers as he worked them back and forth. She could tell he was on the verge a climax as his member stiffened and started to pulsate. He was desperate, so she took it out of her mouth and slowly extracted his fingers from her.

She led him to the bedroom, not by his hand, but by grasping his erect member and pulling him behind her. She eased to the side of the bed and laid face-down, her magnificent derriere dangling on the edge of the bed with her feet barely touching the floor. She reached back, pulled her cheeks apart with both hands and jutted her derriere up into the air and said, "I want it hard baby – real hard."

He positioned the tip of his member gently against her gapping opening, and she said, "Ram it in baby. Ram it hard."

He was a gentle man, so he did not want to hurt her. Yet, as he eased into her, she kept saying, "Ram it baby. Ram it."

She was as loose as a goose in heat and hotter than a firecracker on Chinese New Year. As Rodrigo picked up the rhythm she kept saying, "oh my, oh my. It's so good baby."

He kept furiously thrusting forward and she met each thrust so hard you could hear the flesh pounding through the apartment and Rodrigo's balls were pressed right up firmly against her ass cheeks.

Chablis and the Terrorist
Who Resurrected the Spirit of Che Guevara

Chablis began to shout, "Harder, harder."

Rodrigo moaned with pleasure as he picked up the rhythm and began rolling his head loosely from one side to the other.

"Slower baby. Slower now. Enjoy it, enjoy my deep hole," she said as she turned her head and he bent forward to kiss her. Their lips played wetly and passionately. Their tongues touched each other in a light sparing juicy war. Then their mouths parted and Chablis ground her hips powerfully in a circle motion against his manhood. He let out a soft long moan and his head rose up toward the ceiling and then he collapsed onto her back. All the while, he kept pumping away.

Chablis could tell he was quickly losing control. Anything she wanted to do to him now, he was ready and would let her. She was fantastically turned on by her position of power as she always was. It wasn't the sex as much as the knowledge she had complete control over any man because of her gyrating, mind-blowing derriere that drove them over the edge. She was now experiencing waves of joy as her own stiff stick pumped load after load of hot juice onto the bed.

Rodrigo's passion was almost overpowering. His feelings were warm and tickly and then ice cold in alternation. He felt himself trembling with openness for this new experience with a woman who was like no other he had ever encountered. This was a woman who knew no restraint in passion.

Chablis and the Terrorist
Who Resurrected the Spirit of Che Guevara

His erection was the hardest he had ever experienced. He pounded ever harder, watching Chablis' magnificent hips as little beads of sweat formed on them. She was taking all he had and still pleading for more.

Without realizing it, he reached around and fondled her breasts, squeezing and pricking the hard nipples. Though she had obviously cum, she still wanted more, wanted Rodrigo to keep pounding her. He looked down and watched his member work in and out, in and out, in and out. Staring intently at the enticing vibrations as Chablis met each thrust, he felt her hole spreading wider, inviting him into the chamber where delightful dalliances of deliciousness were furiously pulling at his member now, wanting that wonderful sensation to rock her body as he seeded her. He was now buried so deeply in her that he felt his stomach begin to ache from brushing against her gorgeous cheeks.

He bent over and kissed Chablis' neck, never slowing the rhythmic pounding, and then he realized that he could hold back no more. As his member pulsated violently, she had another orgasm, squirming to get her hole crushed right up against the base of the vibrating member, to press her orgasm into being, up out of her groin and shooting throughout her body. She shook as if she were at the end of the world and falling, falling over the edge into oblivion. Seeing her cum like that drove Rodrigo to the edge of insanity and increasing his pace, sliding up and down the gigantic shaft would not let up as the stimulation was so intense and

Chablis and the Terrorist
Who Resurrected the Spirit of Che Guevara

coming from so many places at once that he could barely tell what was happening until he spurted again, filling her up with his seed to the brim. He could feel it coming back out the opening, squiggling down her crack.

The raging fire of passion subsided and Rodrigo collapsed on Chablis' back, then rolled to her side and laid there staring at the ceiling as she turned on her left side, reached over with her right arm and wrapped it around him. They were exhausted.

Rodrigo left early the next morning and as Chablis was heading for work she got a call from Donald Beckman. "Ms. Chavez, I am Donald Beckman."

"Yes, I know you. I believe we have a mutual acquaintance," replied Chablis.

"We do, yes ma'am. I got a call from him this morning. He is about to do something big."

Chablis was about to get on the IRT, but said, "Wait a minute, I'll go across the street and take a train down to the *Times*. Be there in 10 minutes."

"O.K., I'll leave word at the main desk to send you right up."

Describing Chablis is like describing a Michelangelo work of art. There is a perfection to her that defies description. She is the human Sistine Chapel.

Chablis and the Terrorist
Who Resurrected the Spirit of Che Guevara

As she walked through the revolving door and strode confidently into the lobby, it was as if everyone there, even the women, suddenly were hypnotized into silence. Conversations between people stopped in mid sentence, all eyes scanned her way, heads turned slowly to follow her gazelle like strides. Her cascading long black hair seemed to dance about her shoulders in a waltz of seductive sexiness as she glided to the lobby desk.

One man bumped into the revolving door as his head was strained backward looking at the most perfectly shaped derriere to ever grace a mid-thigh skirt. The wiggle was not pronounced, but the sway said in silent tones of temptation, "Come and get it baby – it is good stuff."

She leaned over the desk. Her magnificent, perfectly shaped ass jutted out like a tempting, tempestuous terminal where the trains to heaven awaited boarding. No doubt, erections were popping up all about as the men there dreamed of dropping to their knees to pay homage to the perfection that was Chablis' ass.

As she leaned over the counter, the desk clerk's eyes tilted downward to gaze upon her apples balcony. Her breasts were not huge, but they were perfectly shaped beautiful love bubbles that seemed to cry out for a man's touch, a man's mouth to savour the tantalizing tastiness of her two brown bean bags that jutted out like two beautiful dark hills in the distance beckoning for the weary traveller of temptation to take a taste.

Chablis and the Terrorist
Who Resurrected the Spirit of Che Guevara

Her voice was as melodious as a nightingale and exuded the sweetness of un-harvested sugar cane. The man sighed deeply as she said, "I have an appointment with Donald Beckman."

Stuttering he replied, "Yes ma'am, he's expecting you" as he pointed to a bank of elevators to his right. "4th floor – city desk."

She smiled and her eye lids fluttered a bit. "Thank you so much."

He took a deep breath and watched intently as she walked to the elevators. Along with 25 or 30 other men in the lobby, his heart was fluttering with awe and desire, and, no doubt, so were the hearts of a few women.

What happened in the lobby was repeated in the City Editor's Room, and Donald Beckman was overwhelmed that he was sharing time with a woman he had read about many times in his own newspaper, but never had the privilege to meet. Her beauty in photographs that had appeared in the newspaper was obvious, but photographs did not do her beauty justice. There was an aura about her, a light that was almost celestial as it seemed to dance about her shining a beacon of beauty that was a guidepost, a graph, a diagram, a map to heaven if only you could wrap your arms around her.

As the City Room got back to normal, Donald said, "So, tell me what you know about our boy the *Spirit of Che*.

Chablis and the Terrorist
Who Resurrected the Spirit of Che Guevara

"Unfortunately, very little.

Donald, who was sitting in a chair beside Chablis, rather than behind his desk, said "I must profess some sympathy for his cause; although, his methods are questionable."

Chablis replied, "I agree, but he has already had a profound effect. Hey, even Nelson Mandela resorted to violence when it appeared all else had failed. Maybe Martin Luther King would have, too, if he had lived long enough."

"True, there is no doubt that it was the fury of the Black Panthers and other violent activists that had more to do with the government passing civil rights legislation than King's civil disobedience. A million black people with extended hands begging for their rights are not nearly as effective as 12 angry black men packing AK-47's. As Mao said, "Power comes from the barrel of a gun."

Chablis very seriously said, "I agree, and having read Marx, I can attest to the fact the rich will not give up their privileged status without a fight. Still, I am afraid that our friend will not be able to maintain his ability to avoid collateral damage. If he keeps this up, some innocents will be killed."

Donald offered a sage observation. "In the fight for justice, innocents often pay the price for that which they will never obtain. A revolution is not a dinner party, or writing an essay, or painting a picture, or doing embroidery; it cannot be so refined, so leisurely and gentle, so temperate, kind, courteous, restrained and magnanimous. A revolution is an insurrection, an act of violence by which one class overthrows another."

Chablis smiled at the depth of Donald's knowledge. "You know your Mao. Obviously, you have read the Little Red Book."

"I may be part of the *Me Generation* that was ushered in with that buffoon Ronald Reagan, but I have grandparents who came up in the 60's. I heard many tales from them about the way they stopped an unjust war through acts of violence. This nation needs people with that kind of dedication to justice today. Now, you stand against government tyranny and you are a traitor. We are supposed to support wars of conquest, torture and the corporatization of the world without protest. Americans are the most easily manipulated and controlled people in the world. Wave a flag, mention Jesus and they all fall in line. This is a nation of robotic believers in their own superiority, and they cannot see that they are the least free in the entire free world. You can't even check a book out of the library without the government knowing about it for fear you might be a terrorist. When I talk to my mom about politics, she is always telling me to watch what I say. She is fearful someone might be listening. This is a nation that lives in fear, and the thing we all fear most is our own government, which has become oppressive."

Chablis really liked Donald. "You sound like a fugitive from the 60's. Burn baby burn!"

Chablis and the Terrorist
Who Resurrected the Spirit of Che Guevara

"Yeah, I suppose I was born about 30 years too late. Anyway, what can we do to get a line on Mr. Che?"

"Well, Donald, I had him in my sights, but I just barely missed him."

"I bet you know where his mom and sister are don't you? It's O.K. I am not asking. In fact, I don't want to know. I am just glad they are safe for the time being from the wrath of the government."

"They were shocked at the revelation, but not overly so, because they knew he was getting fed up. He is, like Che, an idealist, who dreams of a world without hunger, a world where people are not honoured for how much money they have but for the humanity they show. He sees no need for the many to live in poverty while the few live in splendour. I have the same feeling, but I am more of a realist who knows that the world has always been this way and keeps getting worse. There was a brief time in America in the 50's, 60's and 70's when the working man had a shot, but when Ronald Reagan destroyed the unions that was the final nail in the working man's coffin. It's over and nothing the *Spirit of Che* or anybody else does will change things unless the police, the military and a few of the politicians switch sides. There is too much firepower and too much authoritarian fascism in the hands of the tyrants."

Smiling, Donald said, "Chablis, I think you and I are secretly pulling for the *Spirit of Che*."

Chablis and the Terrorist
Who Resurrected the Spirit of Che Guevara

Suddenly, the phone rang. Donald said, "Hello, City Desk."

"Hi Donald."

Donald flipped the speaker switch and nodded at Chablis. She knew it was the *Spirit of Che*.

"Donald, I am like a man in a deep dark hole, slowly moving forward, realizing that my pleasure comes from being in that hole. There is no fear, only the thrill of being inside and enjoying the tightness, the darkness."

Chablis began to tingle and her sphincter muscle relaxed as he was talking in an almost sexual tone, talking as if he was pounding her ass like Rodrigo did. She was getting horny. She could feel an erection growing between her legs. J.J. looked pretty good from a distance she thought to herself. Hey, she had Rodrigo now, she didn't need another man, but........

"I am bringing down the Comstock Brothers today. The Republican Party is going to be short of money from their biggest donors, because the brothers will need all the money they have. The insurance companies won't cover all the damage I am going to do to their empire of greed. This is the day the common man gets his retribution and brings justice to the unjust."

"I suppose it would be fruitless to tell you that you are going to be caught eventually."

Chablis and the Terrorist
Who Resurrected the Spirit of Che Guevara

"Mandela was caught. 30 years later he was President of South Africa. That is why the C.I.A. gave the green light to the murder of Che, if he had lived, he might have been President of Bolivia one day. Murder is the solution America uses to eliminate those it deems a threat. O.K., the tables are turned now. I am systematically eliminating those who are a threat to freedom and justice."

Chablis could not resist, as her sexual sensations had subsided. "J.J., you are not going to be able to avoid capture for long. There is no need for you to disguise your voice to us. Take the handkerchief off the mouthpiece. Go ahead and let the world know who you are. Aaron Adams and I will help you get out of the country. We have contacts in Cuba, one of the last places on earth where greed has not cast its ugly shadow. You will not be able to avoid murdering innocents in collateral damage much longer. We believe in your cause and want to help you escape the wrath of a government with no pity, no compassion. You can do more good alive as a propagandist now than as a dead martyr."

You could sense the delight in his voice. "Why Chablis, you sound like you might have some affection for me. I am a man who appreciates a beautiful woman. What say we go out some time?"

"Sure, how about the Copacabana in Havana?"

"Chablis, Americans don't have the freedom to travel to Cuba. You'd be breaking the law. They might water board you."

Chablis and the Terrorist
Who Resurrected the Spirit of Che Guevara

"Hey, I might risk it for a date with a hot stud like you."

"I'll think about it," were his last words as he hung up.

Just then, the city room runner came in with an envelope, handed it to Donald and the gathered crowd awaited his opening it. He pulled out a large photo of the brothers tied to trees in the wilderness. they were looking fearfully into the camera lens, almost pleading for help. Donald read the accompanying memo.:

I have the Comstock Brothers and their attorney. They will be released when the below power of attorney is exercised by their sister and all their stock is sold and the money distributed equally in cash to the residents over the age of 18 of the following city housing projects. Do it in 24 hours.

- o   *Alfred E. Smith Houses, Manhattan*
- o   *Baruch Houses, Manhattan*
- o   *Breukelen Houses, Brooklyn*
- o   *Bronx River Houses, Bronx*
- o   *Carver Houses, Manhattan*
- o   *First Houses, Manhattan*
- o   *Frederick Douglass Houses, Manhattan*
- o   *Glenwood Houses, Brooklyn*
- o   *Harlem River Houses, Manhattan*
- o   *Marcy Houses, Brooklyn*
- o   *Mariners Harbour Houses, Staten Island*
- o   *Patterson Houses, Bronx*
- o   *Pomonok Houses, Queens*

Chablis and the Terrorist
Who Resurrected the Spirit of Che Guevara

- *Queensbridge Houses, Queens*
- *Robert F. Wagner Houses, Manhattan*
- *Sheepshead Bay Houses, Brooklyn*
- *Soundview Houses, Bronx*
- *St. Nicholas Houses, Manhattan*
- *Williamsburg Houses, Brooklyn*
- *South Jamaica Houses, Jamaica-Queens*

DURABLE POWER OF ATTORNEY

KNOW ALL MEN BY THESE PRESENTS, that we, the undersigned, Harold W. Comstock and Spencer L. Comstock over the age of eighteen ....

The power of attorney instructed their sister to sell all the stock they owned and to distribute the money to the aforementioned tenants in the housing projects listed. All present shook their heads in disbelief that the *Spirit of Che* managed to kidnap the two brothers and their attorney. How it happened shall now be revealed in as much detail as possible, based on eyewitness accounts.

The two brothers were not overly cautious, but they did add an additional bodyguard, so they had three rather than the usual two. They travelled almost everywhere together, so the limousine had the driver and one bodyguard up front and two bodyguards in the back sitting in the jump seats. Now, the brothers were notoriously cheap on personnel, so the bodyguards, though professional were not very well compensated. That would be an error of judgement on the brothers part, an error that would cost them most of their fortune

J.J. had, for several days, watched them closely and noticed that they made it a point every morning to stop at a coffee shop on Park Avenue. They apparently enjoyed the attention they got from normal people who would point them out and fawn over the fact that two billionaires were dining where they were also eating. Typical of the oppressed class, they were enthralled by royalty, as in America, royalty was the wealthy class. Just like the fools who lined the streets to wave at royal leeches like the Queen, King, Princes and Princesses of England, Americans bowed and scrapped before the wealthy as they were considered something special, because they happened to be born with a silver spoon in their mouths. J.J. was about to yank that silver spoon out of their mouths and shove it up their asses.

The bodyguards did not go into the shop, only escorted the brothers to the door. Then a stroke of luck put the brother's attorney Thurston Blakely in the coffee shop at the same time. J.J. pulled the Crown Victoria into a spot on Park Avenue and watched closely as a cop stopped and talked to the chauffeur, but never bothered to write a ticket, because obviously he was told who the car belong to. Billionaires had special parking privileges in New York City, just like the police did. For years, the police had parked their own cars at fire hydrants and in no parking zones to go in for donuts and coffee, but they were part of the privileged class, so it was permissible. After all, those who enforced the laws were not obligated to follow the laws.

The Comstock brothers came out and their attorney got in the car with them. They pulled away, and as they headed for Wall Street, J.J., who had hacked the brothers' cell-phone, gave them a call. "Harold Comstock here, who the hell is this? How'd you get this number?"

"This is the *Spirit of Che Guevara*. I got this number the same way I got to your vehicle last night and put a bomb under the transmission casing, and I can detonate it with one flick of my remote I am holding. Listen to me very carefully and you can continue to live. Make one mistake, one deviation from my instructions and you will never be able to steal money from people again. Go ahead and explain it to those there with you, and make certain there is no stoppage or you are all dead. Go ahead, tell them."

Harold explained to them all what was happening. Then, he put the phone to his ear and said, "You fucking with the wrong people buddy."

"No, I'm fucking with the right people, Harold. You are the one who has been fucking with the wrong people – the workers whom you have gotten wealthy off. "

"We make this country work, asshole. Most people are too stupid to accumulate anything. We make capitalism work."

Chablis and the Terrorist
Who Resurrected the Spirit of Che Guevara

"You make nothing work. You were born with a silver spoon in your mouth. If you had to work on the factory floor, you wouldn't last two hours. Turn the car around and head for Boston Post Road. Keep the phone line open but shut the fuck up until I tell you to talk. Go ahead, get going, now."

J.J. picked the Boston Post Road because it would keep them off the toll ways, and because it led right to the spot where he was going to take them for a little walk in the woods.

Spencer Comstock was frantically texting the police on his phone, telling them where they were, but he had a surprise coming. J.J. told Harold, "Tell your brother to look out the back of the window and he'll see a Jeep right behind you and on the hood is a triangular antenna. Now tell him to look at the text that just arrived on his phone."

All your communications are being rerouted to my phone asshole. Gottcha!

All their jaws dropped and Harold said, "Listen, give us a figure and we'll pay. O.K., you win. You win."

"A figure, well, how about it all. Make a right at the next dirt road. Miss it and you're all dead."

Harold, almost pleading with the chauffeur, said, "Make a right at the next dirt road. Don't miss it. Don't miss it. Slow down."

Chablis and the Terrorist
Who Resurrected the Spirit of Che Guevara

They proceeded down the road with J.J. right behind them. After about 5 kilometres, J.J. told them to stop. "O.K., have the chauffeur and bodyguards toss their weapons out the window."

They complied and then J.J. told Harold, "Have them get out with their hands up. I am holding an Uzi, so I would suggest they do exactly as I say."

J.J. stood by the hood of the Jeep Patriot and told the guards and Chauffeur to take their jackets off and lie facedown. He moved over with some rope, tossed it down in front of one of the bodyguards and said, "Tie them up." then he hollered at the Comstock Brothers and the attorney, "You three out with your hands up."

After making sure the four men on the ground were securely tied up and properly positioned, he turned his attention to the brothers and Thurston Blakely. "You are a bonus Blakely. You got your notary seal with you?"

"Yeah, in my briefcase. I always carry it. You want me to notarize your death warrant, because that is what will happen when you get caught. You're fucking with some important people here."

"You know what Thurston? If I fucked the lowest wino in the Bowery she would be better than you three assholes. You are important in your own minds, but to me you are lower than whale shit," Then, J.J. reached into his pocket and came out with a power of attorney and handed it to Harold.

Chablis and the Terrorist
Who Resurrected the Spirit of Che Guevara

Harold looked down and read it. "You got to be fucking kidding. I am not giving anything to those low-life cretins living in the projects. Those leeches have been living off public askance all their lives."

"Harold, you are right, but you been living off welfare too. You cheat the taxpayers out of their fair share, and make the little guy with no juice pay. You are a leech. You get to deduct your high priced lunch, your golf club membership, the company retreat in the Hamptons, the company yacht, the company airplane. You want to talk welfare, look in the mirror asshole."

Harold, defiantly said, "I'm not signing."

J.J. put a quick burst with the Uzi right at Harold's feet. "Your call Harold. Your fortune or your life. Frankly, I prefer the later, but the ball's in your court."

His brother grabbed the paper from his hand and said, "Give me a pen. My life is worth more than my fortune."

"Smart man Spencer," said J.J. as he handed him a pen.

After Spencer signed, he handed the paper to Harold and said, "Sign."

Harold signed and handed the paper over to Blakely who notarized it and handed it to back to J.J.

Chablis and the Terrorist
Who Resurrected the Spirit of Che Guevara

"O.K., into the woods over there on the right. They preceded forward and stopped at a small grove of spruce trees that were about 30 centimetres in circumference. J.J. pulled out three hand cuffs and tossed them to Blakely. "Handcuff them to a tree, then yourself. He went back to the car and had the four others join them. He lashed them all to a tree and said, "So, you boys take it easy. I'll be back."

The envelope, of course, went to Donald Beckman, and within 24 hours, the money was dispersed. 303,120 residents over the age of 18 in those projects wound up with $47,700 each. Ironically, most of it would be spent foolishly by people who had never had more than a few dollars in their pockets. However, that foolish spending actually gave a shot of adrenalin to the moribund New York City economy, as rather than being tied up to provide great largesse for two fascist capitalists it was released to illustrate what happens when you put money in people's pockets. In fact, one astute newscaster said, "This is an example of what would happen if the minimum wage was raised dramatically. People spend and the money goes right back into the economy. We may not condone the methods used by this man calling himself the *Spirit of Che*, but he certainly provided an example of what happens when people have money – they spend!

Now, back in the field where the seven men were tied up, they had an anxious night with J.J., who brought them some pizza. When he heard that the money had been dispersed, he had a surprise for the

the men. He released the bodyguards and chauffeur and said, "You guys will get a kind citizen to stop on the Boston Post Road. These three assholes are going to be here for awhile." He put the handcuff keys in his pocket and smiled."

The four men walked back with him and one of them said, "Thanks for the fun. It was great to see those assholes squirm."

J.J. got into the Patriot and said, "Sorry I can't give you a ride, but I need some lead time."

The chauffeur said, "No problem man, good luck."

J.J. was actually proud of himself for pulling it off so smoothly and the thought of the Comstock Brothers now being reduced to probably not more than 30 or 40 million dollars in assets was very pleasing, because for them, that was poverty. He picked up the Crown Victoria, removed his disguise and drove back to the city and heard that a group of homeless people had just walked into three corporate owned grocery stores in the Bowery and started taking food off the shelves. The riot squad was sent but there were far too many homeless people joined by others for the police to handle the situation; therefore; they just watched as people made off with food. It was starting. Darkness began to fall and J.J. looked over in the passenger seat and mist was forming outside the fogged up window. He could barely make it out, but it looked like a man in army fatigues and a beret puffing on a cigar.

Chablis and the Terrorist
Who Resurrected the Spirit of Che Guevara

He cruised back into town, stopped by the Lock and Leave and went to his hotel, firm in the knowledge that he had struck a mighty blow against greed. As he lay on his bed looking out at the blinking neon hotel sign that was only partially lit, he reflected back on his transformation to a firebrand revolutionary bent on motivating change in a nation that had deteriorated into a mere shell of its former self since 1980 when the country was turned lock, stock and barrel over to corporate interests to run as they pleased. How ironic that the former head of a union, Ronald Reagan, would be the man who destroyed the unions and along with it, the last hope of the working man in America.

Now, a mighty wind was blowing across the land in the form of the *Spirit of Che Guevara*. It was only a stiff breeze at present, but as it gathered steam it was possible it could be of hurricane force, toppling the hypocrisy of self-aggrandizement, arrogance and greed that had trapped a nation in a downward spiral for so long. Did people have the courage and the intelligence to finally take a stand against the injustice that had paved the thoroughfares of the rich with gold while forcing the middle class and poor to drive on roads filled with the pot holes of despair?

He noticed the neon light began to blink off and on, and in the evening mist that was forming outside his window, a ghostlike figure began to slowly come into view just below the neon sign. It was the figure that had guided him for so long now, the figure of hope for the hopeless.

Chablis and the Terrorist
Who Resurrected the Spirit of Che Guevara

Looking at the figure in a beret and army fatigues, J.J. knew his next move would be his boldest, and it would rival the destruction of the Twin Towers in magnitude. He was prepared to deliver a grand blow in the name of justice. His one man revolution would deliver the *coup de grâce* to the grandest symbol of greed.

CHAPTER 11
FOLDED INTO A TRIANGLE

I shall walk barefoot.
I shall walk in the pouring rain.
Through thorns, despite the fire,
Despite the pain...
I shall buy a bullet, at any price.
For a bullet is all they understand.
They dispersed all my hope
In this uncompassionate land,
And they stole my smile.
Between us there is a money divide.
Between me and them,
There must be war and bloodshed.
So I shall buy a bullet, at any price.
I shall buy a bullet at any price.

What can you do to make things right in a land where there is no will to lift up those who are discarded by a cruel system that exalts only those at the top of the economic ladder. You can hope for change, but without force there is little incentive for change. Those at the top will not give up privilege without a fight.

As usual, the Republicans were frantic that the Democratic President was not acting boldly enough to combat this vile threat to democracy. Attacking the rich was an evil their party could not countenance, because it was the rich who were the lifeblood of the nation. It was the rich who made the economic engine hum and gave people jobs to provide their sustenance. Rich was good!

J. Wayne Frye   263

Chablis and the Terrorist
Who Resurrected the Spirit of Che Guevara

One Republican Senator even introduced a bill to compensate the Comstock Brothers for their loss with money from the public treasury. The very obscenity of such a motion goes to the heart of how sick the American economic system is thought J.J. as he prepared for the final attack in his one man revolution that was now gaining adherents despite the President, the Cabinet heads, the Congressmen and the Senators all railing against a man who was attacking the American economic system.

All across America, movements were gathering steam to force a higher minimum age, to ease rules on voting in a union, to force management to appoint workers to committees to review company policies and give workers a say in how profits were distributed. Even Boards of Directors were beginning to realize that they had to rein in executive pay on order to assure the employees did not openly rebel. Several C.E.O.'s actually cut their salaries, one to $1 a year and a promise to never accept more than one million dollars a year based on company profits. Any excess would be distributed to the workers. Fear was running rampant among the rich as J.J. had planted a seed that was sprouting into a mighty tree with branches that stretched out in all directions, as more and more people started demanding their rights rather than begging for them. One day in Chicago, all factory workers walked off the job at noon and went to the Wrigley Building where they shut down traffic and demanded an audience with the mayor from whom they got an agreement to introduce a $20 an hour minimum wage bill.

Chablis and the Terrorist
Who Resurrected the Spirit of Che Guevara

In America's most liberal and progressive city, San Francisco, 400,000 people showed up at City Hall demanding the city pass a bill to make it mandatory that all corporations with 100 or more employees must set aside for the workers a percentage of the profits each year to be distributed based on their years of service. So progressive was San Francisco that the bill was brought before the council that night and passed without debate.

As all these actions were taking place, Republicans cried that the leaders were giving in to blackmail by a terrorist. Meanwhile, most of the Democrats, except a few of the more socialist oriented ones, joined the Republicans in decrying any movement toward economic justice as a response to terrorism. To quote one Senator, "Economic justice will come if we make changes systematically and patiently with careful consideration. We cannot let one man force us to change the economic system over night that is the envy of the world. Our system may be flawed, but it is still the best hope for mankind."

J.J. laughed at the buffoon who didn't realize that almost no country wanted to emulate the American system that permanently relegated a large part of the population to institutionalized poverty. Rather, most nations followed the European model where high taxes on the rich made for a more equitable society. In America, the worship of the wealthy was so obscene that ostentatious living was actually aggrandized and the rich were afforded the status that was once reserved for European royalty.

Chablis and the Terrorist
Who Resurrected the Spirit of Che Guevara

J.J. composed a letter to Donald as he wanted to make sure the nation was going to be aghast at what he was about to do next.

Dear Donald:

Please see that the public is alerted that the Spirit of Che is about to act again. This action will shake the foundations of a nation that for far too long has elected to let all the good things only flow to those at the top of the economic ladder. I am now not a one man revolution, as others are starting to realize that if you demand your rights rather than beg for them, you are more likely to get results. However, they must never let up, because if they let up, all is lost. One moment of weakness and the privileged class will pounce upon the poor, crushing them under the jack-booted heel of fascism.

Wall Street represents the modern-day plantation, and the workers are the modern-day slaves. The overlords rape hope and they lynch economic fairness. The government does their bidding and drives out anyone who dares cry for justice. They practiced genocide against the Native Americans. They drove out Robeson. They executed the Rosenbergs. They jailed Debs. They railroaded the Scottsboro boys. They exiled Chaplin. They locked up Garvey and the Hollywood 10. They stole Puerto Rico, the Indies, the Philippines, even Manhattan. Stand against America and you pay the piper. Well, America's rich are about to pay the piper now. The rich in America had better go into hiding, because I am coming. I am coming. I am coming.

Sincerely,

THE SPIRIT OF CHE GUEVARA

There was a massive run on gun shops as the rich began to exercise those sacrosanct 2nd Amendment rights that were so precious to Americans who believed the right to be packing was more important than freedom of speech. Guns were the whip cream on apple pie, the hot fudge on a sundae. Why guns were as American as love of Jesus. The governor deployed the National Guard to Wall Street to protect the tycoons, as they were essential to America. Forget about the social workers, the teachers, the fast food workers, the factory personnel, the people who really made America work. It was the tycoons who were the most important. Those who shuffle money from one bank to another, who buy short and sell long, who corer the market on pork bellies – those are who really count in America.

J.J. just sat back in his hotel room watching television, enjoying the spectacle that was taking place, all because one man decided to go to war against the privileged class.

All over the world, when people marched for democracy, which was the catch American phrase for embracing unfettered capitalism, the USA hailed the bravery of the people. It was called people power. Now, America was about to get a dose of democracy. It was about to witness people power in the homeland.

Chablis and the Terrorist
Who Resurrected the Spirit of Che Guevara

It was Thursday morning, and as the National Guard stood lined up along the sidewalk side by side to make certain the titans of cash were protected, many people avoided going to work as they feared a great calamity from the *Spirit of Che*. That day was also a red letter day for Chablis, as, although she was still trying to locate J.J., so she could spirit him out of the country and get him to safety, she was excited because Rodrigo was due back in town.

Making sure that she was not being monitored, she called J.J.'s sister and mom from a pay phone using a sound activating diverter just in case the government had men with high powered listening cones near her. Obviously they did, as she spotted a van on the corner across from the phone booth. There was a large cone on top, so they were monitoring her calls, even from public booths. However, she had the technical equipment to make certain they could not listen in. She hooked up the device to the phone and dialled, routing the call through Mozambique. She made her call quickly and informed them she still had not found J.J. but that she was close, real close. She also told them a composite photo had been circulated and broadcast on television, so he was not likely to surface.

Keita laughed and said, "He was an amateur actor. He has the ability to completely change his appearance. The composite they are showing isn't even accurate. He wore a putty nose to work for years. He was planning this long before I was fired by Kimberline. No one but us really knows what he looks like. He has lived in disguise for years."

Chablis said, "I'll be up with a composite sketch book in a couple of days. I need to know his real appearance if I'm going to get him out of the country. See you soon. Got to go before they manage to trace this call. Bye."

She hung up, placed the mouthpiece of the pay phone next to her cell-phone and turned on a loud screeching noise to give the listeners in the van an ear ache. She stepped out of the booth, walked across the street and knocked on the back van door. Joe Harrington opened it and she said, "Fuck you and fuck every spying fascist working for this lousy excuse of a democracy. You assholes wouldn't know what democracy was if it bit you on the ass."

As he started to make a retort, she turned and walked away. She gave him the middle finger as she did, moving up the street with that normal provocative sway that was causing a disturbance. She noticed a large crowd gathering in the nearby park and sauntered over to see what was going on. A man on a dais was shouting to the crowd. "Form up and walk to Wall Street where the National Guard is protecting the oligarchs of America. We want the voices of the people heard. We don't want the National Guard in our streets. If this is a free nation, then there is no place for armed troops in our streets. It is time that the government served all the people, not just the rich. This nation is at a crossroads thanks to the *Spirit of Che Guevara*, whoever he is and where ever he is. Let's go."

Chablis and the Terrorist
Who Resurrected the Spirit of Che Guevara

Since most of the police force was assisting the National Guard on Wall Street, there was little crowd control from authorities to keep the people from leaving the park and spontaneously flooding onto the street. As they moved toward the Financial District, more and more people began to join them until the crowd swelled to over 20,000 people, then 30,000, 40,000 as clerks left their jobs in office buildings, simply walked out without asking permission. Retail workers in department stores, fast food restaurants all filed out in mass until the crowd swelled and swelled to well over 200,000 people. Some drivers parked their cars, got out and joined the march. Almost all cabbies honked their horns in support as makeshift signs were made and hoisted high proclaiming, *End Greed, People Power - Not Money Power, No More Money for War – Use It to Help the Poor.*

As the crowd moved onto Wall Street, the National Guard, had their guns cocked and ready, as protecting the rich, the money changers in the temple of greed was their assigned duty. The crowd walked up to the cocked guns and pleaded with the young soldiers. "Join us. Do not defend the money changers in this temple of greed. Put down your guns that protect the rich and join those like you, people who work for chump change while the rich horde their bars of gold."

There were no leaders of the march, only the occasional spokesperson who would arouse the crowd. One stood on top of a car and shouted at the frightened guardsmen, "Put you guns down and you can be part of the solution rather than part of the problem. This can be the beginning of fairness and justice. If you fire a bullet, you are not just killing us. You are killing yourselves. You are killing the chance to be truly free of those who have kept us all in chains for too long, now."

As guardsman after guardsman began to lay down their guns, many of the officers included, the commanding general stepped forward and took aim at the man on top of the car. Suddenly, his second in command grabbed his hand, and the bullet was fired aimlessly, hitting a building on the opposite side of the street. As the crowd screamed in fear, the soldier took the gun from the dumbfounded overpaid war monger and said, "These people have done nothing but demand justice. I will not allow you to murder one of them. We are supposed to defend democracy not destroy it."

He signalled for all the soldiers to put on their safeties and lower their guns. The crowd let out a mighty cheer and began to chant "join us, join us, join us."

As television cameras rolled and live coverage was being followed in the Oval Office, the President slammed his hand down on his desk and shouted, "We can't have this. This is anarchy. Call out the 87th Airborne immediately and put some real soldiers in there and give them direct orders to stop this rebellious rabble from taking over the economic hub of this nation. Anarchy! It is anarchy. I'm declaring marshal law."

Chablis and the Terrorist
Who Resurrected the Spirit of Che Guevara

One of his advisers, maintaining his calm, said in a very precise manner. "Big mistake, Mr. President. These people are just exercising their rights, and if you come down too hard, similar demonstrations will pop up all over America."

Just then, another adviser pointed at the television and said, "No, you need to get a handle on it now, look."

Suddenly, the news began to flash from one affiliate to another as all over America, spontaneous demonstrations were breaking out as people were marching in all the large cities to the financial districts. In Denver, over 300,000 people were marching down Arapahoe Drive, simply going to City Hall to demand an audience with the mayor. When he refused to come out, they boldly overwhelmed the police and walked into City Hall where a shaken mayor, who was trying to skip out the backdoor, was apprehended and forced to appear before the crowd who chanted, "Down with greed. Down with injustice! People power not rich power."

As police tried to recue him, shots were fired, and demonstrators begin to fall from the hail of bullets, but before they realized it, the people had seized the police and taken their guns. Rather than kill them in rage, they shouted "People's Court and justice will prevail." The police, notorious intimidation, were surrounded, and for once, their arrogance was stayed. The people were now in control of their own destiny.

Chablis and the Terrorist
Who Resurrected the Spirit of Che Guevara

As all this was happening, J.J. sat in front of his television, realizing that the revolution in America had finally begun. These people would be assailed as anarchists, but they were, in fact, true patriots who had stepped forward and demanded justice at long last. A sleeping giant had been aroused – the American public.

As demonstrations spread across America, the moneyed class was demanding action from all levels of government, which was there to protect the rich. Their campaign contributions were supposed to buy them protection from the masses that had lived under the delusion of democracy. Mass mobilizations began, putting the militarized police on the streets, along with Army and Marine troops that were told to restore order at any cost. So far, not a single authority had been killed, and they had systematically begun attacking demonstrators. Yet, it was the demonstrators who were labelled anarchists not the culprits of greed.

As this was going on, J.J. got dressed and prepared for an act of sabotage that would rival Hiroshima in intensity. This act would involve the killing of innocents unfortunately, but it would take one dramatic act to solidify the rebellion and unite the opposition. Chaos would have to reign if change were to be truly effectuated.

Chablis had been caught up in the demonstrations, but she had a 2:00 o'clock date with Rodrigo, so she made her way to the Hunter College Café on Park Avenue where they had agreed to meet. Once there, she noticed the place was almost empty, not just of customers, but of workers. Obviously, they had left to join the demonstrations.

Chablis was afraid, because she had been deeply in love twice, and both times it had ended tragically. She wanted to be careful with Rodrigo, but she found herself unable to restrain her emotions. Still, the fear was there. Just how much did she know about him?

Happiness is an elusive commodity,
and when you are lucky enough to find it,
you are often living on the edge of a precipice
for deep within is the fear that you might lose it.

Nothing is forever, as permanence is as elusive
as efficiency and competence in government.
So, grab affection with great verve and gusto.
Don't let fear keep you from loving.

Remember that when one door closes,
another door will, in time, open.
You must be willing to accept that fate,
whether good or bad, will play its tune.

"So, Rodrigo, are you prepared for the coming revolution," said pensively solemn Chablis as she eased into the booth.

Rodrigo, himself in a seemingly pensive mood, replied, "Revolution is a state of mind as much as it is an action. This fellow calling himself the *Spirit of Che* is a catalyst that has lit a fuse that will not go out until it causes an event of cataclysmic proportions."

"So, you believe him when he says he is about to unleash violent fury that will shock the nation?"

"Everything he has said he will do so far, he has done. I believe the man is capable of an apocalyptic act."

Chablis, looking extremely troubled, said "Apocalyptic? What kind of act would qualify as apocalyptic?"

Shaking his head, Rodrigo said, "I would say an attack on the White House, Congress, and the stupid conservative dominated Supreme Court that has for years sided with corporations against the people and diminished people's right to vote, maybe an attack on the Commerce Department that is just an arm of big corporations. Hey, he might even go after Wall Street, maybe detonate a nuclear bomb in the real heart of American greed. Of course, his sensitivity so far precludes any act that would involve massive collateral damage to innocents."

"So, we should be prepared for something dramatic?"

"Chablis, you know how easy it is for a fairly intelligent person to make a nuclear bomb if he has the materials for it? If you make the right contacts in this country, if you have the right amount of money, you can get anything. As Lenin said, 'the capitalist will sell you the rope you are going to hang him with.' Greed is so rampant that there is no limit to what a man with money can get, and remember, the *Spirit of Che* got a lot of money from Kimberline."

"I saw the money, There wasn't that much, not enough to buy material for a nuclear bomb."

"How do you know how much he took? You only saw what was under the mattress. He might have gotten more and hidden it elsewhere."

Quizzically, she replied, "That is possible, I suppose. He said he got 3 million."

Rodrigo leaned over the table and whispered, "I'm actually pulling for the guy. I see him as the last hope for the working men and women of this nation. He has aroused a passion within the downtrodden for justice. He has resurrected the anti-establishment fervour that has been dead for far to long in this nation."

Maybe you are right. Hey, I just want to get him to safety. I promised his mom and sister I would do all I could. So far, he has killed no innocents, but I am fearful of what might happen if and when he does. He already has a bull's eye on his chest, as every government agency - federal, state, local wants this guy dead."

Rodrigo almost had tears in his eyes. "Chablis, maybe he doesn't want to get to safety. Maybe he is so dedicated to righting the wrongs perpetrated against the working people in this country that he wants to die as Che did, fighting until his last breath to lift up humanity from the evil of corporate capitalism. To free humanity from the system of greed that has spread from this country all over the world. There are worse things than death Chablis. Death is the end. After death there is nothing. All suffering ceases, but as long as you live under the tyranny of this nation's commitment to aggrandizing greed as an enviable trait, then you are already dead unless you are part of the 1% who ride to their splendorous lives of excess on the backs of the working people." He looked up at the television that was on the wall in the booth behind them and pointed to it. "You see, all over America today people are taking a stand. I do not know how long the authorities will permit it to continue, nor do I know if once the repression is violently applied by the fascists who run things if the people will roll over and give up as they always do, or continue to fight, but an awakening has occurred because of the man calling himself the *Spirit of Che Guevara*. Don't find him Chablis, regardless of your promise. Let him, as long as he can, continue to rouse the passions of the people to stop their complacency, to put aside their video games, to stop worrying about what the media whores like the Kardashians are doing, to realize that the lives of the rich and famous are not as important as the lives of people who make a difference every day by reaching out with the hand of compassion to stir people to realize that every rich person is taking from society not giving. This man is motivated by Che Guevara who was called by Jean-Paul Sartre, the most complete human being in all of history. To die as Che did, for the poor of the world, who have no champion, is the noblest death a man can have. He linked his destiny to the destiny of the poor. He was the Jesus Christ of his day, and like Jesus, he was crucified by the Pharisees of deceit. Like Che, this man J.J. has amazingly transitioned from quiet bourgeois complacency to fiery rebel. It is a voyage from reality into myth. He is myth now, but the man was greater than the myth. In 1968, the great year of political, cultural and social revolution that followed his death, the slogan "Che lives" appeared on walls from Paris to Prague, Berkeley to Belfast and anywhere else that the old order seemed under threat by what felt like an unstoppable wave of youthful opposition. But the establishment conquered the movement and complacency set in."

Rodrigo was aroused now. "It is not difficult to deconstruct the power of the man and his myth. There is no myth around his revolutionary comrade Fidel Castro, who made the mistake of staying alive. Che Guevara, by contrast, died young. Had the CIA let him live, his star may not have shined as bright. He was the ultimate warrior, who had made real the aspiration that, against all the odds, things could actually be changed. Ordinary people could triumph over their masters. Even as a member of Castro's elite after the revolution, he refused the privilege and luxury granted to other Cuban leaders, insisting on drawing only the average wage, because he was everyman. He saw privilege as the evil it is."

Chablis and the Terrorist
Who Resurrected the Spirit of Che Guevara

Chablis was fascinated by Rodrigo's knowledge of Che Guevara. He continued his impassioned oration. "His words are as valid today as they were when he originally spoke them. It is indeed better to die standing than to live on your knees. We all, if we are revolutionaries, have a rendezvous with history, and we simply cannot permit ourselves to be afraid. Even his execution was a lesson in devotion. Che knew only his body was dying. He told the killer that he was shooting a man, but the ideals would live forever. Truth is, Che Guevara was more than a man. He was the modern day Jesus, and though he was buried, he has been resurrected time and time again, enlisted in the battle for justice and hope."

Rodrigo displayed political passion as Chablis had rarely, if ever, seen in anyone as he continued. "They who captured him were awed by the aura of peace and determination in a man they had been told was the anti-Christ. Finding someone willing to pull the trigger and end his life was not easy. Those in command were scared to execute him. Even the C.I.A. agent who was sent by Washington to make certain his life was terminated could not do the job himself. They found an ignorant, poor country recruited soldier who had been brainwashed by American propaganda to do the dirty dead. Ironically, Che, at a conference a few months earlier had written his own epitaph when he said wherever death may surprise us, let it be welcome, provided that this, our battle cry, may have reached some receptive ear and another hand may be extended to wield our weapons."

Chablis and the Terrorist
Who Resurrected the Spirit of Che Guevara

Rodrigo was fiery with passion as he continued. "When they killed him, they cut off his hands for identification. His captors instructed some local nuns to wash his face, tidy his hair and beard, then photographed his corpse. But the image which circulated the world did not have the effect intended. He lay there like the crucified Christ, taken down from the cross to be placed in a tomb. Yet, he was resurrected in a way that made him more powerful than before his assassination. He looked, like Christ, at his killers and forgave them, proclaiming that he who dies for an idea truly lives forever. He was given eternal life by those who thought they were slaying him."

Chablis began to get tears in her eyes. She looked directly into Rodrigo's eyes and said, "You have a great passion for the downtrodden. Maybe that is why I love you, Rodrigo."

"I wish I had time to show you some passion right now. You are arousing my libido."

Smiling, she said, "So, your compassion arouses your passion. My sphincter muscle is twitching you know."

"Chablis, I am like a man in a deep dark hole, slowly moving forward, realizing that my pleasure comes from being in that hole. There is no fear, only the thrill of being inside and enjoying the tightness, the darkness." He seemed to catch himself, as what he had said was a red flag, and Chablis, for a second, reflected not on what he said, but how he said it. She had heard something like that before.

He picked up the check the waitress had placed on the table and began playing with it. He placed it by his plate as Chablis stared at him.

He looked at her longingly and said, "No matter what happens, Chablis, always remember that I love you. I am an imperfect human being, but I am perfect in the love I have for you. I have never known a woman like you."

Giggling, she looked downward and said, "Well, I am sure of that. Not many women have what I have between their legs."

Shaking his head, Rodrigo said, "Don't demean yourself with cheap jokes. I know you are 100% woman. Myerson made a fatal mistake that day in the coffee shop when eh demeaned you. He paid a heavy price for that.

Rodrigo knew he had made an outright admission when he bought up Myerson, but he reached over, took her hand in his and said, "Chablis, I am on a journey that is long and arduous. I may not see you for awhile. Who knows, if fate intervenes, I may never see you again, but always remember that I carry you within my heart forever."

Fearful, she began to fret over what he had said earlier, and then she knew where she had heard the oration about the hole. He leaned forward and so did she. He kissed her on the lips for the last time, got up and without another word between them, he walked out of the restaurant."

Looking at him from behind, she recognized his gait. She would not chase after him. It was not what he wanted. He was about to unleash Armageddon, but she would not stop it, no matter how catastrophic it might be. She was on his side now, the side of righteous indignation. She looked down at the check laying beside the money he had placed on the table. Then, she knew for sure who he was as she looked at it, folded into a triangle. △

EPILOGUE
AND WAITED, AND WAITED, AND WAITED

Chablis expected a cataclysmic event soon, but the next morning, the *New York Times*, in an article under Donald Beckman's by-line ran the following:

TO: My Compatriots Who Fight for Justice and Those Devils of Greed Who Oppress the People
FROM: The Spirit of Che Guevara

I am still present though I may not be seen. I am like the wind that floats over the desert of heated discontent. The sand may sting my eyes, but it does not blind me. I see the oasis of hope in the distance and it is so beautiful and peaceful – a place where man is freed from greed and lives in utopian harmony. The lions still roam on the outskirts of the oasis, roaring with hunger to destroy that which they cannot understand, but united, those who dwell in the Oasis of Hope will withstand any onslaught of the greedy, for those within have justice on their side!

I, then, am here to float over the land, and like Jesus, who said he came not to bring peace but a sword, so am I ready to bring down the sword on those who defile humanity with their insidious greed. I have said that I am capable of a cataclysmic act of Biblical proportions, and I have my hands on the button of destruction. So, to the rich who do not heed Jesus' admonition to give all they have to the poor, keep looking over your shoulder for the Spirit of Che Guevara stealthily is

J. Wayne Frye 283

stalking you. To an uncaring government that only serves the wealthy in a nation that worships at the altar of greed, be vigilant and do the right thing, for the Spirit of Che Guevara is watching you.

If you wish to express what all future generations must be like, look to the Spirit of Che Guevara. If you want your children to grow up with compassion for the downtrodden, be like Che. If you want to educate all, then, like Che, make education free and readily available for each citizen and be sure that they are educated in Che's spirit. If you believe healthcare is a human right, then demand it be available to all unencumbered by the profit motive. If you believe all work is dignified then in the spirit of Che demand a fair wage for a fair day's work. If you believe all are entitled to shelter then tear down the monuments to ostentatious living and let everyone be afforded the dignity of a safe and secure home. If you want a society without the stain of greed and envy, then be like the Spirit of Che Guevara.

Sincerely,

The Spirit of Che Guevara

All across America, corporations were so fearful of the aroused public that they started cutting executives salaries in some places to ward off proposed laws that would cap all pay at no more than $500,000 a year. Corporations willingly reduced profit margins to satisfy a public that was demanding fairness and an end to corporate greed.

Chablis and the Terrorist
Who Resurrected the Spirit of Che Guevara

City after city, county after county, state after state passed higher minimum wage laws so rapidly that the federal government was shamed into raising the minimum wage, even with the majority of Republicans, although reluctant, supporting it. Yes, what was happening was not the result of a sudden respect for the working man, but fear by the privileged that their empires would be totally destroyed if they did not effectuate change to placate an aroused public. And whenever there would be waffling, suddenly a letter from the *Spirit of Che* reminding the powerful that his finger was still on the trigger of a tempest of turmoil would arrive on Donald's desk and its publication would warn the privileged that they were in a tenuous situation, wavering on the edge of a precipice over a pit of fiery retribution.

It was not their magnanimity of heart that kept the rich compliant, but the fear of a public that was no longer begging for justice but demanding it. Politicians were even forced to lower their salaries and cut back on their parsimonious benefits; otherwise, they would face a public that would hang their lying, cheating, hypocritical asses on any tree available. No longer did the people fear the government. Now, the government feared the people!

In churches, parishioners started putting up images of Che after his execution next to images of Christ on the cross. How ironic that there was an instant movement to canonize Che, a fervent non-believer, as a saint in the Catholic Church.

Chablis and the Terrorist
Who Resurrected the Spirit of Che Guevara

There seemed to be new vigour and hope in a land that had lost its way. However, the people heeded Che's advice to be loyal to the country always, but loyal to the government when it deserved it. And, in the new America, the government was ever vigilant in its pursuit of fairness and justice, because it feared losing the loyalty of the people who now refused to bow before the privileged and demanded a new fairness and an end to nepotism. So fearful of the stain of privilege and the disdain for royalty, even the President insisted he no longer be referred to as Mr. President, because it bespoke of royalty and in America no one was royal. Within a year, the royal leeches of Europe had all abdicated and been forced to return their ill-gotten fortunes of privilege to the public treasury. In Saudi Arabia and other despotic kingdoms, the oil sheiks were disposed, their wealth confiscated and a people's tribunal put in place to mange the money and distribute it fairly to all. Old animosities between tribes began to diminish and the harshness of the Koran punishments were dismissed as out of step with true justice. Christians all across the world insisted on abrogating any antiquated finger-pointing at alternative lifestyles, because it was obvious Jesus was nonjudgmental and if the church was to imitate him, it must open its heart and embrace all who seek acceptance.

Each day, Chablis stopped for lunch at the Hunter College Café where she had last seen Rodrigo. She hoped he would walk through the door, maybe in one of his disguises and come over, take her hand and whisper, "I love you." As Rodrigo, J.J., the

Chablis and the Terrorist
Who Resurrected the Spirit of Che Guevara

Spirit of Che or anyone else he might be disguised as she would welcome his love. She sipped on her coffee and waited, and waited, and waited.

THE END

Don't Miss the Original
Chablis Louise Chavez Adventure

Chablis: Avenging Angel for the Forgotten
In the City of Lost Hope

AND COMING SOON

Chablis and the Manila Aswang
That Danced with the Devil

Also Available from Fireside Books,
The Adventures of Chablis' Partner, Aaron Adams,
In These J. Wayne Frye Thrillers

Fall From Apocalypse
Armageddon Now
Something Evil in the Darkness at Hopkins House
When Jesus Came to Jersey as the Son of Thunder
When Jesus Came to Canada to Lead an Indigenous Rebellion
The Girl Who Stirred up the Whirlwind
The Girl Who Motivated Murder Most Foul
The Girl Who Said Goodbye for the Last Time